Dream for a Sinner

by

Lynn Shurr

A Sinner's Legacy, Book Six

This is a work of fiction. Names, characters, places, and incidents are either the product of the author's imagination or are used fictitiously, and any resemblance to actual persons living or dead, business establishments, events, or locales, is entirely coincidental.

Dream for a Sinner

Contact Information: info@thewildrosepress.com

Cover Art by *Diana Carlile*

The Wild Rose Press, Inc.
PO Box 708
Adams Basin, NY 14410-0708
Visit us at www.thewildrosepress.com

Publishing History
First Champagne Rose Edition, 2019
Print ISBN 978-1-5092-2706-8
Digital ISBN 978-1-5092-2707-5

A Sinner's Legacy, Book Six
Published in the United States of America

Jilly grasped his hand. “One of my favorites. Let’s dance.”

Trapped again. When the song started, he saw trouble as big as a Texas tornado approaching Josee. A massive guy, who had six inches and a hundred pounds on him, shoved chairs out of the way to reach her. Judging by his drunken sway, he wanted to dance in a big way, whether capable or not.

Josee shook her head, gave him a pleasant smile, and returned to her conversation. The big dude grasped her slender wrist hard. Trin winced, knowing she’d bear bruises tomorrow. This jerk yanked Josee from her chair. Over the music, Trin heard him bellow, “I ain’t good enough to dance with you when you show your near naked body on magazine covers.”

Josee stomped his instep with her boot and pulled free. She lost her balance and struck the edge of the table. Empties crashed to the floor. Beer flowed from the full bottles into the sawdust. Trin shook loose of Jilly. “Sorry, gotta help her.”

He dodged the dancers and followed the aisle the brute had carved between the chairs. Josee’s assailant stooped and grasped a broken longneck, its edge jagged and sharp. “See if you’re so pretty after I mess you up.”

Trin grabbed his bulging arm and drew it back with all his strength. Flinging him off, the thug pivoted. “You want to fight me for her, you pansy geek?”

“Yeah, yeah, I do, asshole.”

Vaguely, he heard Josee say, “No, Trin! Here come the bouncers.”

Too late.

Praise for Lynn Shurr

"Shurr is a wonderful storyteller."

~The Romance Studio

~*~

"Lynn Shurr's delightful New Orleans Sinners series is sure to please both non-sports fans and sports fans alike. Do yourself a favor and dive into the world of the Sinners."

~Farrah Rochon, USA Today best-selling author of the New York Sabers football series

~*~

"The author has created a family full of surprises with the Billodeaux bunch. After reading just one book, I am eager to read more about this colorful family."

~Rachel's Willful Thoughts, The Romance Reviews

~*~

"Very easy reads, well written, combined with conflict, believable plots and secondary characters that make the plot come alive."

~Jane Lange, Romances, Reads and Reviews

~*~

"I love how deep and well-written the characters are."

~Juliette Brandt, Paperbacks and Frosting

Dedication

For Joann Meinholz Fritz,
an old friend rediscovered

A SINNER'S LEGACY

The Children of Joe and Nell Billodeaux
who fulfilled the prophecy that they would have
twelve offspring, this way, that way, all ways.

1. Dean Joseph Billodeaux - Joe's illegitimate son by a one-night stand with a woman who planned to shake him down for money. He is adopted by Nell who believes she cannot have children of her own. Current Sinners quarterback. (*Wish for a Sinner* and *Son of a Sinner*)

2. Thomas Cassidy Billodeaux - a redheaded son who enters the family through an open adoption with a teenage mother. His birth father is Joe's no-good cousin. He is a kicker for the Sinners. *(Wish for a Sinner, Kicks for a Sinner, She's a Sinner*)

3. Jude Emily Billodeaux - twin of Ann, conceived by in vitro fertilization using eggs purchased from Nell's sister, Emily. (*Wish for a Sinner*)

4. Ann Marie Billodeaux (Annie) - Jude's quiet twin. (*Wish for a Sinner, The Heart of a Sinner))*

5. Lorena Renee Billodeaux (Lori) - First of Nell's little frozen babies to be born, one of the triplets. (*Kicks for a Sinner*)

6. Mack Coy Christopher Billodeaux - Second of the triplets to be born. (*Kicks for a Sinner* and *Dream for a Sinner*)

7. Trinity Billodeaux - Youngest of the triplets and named for the Father, Son, and Holy Ghost, smallest of the three and in need of a powerful saintly help to survive. (*Kicks for* a *Sinner*)

8. Xochi Maria Billodeaux - child of Joe's no-good cousin by a young Mexican woman. She is Tom's half-sister and is adopted into the family after the terrifying deaths of her parents. Her name means “blossom” in Aztec. (*Kicks for a Sinner* and *Sister of a Sinner*)

9. Teddy Wilkes Billodeaux - a child with spina bifida abandoned by his mother at Nell’s health care center and adopted by the family. He believed himself to be Joe’s natural son. (*Paradise for a Sinner* and *Never A Sinner*)

10. Anastasia Marya Polasky (Stacy) - daughter of Nell’s sister, Emily, and a bogus Polish prince. She becomes a ward of the Billodeauxs upon her parents’ deaths but is never adopted by her own wish. She arrives on their doorstep the same day as Teddy. (*Paradise for a Sinner* and *Son of a Sinner*)

11. Edith Patricia Billodeaux (Edie) - a normally conceived child, twin of Rex. (*Love Letter for a Sinner*)

12. Rex Worthy Billodeaux (T-Rex) - Edie’s twin brother and future Sinner’s quarterback, maybe. (*Love Letter for a Sinner*)

Chapter One

With his hands locked behind his head, Trinity Billodeaux stretched his modest length out on the lounger of Teddy's new patio. His brother had chosen the location of his rambling ranch-style home well. Situated on a ridge created by a once mighty river, the house had a view over two pastures dotted with white cattle, red horses, and a passel of ponies right down to the edge of the placid brown bayou fringed with clumps of cypress trees. A low brick wall enclosed three sides of the patio, leaving one side open for a paved ramp. An overhang provided shade on this hot June day, but he wore his prescription sunglasses anyhow since they were less geeky than his usual eyewear. A couple of picnic tables sat in the sun near a built-in grill and what his sister-in-law, Jessie, said was a bread oven.

Trin reached out an arm and took a swig from a cold beer. "This is the life, huh, X?"

On the other side of a mosaic table sporting a cheery yellow sunflower in its center, now obscured by the chilled six-pack, Sinners' football player X-avier Hopkins relaxed with his long running back legs reaching to the end of his lounger. He freed his second beer from its ring and popped it open. "Sho is. Teddy built a real nice place here for his family. It's modest but has everything needed just like the man hisself. I wanted to get my mama a place in the country, but she won't leave the hood. Her church and all her friends are there, she says. Best I could do was get her to move into a gated condo complex just across the road. At least, it's out of the high crime area, so she's not likely to get robbed or hit by a stray bullet."

That sobering statement made Trinity Billodeaux appreciate Lorena Ranch, his dad's acreage, all the more. "No worries about that here with all the security Knox Polk has built into the surroundings. I like this house because it makes me, the runt of the Billodeaux men, feel tall with all the cabinets lowered to wheelchair height. Even with his spina bifida, Teddy is only an inch shorter than me, and he was adopted."

X-avier studied Trinity for a moment. "I'd say you about average height. Me, at barely six feet, I'm considered short for a running back. We all got our physical challenges. Shouldn't stop us from getting what we want." Sweat beaded on his mocha-colored forehead and deflated his carefully fluffed fro some. He rolled the cold can of beer over his brow. "When you think they'll get back—or did we show up too early?" He checked a massive sports watch on his sinewy wrist. "It's past six."

"Note on the door said they needed to step out for a few items and would be back soon, but I've observed my brothers with their kids and wives. A guy goes to the store alone, gets in, picks up what he wants, and gets out. Drag along the wife and two kids, and you can triple the time it takes to buy so much as a carton of milk. That is not the life."

X raised his eyebrows in his rather narrow face that went with his lean and fast as a whippet body on the playing field. "You don't want to marry someday?

Right now, I'm just fooling around enjoying my fame and my Super Bowl ring, but one day I want to settle down and give my mama those grandchildren she wants."

Trin raked his unruly black curls, damp and growing tighter with the heat and humidity, off his neck. "Sure, you can get any woman you want when you're ready. Computer geeks aren't so lucky."

Again, he earned X-avier's scrutiny. "You not so bad. Looks like you been working out a little and got a nice tan, not pasty like most nerds. But when was the last time you had a haircut? I'll bet not since your sister Annie's wedding back in December. Right, you didn't get one then either."

"No, I think I've had a haircut since the wedding. Hey, my brother Mack has his hair all down around his shoulders, and people think he's sexy. Besides, this isn't a tan. It's the Billodeaux olive complexion you're seeing. It will get darker since I'm on pool patrol when Camp Love Letter starts tomorrow along with the computer workshops I'm giving. So, I have been working out a little. Don't want to look puny on lifeguard duty."

"Like a bunch of poor crippled and sick kids are going to notice." X's face displayed an a-ha moment with a flash of white teeth. "Somebody else gonna be around you want to impress?"

"Nope."

"Let's play a little game. If you could have any woman in the world, who'd you want to do?"

Trin took the high road. "I don't do women."

"Didn't think you swung that way," X-avier said with a teasing glint in his dark eyes.

"Come on. You know I'm not gay. I mean I'd make love to a woman, not do her. My mom would let me have it for playing a game like this."

"Mine, too, but women play it all the time. I know for a fact since a few female fans have told me I'm at the top of their list."

Now that was a man with a smug smile, Trin thought. He wasn't at the top of anyone's to do list. "Are you fulfilling their dreams, X?"

"My mama also said a gentleman don't kiss and tell. Come on, think about it. Who's the first to come into your mind."

Under pressure to prove his manliness, Trinity blurted out the truth. "Josee Riley."

"The model, leggy, blonde, and bodacious, the one on the cover of the last swimsuit issue. You do aim high. Say, wait a minute. Wasn't she at Annie's wedding?"

"Yep, she's Connor Riley's daughter. He was my dad's favorite wide receiver back in the day. I've known her since she was a baby and danced with her more than once, but she hardly notices me with all my six-foot-plus brothers standing in the way. She's close to that height herself and always wears high heels. Whenever I dance with her, I want to rest my head on her shoulder."

"Don't do that, man. She'll treat you like her baby brother."

"I wish. Arjay is way taller than she is and plays football. I don't stand a chance. I'm not slick with women like you."

X-avier mimed an offended expression. "I am not slick. I am sincere. That's the secret. I never tell a woman something I don't mean. When I hit on Jessie, I told her I admired strong women who could give a good massage. Totally true as she was working a cramp out of my leg back when she was a trainer."

"You hit on Teddy's wife, a woman in a wheelchair!"

"Didn't know they was a couple at the time. She set me straight fast enough. But sure, Jessie is a beautiful woman, chair or no chair, and I do not discriminate against the disabled. Besides, I think I gave her confidence a boost she needed since that accident crippled her."

A red van rigged for the handicapped turned onto the long drive that led to the house. Its bright color flashed between the thick trunks of the live oaks that shaded the way. Trin got up and watched its progress. "Here they come. Prepare yourself to be hugged."

"By Teddy?" X-avier questioned as he also stood up to greet the family.

"Nope."

The first one out of the van was Teddy's adopted daughter, a few months shy of two, racing her way up the ramp like a puppy toward an open gate. Her mass of black curls fanned out behind a red headband that matched the little sneakers hitting the concrete. Her startling blue eyes, so much like Teddy's since she was actually his niece, were set in a honey-colored face that homed in on Trinity. "Unc Trin, we home!" She roped her arms around his legs to deliver that hug. "Up!" Lizzy commanded.

"How far up?" her uncle teased. He raised her above his head and spun around a few times. She held out her arms and shouted, "I an airplane! Down now."

Trinity brought her in for a landing. The second her feet hit the ground, Lizzy embraced X-avier's legs. "Hiya, X. You gonna play music for us?"

"Right back at ya, Dizzy Lizzy. If I do, will you sing along?"

Lizzy nodded. "I sing wit' you at Annie's wedding. I throw flowers, too."

"You remember I DJ'd for your Aunt Annie. Well, bless your heart. But we don't need no flowers thrown tonight, baby. Save them for Uncle Trin's wedding."

Trinity snorted. "They'll be turned to dust by then."

The rest of the family joined them, Jessie in her wheelchair holding their three-month-old daughter, May, in a sling that left her hands free. Trin blurred his eyes and deleted the wheelchair. Big hazel eyes, light brown hair streaked with blonde, a perfect face with a cute nose and delicious lips, she truly was beautiful. He felt a bit ashamed for not noticing before X pointed that fact out to him.

Teddy clomped behind on his armband crutches, a diaper bag slung over one shoulder, his fine blond hair flopping in his pale face, his ever-present smile in place. "Sorry that took so long. Jessie noticed Pommier's bakery had the red light on for their hot French bread, and I had to stand in line for that before we even got to the grocery. I only wanted to pick up some beer. Now I see you've brought your own. Anyhow, the steaks are marinating in the fridge. Jessie already made the salad. The potatoes are twice-baked and just need to be heated in the microwave. We'll get this show on the road fairly quickly."

Teddy took a remote from his pocket and aimed it

at the sliding glass doors that gave access to the interior. They opened almost magically. Jessie rolled ahead. “Ladies first. This one needs a clean diaper and a feeding. Come on, Lizzy, go potty.”

“Don’t need to potty.”

Trin gave her a wink. “Big girls go potty.”

“I go potty.” She followed her mother inside the cool roomy space of the large living room, free of clutter that might get in the way of a wheelchair, and boasting a large fireplace totally unnecessary in the Louisiana climate but nice to gather around.

“Give me a hand by getting the groceries, guys. Four kinds of ice cream are melting in the van because the girls couldn’t make up their minds which they wanted. Then meet me in the kitchen. You can come in through the front door. I’ll unlock it.”

Trin and X followed the path to the drive and loaded up with bags containing the long loaves of bread, the endangered ice cream, carriers of bottled beer, and an array of other groceries. They hauled it all in one trip, entering through the stepless portico beside the two-car garage. An open floor plan, the kitchen sat to the right of the entry. Teddy, in a great balancing act with one thing stacked atop another, had already removed the pan of steaks, the bowl of salad, and the potatoes from the fridge to a low counter. He spread the food out in a line and removed a bread knife from a drawer.

“Ice cream goes in the top drawer of the freezer. Hand me those loaves and get the butter out, Trin.”

He put the bread on the counter and held up the bags still ringing his arms. “Where?”

“Ah, wherever it fits. Just leave the dry stuff on the

counter. We'll get to it later." Teddy sliced the loaves lengthwise and slathered both sides with whipped butter. He shook on garlic salt from a spice rack. "This will be worth the wait. Hey, X, nuke those potatoes in the microwave for two minutes each. Got to get the bacon bits nice and warm and melt the cheese in the mixture."

Stripping the plastic wrap from the salad bowl, Teddy rummaged in one of the bags for premium steakhouse dressing and tossed some with the greens. Trin admired his ability in cooking. He'd never learned how and mostly ate in the cafeteria at Hartz Technology, often taking some meals home for his dinner. Teddy, wanting to be independent of others, had taught himself to make plenty of easy dishes.

Jessie returned with the children. "I do love a man who can fend for himself in the kitchen. Here we are, Daddy, all nice and clean. Lizzy went potty."

Teddy applauded, and after a shrug, so did Trin and X. "Did you wash your hands, Liz?"

She nodded and was rewarded with the duty of carrying four wooden bowls out to the picnic table while Trin toted the salad. X-avier loaded the warmed potatoes onto a platter and followed. Teddy managed the pan of steaks. Jessie snagged a caddy of cutlery from the counter, checkered napkins from a drawer, and joined the procession. While Jessie set the table, Teddy turned on the gas and heaved the steaks onto the grill. They were the thick-cut rib eyes all the Billodeaux men, including Trinity, preferred, leaving no doubt Teddy had been raised as one of them.

"How do you like your steak?"

Trinity said, "Medium rare, pink but not bloody."

X preferred his charred. Teddy sent Trin back for the bread and a shaker of parmesan. "Bring the bottle of Dad's hot and spicy sauce. Someone might want it."

While the steaks sizzled, Teddy splayed the loaves of bread butter-side down and placed them on the grill. A few flames shot up as the spread dripped into the fake charcoal. He flipped them swiftly, each loaf beautifully marked with grill lines. A minute later, he placed them in a long basket rummaged from a nearby storage cabinet and showered on the parm. He found a platter in the same space and removed the medium rare steaks. X's choice remained until well done. Trinity envied his brother's deftness and his grill. His own was a small hibachi on the balcony of his apartment. He didn't possess the beautiful wife and pretty children his handicapped brother had either.

Shaking off the feeling he never would, Trin distributed the three remaining beers while Jessie helped herself to a canned iced tea from the minifridge in the outdoor kitchen. They gathered around the picnic table with Jessie on the end, the baby so blond it seemed almost bald still nestled in its sling. May's big hazel eyes zoned in on her mother's chest, and she began to fuss and root.

"Mind if I nurse her while we eat?"

"Uh, no," Trin said. "Most natural thing in the world, right X?"

"Ah, yeah, very natural." Still, both men raised their eyes skyward as Jessie released a breast, offered it to the baby, and covered both with the light cotton blanket lining the sling.

"Good, because I'm as hungry as she is." Jessie tore off a piece of bread and set it beside the perfectly cooked steak spurting red juices when she cut into it. Each claimed a potato and passed around the salad. Lizzy, perched on the end of the bench nearest Jessie, ate tidbits from her mother's plate.

"Pass me some of Joe's Hot and Spicy Sauce," X-avier said.

"You sure? You're sweating already," Teddy jested.

"I love this stuff, but it's not for wimps." X doused his meat. "Anyone else?" None of the others fell for the challenge.

"Good thing someone likes it since the proceeds go to support Camp Love Letter. Connor Riley's sweet sauce sells better, but I'd never say that to Joe. Breast change," Jessie warned.

"Would you look at that view," Trinity said, averting his eyes. "Yeah, camp starts tomorrow. What have all of you been drafted to do? I'm giving some computer workshops in the pool house, doing a life guard shift, and helping Edie with the newsletter like old times when Teddy and I did it as kids."

"I love helping, but Annie and I got a pass since we both have small babies," Jessie admitted.

"I'm scheduled for wheelchair basketball, horseback riding, and dragon boat captain since you grabbed all the computer stuff, Trin. X, this is your first year. What does our mom have planned for you?

"Well, I suck at computers, don't swim, and stay as far away from horses as I can. It's their ugly, yellow teeth and big feet. I'm down for the football toss and catch, bonfire jam session, and making all the ladies feel special. Those are my talents, but I really think we should help Trin out with a certain babe. Make him our project. Sing his praises."

All eyes swiveled toward Trinity. He restrained his urge to stab X in the ribs with his steak knife. "I can get my own woman."

"Not what you said befo'," X reminded him.

"Who?" asked Jessie.

"Gotta be Josee Riley. He's been crushing on her since she turned sixteen and went into modeling. Before that, Josee was only the kid who tagged along after the triplets, always pretty though. She's here for a week—makeup classes for the moms and older girls, I think, and just being one of the featured celebrities, mixing and mingling."

"Thanks for sharing, Teddy. Fat chance I have since Mack is coming, too."

"No. I met her at Annie's wedding, and she seemed very down to earth and friendly to everyone, not the stuck up 'don't hate me because I'm beautiful' type at all. Mack is mostly show and no substance. You should let her know how you feel. We'll all help you get time with her," Jessie said.

"To give the man credit, Mack is an awesome wide receiver and a ladies' man like some other people I know." X-avier polished his nails on the tight black Sinners T-shirt he wore. "But I think we can clean this boy up some and work on his lines, ya know. Be almost as good as winning a Super Bowl if we can do it, a real challenge."

His complexion might have been olive, but Trin knew his face burned red by its sudden heat. "I don't need help."

"Yes, you do," three positive voices answered in unison.

Jessie bailed him out. “So that’s settled. Dessert, anyone? Four kinds of ice cream: vanilla, chocolate, mint chip, and cherry.”

“Choc-late,” Lizzy screamed.

“My choice, too, baby girl. Most of the time.” X wiggled his brows at Jessie.

“Hey, my wife, mother of my two children, off the market.” Teddy spoke up.

“Yeah, and that’s a damned shame. Come on, Lizzy, let’s get that ice cream.” X offered the little girl his large hand and off they went to the kitchen.

“He does have a way with the ladies of any age. And I have none.”

“You’re great with Lizzy. Don’t put yourself down, Trin. I think I want the cherry. I know Teddy will go with mint chip. We’ll all help ourselves.” Jessie pivoted her chair and went to join the others with her husband pounding in her wake. That left Trinity sitting at the table, dreading tomorrow.

Chapter Two

Ah—the controlled chaos of opening day at Camp Love Letter. Knox Polk guarded the gate, checking off each family as they arrived and double checking them against family photos. The line of vehicles moved down the oak-lined lane to the big house with its white pillars and wide verandahs. Once parked, each family received the key to one of the cottages that dotted the ranch: two bedrooms, a full bath, a small kitchen stocked with breakfast items and snacks, and a living room with a foldout sofa in case the family needed more sleeping space, plus plenty of board games and decks of cards for rainy days. No televisions as the goal of the camp was rest, relaxation, fun, and freedom from external worries.

So it had been as long as Trin could remember. He did his part at registration, guiding the participants to their places and helping to haul their baggage if needed. All the while, he kept an eye out for the arrival of Josee Riley. Teddy had offered him and X their two spare bedrooms since the children currently shared one in the new four-bedroom home, but they'd declined and stayed with his parents in the mansion.

Trin slipped all too easily into his old bedroom where he'd once overstayed his welcome, being the only one of the older children needing a push off the edge to leave the nest. "Trinity," Mama Nell had said.

"A young man needs a place of his own to spread his wings and, um, entertain." That was his mom, the psychologist, putting it gently that he needed to go out into the world and seek a mate. He made an excellent salary as a game coder at Hartz Technology and really had no excuse to linger. Off he went to get a condo in Lafayette, certain in the knowledge that a bedroom at the ranch waited if he needed it. Right now, he did need it because his old room sat just down the hall from the one assigned to Josee, his sister-in-law Stacy's former princess lair, all gold and white. How fitting for his dream girl.

The big problem lay in the fact that Mack's room stood between hers and his. Mack would know his every move. They'd share a bathroom. Every day, he'd have to face his brother's ripped body in the mirror as they shaved at the dual sinks because Mack seldom wore more than his boxer briefs to bed, if that. He'd be there in his droopy pajama bottoms comparing chests, Mack's defined and waxed, his narrow with a dark thatch of hair between his barely noticeable pecs. Nothing like starting out the day demoralized.

Yes, his wide receiver brother had to work in time spent at the camp between voluntary training sessions, minicamps, and then training camp just before the preseason games started. But why this week? Why not after the Fourth or any other time? Trinity swore Mack existed simply to show him up, and he didn't have their third triplet, Lorena, to provide a cushion between them. Actually, his sister was the first born of the three, six feet tall and nearly as athletic as Mack, but currently off playing beach volleyball with the amazing Maisie Morton in Australia. She'd always been the buffer, calling Mack the brawn and Trinity the brains of the trio. He'd have to say Lorena was the heart and soul. He missed her mightily.

When Mack mocked Trin's poor vision, so bad contacts couldn't correct it, Lori suggested he wear Harry Potter style glasses to show he was a wizard with computers. Later, she'd been the one to say he should switch to the Clark Kent type as he grew older. When Mack mentioned one more time that Trinity's adolescent growth spurt stopped at five eight and Trin attempted to slug him, knowing he'd be flattened, Lori stopped the blow and told Mack she'd black his eye if he ever compared their heights again. After all, he'd been born last, the runt of the litter, though Lori never said so.

"Jeez, Mack, our parents named him Trinity because he needed all the help the Father, Son, and Holy Ghost could give him to survive in the days after his birth. It's a miracle he lived." A powerful name, they hadn't given him a middle one. Mack had two—Mack Coy Christopher Billodeaux—because their Mawmaw Nadine insisted he needed a saint's name in there somewhere. Mack had more of everything. Certainly, Josee would notice.

Trinity returned from hauling luggage and passed X-avier pushing a wheelchair containing a girl with a sunhat pulled low over her bald head. "Used to push my granny in a chair like this, but you way prettier," he jawed. Trin caught the girl's eye roll, one X couldn't see. "And you bald like my granddaddy, but he ug-lee. You rock bald. He don't." Now, the girl smiled just a little. X did have a way, yes, he did.

Funny how they'd become friends, meeting first at

Teddy's wedding where X did the DJ honors and some singing as well. How he'd envied the guy's glibness and ease. He'd said as much to Teddy who introduced them and suggested X could give his brother some pointers on the social graces. X-avier had tried. Number one was get a good haircut, which he'd ignored. X hung out with him some after the college football season ended, mostly the two of them playing video games on Trin's awesome setup. He'd asked how come the football phenom, sure to be drafted in the spring despite playing for a small college, wanted to be his pal.

X answered honestly enough. "You a Sinner. I want to be one. The Sinners are tight, so is your family. I like that."

His reply, "I'm no more a Sinner than Teddy is with his handicap."

"Oh, no, you one of them in your heart. Bet you never miss a game, would help any one of them. Besides, I get tired of jocks. Most ain't got no culture."

"You think I do?"

"Sho—and the best gaming system I ever saw. Let's play."

During the offseason, X left his condo and night life in New Orleans and stayed with his mama in the next town down the road from Chapelle. He took her to church on Sundays and out to dinner afterward, but strangely, he liked to spend time with Trin on Saturdays just playing games and talking, good for both of them since most of Trin's friends were nerds and not jocks. Whatever, it worked.

Still thinking how X had made that girl smile for all her troubles, Trinity returned to the check-in area—and there she stood, one hip cocked in model fashion,

Josee Riley talking to his mom. She wore little makeup and had drawn her nearly white blonde hair up in a high ponytail looped through a black Sinners cap. Oversized sunglasses disguised her remarkable blue eyes. Her perfectly plump, kissable lips opened in a smile over perfect teeth. “Hi, Trin,” she said. “Looks like we drew the same slot this summer.”

“Yeah, what a coincidence.” He forced himself not to stare at his feet when he told that lie. In truth, he’d asked his mother to give them similar schedules to which she’d replied, “You can’t do better than Josee—if you can get her.” Why did everyone see right through him?

“Need any help with your bags? I guess you brought a ton of clothes.”

“A misconception about models. No, my single suitcase is already in my room, but I do have a large makeup case you can lug to the pool house. I’ll be doing makeovers in one area while you teach the kids some computer skills in the other.”

He hoped he could keep his mind on computer skills if she set up anywhere in the vicinity. “Sure, where is it?”

“In the gold and white bedroom. I’ll show you.”

As if he didn’t know where that might be. Trin saw his mom’s brows raise, but she didn’t say he’d lived here all his life and knew very well which room she meant. He followed the sway of Josee’s hips, not too large, not too skinny, encased in snug, distressed, pale blue jeans, into the mansion and up to the second floor via the grand central staircase in the foyer. Hadn’t they both ridden down the polished surface of its railing for fun as kids? She took a right in the hallway and almost to the end where the elevator once used by Teddy sat. Wondering why he hadn't walked beside her except for the great view he'd had of her rear, Trin trailed Josee into the princess room like a loyal servant waiting for a command.

His mind immediately leapt to imagining the woman of his dreams stretched out on the golden bedspread with her hair loose and straight down to her waist and not much else covering her body, slim except for her full breasts which he knew she'd inherited from her mother, not paid for from a plastic surgeon. Not that he'd ever seen Josee fully naked—just close to it in those swimsuit issue pictures and the bikinis she wore around the pool. He quickly stepped behind a large, black case with many drawers to hide his rapid arousal. The guys he worked with on projects always said his imagination was the best for creating new scenarios. Now, he had to tamp that talent down.

"This the case you want moved?" He raised it by the handle and hoped Josee noticed his new and improved muscles bunching from the sleeves of the red Camp Love Letter T-shirt issued to everyone on the first day. The heart of the logo rested right over his own, rapidly beating, while hers spanned over her chest, perfectly calm.

"Um, yes, but it has wheels and is very heavy. I had to bring makeup for all sorts of skin tones, not only mine. All of my stuff fits in that little bag in the bathroom. No need to strain yourself."

"It's no strain at all." Okay, it was. She didn't need to know that.

"Please put it down before you get a hernia, Trin."

A third voice intruded. "I thought I heard people

talking over here. You need some help with that, bro?" Bad boy Mack Billodeaux leaned into the doorway, filling it with his height, his brawn, his thick mane of black hair, his father's killer smile.

Trinity set the case down. "No, it has wheels. I'm taking it over to the pool house for Josee's workshop."

"I don't need to use the wheels." Mack tugged at the handle still possessed by Trin's slim keyboard fingers.

Josee seized one wrist each and removed their hands. "We're using the wheels. In fact, I can manage by myself. One of you call the elevator for me."

Fat chance he had of getting around Mack and out of the room to do that service first. Mack pivoted and dashed for the elevator button as if he had a big score to make. Josee put out a hand to prevent Trinity from making a race of it. "You wheel the case. It doesn't take two to press a button."

The thing steered awkwardly, but the lift waited for them with Mack inside holding the door open. The cab wasn't large. The three of them and the cumbersome case filled it. Once down, they took the exit to the outside path rounding the house. Mack batted at his hand as if he tried to strip a football. Trinity hung onto the handle, not about to give it up. As they approached the staging area, he spied X-avier with a huge, welcoming smile on his face.

"Hey, Mack. Nice to meet you off the football field." X held out a friendly hand. "How about giving me an assist with the family of four kids and a mountain of luggage?"

"I guess I can do that. Josee, see you later." Mack didn't catch the broad wink that said X-avier had already put his play into motion, giving Trin time to spend with the dream girl.

They continued on to the pool house with the case wobbling erratically and sometimes straying off the path and getting caught in the grass. Trin manfully heaved it out each time. Finally, Josee added her touch to the handle and said, "Let me help steer. Between the two of us, we can do this."

Their pinkies touched on the grip. Did Josee feel that jolt, the same one that went all the way to Trinity's groin. No telling with women, but probably not. Men goggled as she passed, and one little boy piped up, saying, "You a pretty lady." Josee smiled her cover girl smile and told him he was a very handsome boy. She did things like that, accepted compliments gracefully and returned them, a skill X said he should be working on, but he couldn't come up with anything great on the spot. All that came to his lips was, "That's nice of you."

Josee shrugged her perfect shoulders, not too broad, not too thin. "I like children. They say what they mean."

"Yeah, Jessie says I'm good with kids." Wait, what? He'd given himself a compliment, not her.

She replied neutrally, "I'm sure you are."

How many times had X drilled into him to make the conversation about the girl, not himself. "No talkin' about computers, how Mack picked on you as a child, how much you get paid. Boring, pathetic, and she'll think you're lyin' about your income like guys who claim to be surgeons."

Not paying attention as he struggled with his gaffe, one of the wheels of the obstinate cart ran over his big toe. He sucked up the pain he deserved.

"Did you injure yourself?" Josee turned to him with concern in her voice.

"Nope, just fine." Jesus, that hurt.

They reached the pool, as blue and calm as a mountain lake, no swimming until tomorrow when dozens of kids would break its surface sending up waves and spume from their play. Those unable to jump in on their own had access to a ramp and a hoist if need be. Camp Love Letter tried to accommodate all its guests. Trin reached over the fence and opened the latch set high enough to thwart small children. They waggled the case to the roomy pool house and over the threshold.

He took an unmarked key from a peg board and opened a closet that already held six laptops on a high shelf. "We should stow this here to keep children out of it."

"Good idea. I loved getting into my mother's makeup when I was little. Once I wrote all over her bedroom walls with red lipstick and decorated myself head to toe. It didn't come off of me very well or the walls. I cried, thinking I'd be spotted for life. Mom said just for a few days—and I'd have to help repaint the wall as a punishment—but it was fun. However, she'd made a point. If you make a mess, you clean it up. I wish I'd listened to her more often."

"Sounds very much like the Billodeaux code of conduct. We mucked out a lot of stalls. Even Teddy had to take out the trash and help in the kitchen if he got into trouble, which rarely happened. He was a lot less bother than the rest of us."

She agreed. "Always positive, always a smile on his face."

"How do you see me?" He'd done it again, turned the conversation toward himself. Too late now.

"Highly intelligent, very imaginative."

He couldn't help himself. "How about Mack?"

"Sexy as hell, but immature."

Satisfied, Trin did try to turn the conversation back to her. "I think you are beautiful inside and out." Again, not very original, though he meant it.

"Thanks. The first is an accident of nature, but I do work on the second. What's next?"

His great imagination prompted him to lock the pool house door. Plenty of yoga mats and towels around, enough to make a bed, stretch out, get naked. He said, "Lunch with the guests. First day is always hotdogs and hamburgers, chips, and watermelon for dessert." He headed outside before he acted on his fantasy.

"Sounds good to me."

"I didn't think you'd eat stuff like that."

"What, real food? From time to time, then I exercise it off. Frankly, it was easier when I was younger. I could eat anything I wanted and never gain an ounce, but it's getting harder. Really, I'm near the end of my career and believe that might be a good thing."

"But you're still gorgeous. Why would you quit?"

"I might have a few years left, but once I reach thirty, it's over. I'd rather leave on my own terms while I'm still on top. The swimsuit issue photographed in Samoa helped me to decide. On the way back, the old lecher who did the photography hit on me, a guy named Dexter Sykes. He used to be my mother's partner until he took credit for some of her work back before she met my dad. He also took pictures of her nearly nude, just covered in sand, and replicated that pose with me. Being under contract, I couldn't refuse."

"Hey, I saw those photos of your mom. Sorry to say they're still all over the internet. Just search Stevie Riley, and they pop up." He'd seen Josee's and cut them out of the magazine.

"And you've done that?"

Trin could see he'd dropped a few feet in Josee's estimation. "Mack did it too! I mean years ago, we both had kind of a crush on your mom, so tall, blonde, and Nordic," he blurted out. "Sorry, teenage guys do that sort of shit."

"I'm aware. I have two brothers. When Mom objected to my going into modeling at the age of sixteen, she warned me about getting involved with male photographers, but I insisted and got my dad's consent to sign with the Amberello Agency. He said I had to make my own decisions. I think your dad might have swayed my mother, too, though I don't know how."

Trin nodded. "Yeah, an agency created by one of my father's old girlfriends and your mother's former boyfriend." He'd carefully not used the term lovers, the truth of the matter.

"How do you know all this?"

Trin wiggled his fingers as if he typed on a keyboard. "I'm good at research."

"But why would you…?"

Saved by the bell, or rather the triangle that clanged signaling lunch. "We'd better move, or we'll be at the end of the line." He took off in his athletic shoes so fast the long-legged Josee in her high wedge sandals barely kept up.

Why would he? Because he wanted to know everything about Josee and her family down to the last detail. Anything that would give him an edge with her, and what had he chosen to reveal? That he'd lusted after her mother once upon a time.

They arrived late at the barbecue pavilion. Mack stood at the head of the line ready to enter and fill his plate. He waved in their direction as if he were about to make a sensational catch. "Josee, I'll let you in ahead of me."

"Children first," she called back. "Save a table for us."

She'd stayed with him, not marvelous Mack, a miracle right here before his near-sighted eyes disguised by prescription sunglasses. Josee spoke to those both in front and in back of them as they inched forward. She let some of the kids into the line. Trinity had no problem with that, more time to spend with Josee.

Once inside, she selected a cheeseburger heavily topped with tomato, lettuce, a little onion, but no mayo or ketchup, pickles on the side, no chips, and a Diet Coke. Trin dressed a burger with ketchup and mustard only, added pickles, snagged a hot dog with mustard and relish, two bags of Zapp's chips in case Josee changed her mind, and the same Diet Coke, usually his soft drink of choice, along with Mountain Dew. See, they did have one thing in common.

Mack had saved a table among the many rented for Camp Love Letter. A paper plate with two loaded burgers reserved the place next to him. A single can of Coke rested across the table. As Josee approached, he removed the burgers and motioned to the spot. “You’re the can of Coke, Trin. Should be Diet, I guess.”

With no choice left, Trinity went to the opposite side of the table while Josee slid in next to Mack. Mack attacked his two burgers and a brace of hot dogs. He washed them down with the full-leaded Coke and snagged his brother’s extra bag of chips. “I’m training. I need the calories,” he explained/boasted to Josee. “Trin sits on his butt all day to make a living.”

“Yet, he is still so slim.”

“Yeah, he has the metabolism of a hummingbird.”

“I love hummingbirds.”

“Yeah, great birds. They can fly backward,” a new voice added. “Mind if I take a seat?” X-avier sat down across from Josee before anyone answered and offered his hand across a pyramid of hot dogs. “I don’t think we’ve been properly introduced. X-avier Hopkins. Call me X.”

“Also known as the Missile. I do watch the Sinners games whenever possible. You truly made a difference on the team this year and helped them win the Super Bowl. Josee Riley.” She grasped his hand and shook it lightly.

“Way more famous than me.”

“Not for long, I think.”

“Thank you. I’d like to last long enough and make enough touchdowns to be in the Hall of Fame one day.”

“That’s my goal, too. Trin, do they have one of those for computer geeks?” Mack taunted.

No good retort came to mind, but X dove in to save him. “You got anything going on after lunch, my man? I need to go into town for a few things. Maybe you could show me where to find them.”

"Usually my mom has a stockpile of…" Trinity got an elbow to the ribs. "Ah, no, my first computer class isn't until two. I have two back to back."

"Great. Soon as I finish eating, we'll get on the road. Wouldn't want to make you late."

Mack didn't miss his chance. "How about you, Josee? I'm lifeguarding at the pool. We can hang out unless you need to be somewhere."

"My makeup class starts at two also. I might as well be in the area."

Brinsley, the British Billodeaux butler, approached and offered around a tray of watermelon slices. Wearing sandals with socks, Bermuda shorts, and a Hawaiian shirt wild with tropical flowers, he'd loosened up considerably since joining the family. However, his presentation had not. "Would you care for some fruit, Miss Josee, Mister Mack, Mister Trinity, Mister X-avier?"

Josee selected a wedge and thanked him. Mack took a piece and spit out the first seeds he encountered. He finished his in a few big bites while Trin still picked at his portion with a plastic fork. "Why don't we mosey over to the pool? That's what they say in Texas where I play for the Cowboys."

"Yes, as I am well aware." Did Trin detect a bit of coolness in her reply? He hoped so.

Mack offered Josee a hand up that moved to her shoulders as they walked away. Sadly, she didn't push it off.

Trinity scowled at X. Wasn't he supposed to be helping him get time with Josee? In response, he received a big grin and another poke under the table. He waved away the offer of watermelon. "Don't like it much. Imagine that." X-avier polished off his mound of wieners and two bags of chips. "Let's go."

"Where? What do you need? I swear my mom has enough supplies to survive nuclear war."

X-avier cocked his head and studied Trinity. "Know a good barber in Chapelle?"

"We've got a barber or two. How good they are, I can't say."

"That's obvious."

"You getting rid of the fro?'

"Nope. We'll take my car."

Chapter Three

Xavier drew his red Camaro alongside the high curb in front of the shop with a traditional striped barber's pole. On this somnolent summer day when the heat raised the tar bubbles in the street, not many cars competed for parking space. "Mind you don't scrape my paint on the cement, Trin."

Trinity wormed his way out through the narrow space left between the car and the curb.

They took the three sagging wooden steps up to the raised frame building and woke Ike, the barber, from a midday snooze in one of the three chairs awaiting clients. Rather than giving them a pleasant *Bonjour*, the elderly man eyed X-avier and said, "Me, I don't do those fades or carve thunderbolts in nobody's hair."

"Fades are over, man. Fros are back." X-avier drew a pick from a pocket and fluffed his hair. "I am in no need of your services. This young man is." He pushed Trinity forward. "I'm thinking clip up the sides and leave the curls on top, like a young Tony Curtis."

Behind his bifocals, the barber's faded blue eyes lit. "You know Tony Curtis?"

"Sure. *Some Like it Hot*, *Boston Strangler*, great movies. But we don't want the strangler look. Leave some curls to dangle over his forehead."

Ike pressed Trinity into one of his vacant chairs and unfurled a cape with a snap. He picked up a comb and drew it through Trin's mop with relish. "I know these curls. The boy got his first cut here with me. Inherited those curls from his daddy." Ike gestured with the comb toward a wall full of Joe Billodeaux photos in his football glory days, all autographed, and a few of his brothers, Dean, Tom, and Mack, too. "His daddy always keeps his cropped short, but this boy, he don't come in here often enough. Take off the shades, son."

Trin removed his glasses. His face in the mirror blurred as Ike started clipping away at his forest of hair. "Hey, don't I have a say?" He half rose from his seat. "Maybe I like my hair the way it is."

"You don't want to be Mack or your dad. You want your own look," X-avier asserted. "Ike here knows what he's doing. Let the man work."

Ike pressed his customer back into the chair. "*C'est vrai*, the truth." The barber continued to clip. Mounds of curls fell to the floor. "Tony Curtis," he murmured, shutting his eyes for a moment, which did not reassure Trin, staring hard at him in the mirror.

"Leave it kind of high on the top. Give the man an extra inch or so of height," X-avier directed as he flipped through the *Playboys* hidden under the *Field and Stream* magazines on a shabby table placed between waiting area chairs. He held one up that Trin really couldn't see. "This has old Vargas girls illustrations—vintage."

"*Mais*, yeah, the man knew how to paint the ladies, better than the photographs. Say, ain't you the Sinners' Missile?" Ike chatted as he evened the curls on top. He paused to tap his forehead with the scissors. "X somebody."

"X-avier Hopkins at your service." He executed a

small bow from his place lounging against the wall as if he feared the aged wooden chairs wouldn't hold him upright.

Ike and X were having quite the love fest. Trin felt nearly as left out as when Mack cornered Josee at lunch. He only hoped the barber didn't become so distracted with his friend's charm that he made a bad, irreparable snip.

"I like your style, X. Respectful." Ike massaged some kind of goop into Trin's hair, making his curls stand on end. He sculpted a few to dangle over his customer's forehead. "Not many of my regulars use this stuff. I'll throw in a tube of it in exchange for an autographed picture if you got one."

"Oh, I got one—out in my car."

Trin threw him a desperate "don't leave me alone" glance, but X went on his way and returned with the photo. He found a pen near the cash register and wrote on it. "To Ike, the best barber in Chapelle. Yours truly, X-avier Hopkins," he read and offered it to Ike.

Ike wiped his hands, studied the inscription, and laid the picture aside to finish his job. "Nice, gonna go on my wall." Ike powdered Trin's neck and removed the cape. He spun the chair toward X for approval. "All done. I made you a new man. Don't be so long next time, Trinity Billodeaux. Twenty dollars."

Trin replaced his glasses, not sure he liked the new man, and grubbed in his pocket for his wallet. He guessed he had to pay for it regardless.

X-avier beat him to it. "Now that's a forty-dollar haircut if I ever saw one." He handed over the bills. "If I decide to dump the fro, you're my man, Ike." He left the elderly barber smiling.

Out in the glaring sunshine, Trinity grumbled, "I can pay for my own haircuts," as he eased into the Camaro again. The interior had heated enough to bake bread on the dashboard. "I hope this stuff doesn't melt," he said regarding the tube of gel Ike had pressed into his hand on the way out.

"Wouldn't know. Not my style, but I think it's yours. Let's go see what Miss Josee has to say about it." X ramped up the air-conditioning.

He swore his topknot didn't move as the blast of cold air hit his face. Yeah, what would Josee think of the new Trinity Billodeaux?

****

He sort of hoped he'd find Josee lounging in a very brief bikini by the pool when he went to set up the laptops for his class. No such luck, but maybe better than having Mack showing off his manly perfection in a Speedo ogling her from the lifeguard stand. He found her inside dragging dividers into place to separate her makeup area from his computer tables.

"Let me help you with those, but I don't think they're necessary. I'd like to watch you transform people, and my kids will be so engrossed they won't be looking at anything but their screens." He switched out his sunglasses for his geek glasses. It had to be done.

"Women want their privacy when they are having a makeover. Speaking of which, you've gotten one of your own. You remind me of somebody, but I can't think of who." Josee cocked her head, pondering.

"It's only a haircut. I get them all the time." Now, he'd outright lied to her. He often forgot, hadn't even remembered for Annie's wedding.

"A new style, then. I like it." She sniffed his neck.

"Baby powder?"

"No, no! Ike always dusts customers with talcum after a cut, but I'm glad you approve."

That settled it. He'd be Tony Curtis forever if Josee liked the look. Her assessment gave him new courage. "Ah, you want to go to the movie with me tomorrow night in the home theater? It's the one about the lost clown fish with the deformed fin. Mom always shows films about overcoming adversity during the summer. There will be popcorn."

"Sounds nice. I love that movie, but Mack asked me to go to a place that has music and dancing on Saturday night. Maybe the next movie." She left him with a smidgen of hope.

Their class members, some on crutches, some in wheelchairs, some under their own power, began to filter into the pool house. They milled around waiting for directions.

"The next one is the sequel, the Dory movie," he said before turning to his class. "Computer kids over here. Take a seat in front of one of the laptops." Trin moved fast to remove a chair for a boy in a wheelchair, not needing it.

"I'd like to see that movie. My class, assemble behind the dividers."

Was that a date? He wasn't sure. He had five little boys and one girl to settle. Her group consisted of older girls, some teens, and their mothers, tired and washed out from caring for a special needs child, plus one unaccompanied boy obviously bald under a ballcap pulled low over his eyes. They filed behind the dividers.

As he showed the children the very basics of

computers and explained the terminology, he heard plenty of oohs and aahs from Josee's area. He set his up with e-mail addresses and had them send notes to each other to get the hang of it. While they were engrossed, he peeked behind the divider, caught Josee's eye, and was ordered out. "We'll show you when we're done." She appeared to be giving a haircut. Maybe next time, he'd ask her to do his.

He went back to his students and directed them to a few simple games that came with the software to develop their skills with the keyboard and wireless mouse like tic-tac-toe and hangman. He figured they were too young for solitaire and would find it boring anyhow. They explored some search engines and clicked on safe and interesting sites he knew. When their session ended, he gave them handouts about what they'd learned and encouraged them to keep in touch with each other through e-mail. He also warned them of some of the dangers of the internet and made them pledge to tell their parents if a stranger tried to contact them or they got into a site that made them uncomfortable.

As his mom had asked, he'd made a checkmark next to each name if the child did not have access to a computer. Many were homeschooled because of their illnesses and had financial difficulties that didn't allow for electronic luxuries. He surmised that they'd be getting a surprise in the mail after getting home courtesy of Camp Love Letter, but the always practical Nell did not want kids signing up for the class just to get a free computer or encourage them to lie if they already had one. Smart woman, his mom.

The members of Josee's class began to file out

from behind the dividers. Some appeared self-conscious, others radiant with joy. Worried mothers had their faces softened with a few wisps of hair covering the wrinkles on their foreheads and the gauntness of their cheeks. Gone were the dark circles under the eyes. Cheeks glowed a healthy pink on all of them, and formerly dry lips shone with gloss. The teen girls had gone for more dramatic looks with extra eye makeup and lip liner.

Clutching his ballcap, the boy came out last. He had hair now, a brown wig cut to suit his face, eyebrows feathered on with pencil, and more color in his face. He alone did not carry a hot pink plastic bag with Josee's name splashed across it diagonally in silver lettering, but an eyebrow pencil jutted out of the top of his shirt pocket. As if needing validation from a man, he turned to Trin. "You think I look okay, not girlie or anything?"

"You look fine. And don't worry, your hair will grow back. Miss Nell was a cancer patient as a kid, and she has plenty of curls now."

The boy threw an envious glance at Trin's mop top. "I'd like to have hair like yours."

"Believe me, curls are a curse. I hope you get something better."

The kid smiled with slightly shiny lips, not gloss, but maybe lip balm. Josee had come prepared for any need. She appeared behind the boy and gave his shoulder a squeeze. "My most successful makeover. Remember light, feathery strokes for the eyebrows, not hard lines. You were very brave to come to the class alone, Reed. Now, go show your mom how great you look."

“She’ll cry.” Reed came in for a hug. “I think I’ll love you forever.” Josee returned the embrace before sending him on his way.

Trin felt a twinge of envy. He turned to straightening up his table, putting down fresh handouts for the next class, and placing pencils in a basket to clear the space. “I have an older group next. You?”

“About the same, no boys though. I guess most of the guys who lose their hair just try to go with the biker look.”

“Nice of you to give them free cosmetics.”

“Oh, I get a ton of samples from the company in exchange for endorsing my product line. Sometimes I have wigs left over from photo shoots when they want me with short hair or a different color.”

Repressing the urge to stroke her long, blonde ponytail, Trin said, “I can’t imagine why they’d want to do that.”

“Yep, every man’s fantasy, a woman with long, blonde hair.” She swished that ponytail as she shook her head.

“I’d love you even if you went bald.” What a slip. He hoped she took it as a compliment, not a declaration of his feelings. Not time for that yet.

“That’s sweet. Here come our next groups. See you after.”

“It’s Fish Fry Friday tonight and the bonfire with singalong afterward. X-avier is running that. You coming?”

“Wouldn’t miss it. Maybe we can eat together again.”

“Positively.” All around, a great day even with the Tony Curtis haircut.

Chapter Four

Wearing a shower cap to preserve his haircut, Trin stepped out of the shower and girded his loins with a towel. He made an oval on the moisture-clouded mirror surface. Leaning in close, he inspected his face and smiled at his black scruff, wondering if he should shave or go for the tougher look. He might not have big muscles, but he could probably compete in a beard-growing contest with any of his brothers, except Teddy who had facial hair so light it rarely showed.

The happy from yesterday held overnight. Josee had dinner with him—and Mack because he'd horned in again. She did eat the crispy catfish with some slaw, avoided the potato salad, and accepted a diet drink with ice cream for dessert. He kept track of these details in case a real dinner date loomed sometime in the future. Maybe he'd order for her, exactly the foods she liked.

Josee could sing, at least better than he did. She joined in enthusiastically as X played guitar and led the campers in easy songs with the bonfire blazing behind him. Now, that man had a voice. Trin wasn't jealous since he knew X wouldn't go after the woman his friend adored, even if the running back did tease Teddy by flirting with Jessie. In a flash, Jess lost control of Lizzy who slid from her lap and dashed toward the fire. He'd grabbed the toddler before she came to any harm, but Lizzy really hadn't been heading for the light. She demanded to be put down by X to make a request. "Sing Lizzy song, X."

"Not sure I know that one." X-avier glanced toward Jessie for help.

"It's something I made up when she was a baby—just the old folk song *Little Liza Jane*, but I changed the chorus to 'Oh my Lizzy, li'l Lizzy Jane.' You get the idea."

"Sing," Lizzy demanded with a pat to his knee.

X did, getting the crowd to join in the chorus. When Lizzy insisted, "Again," he repeated the performance, but Teddy rolled up and whisked his daughter away before she could request another encore. "Come on, Lizzy Jane. Bedtime. Mommy will sing it to you at home before you go to sleep."

"Okay." She followed that with a yawn. Teddy's family moved toward their house.

"That was so dear," Josee remarked when he returned to the blanket where they sat. "You were really quick in heading Lizzy off. Everyone thought she was attracted to the flames."

"Turned out she wasn't, so not a hero tonight."

"Maybe another night."

Time to make a move, but when he slid his arm behind her back, he encountered Mack's hand making the same gesture. They tussled for dominance in the dark. Neither won.

"Cut it out, you guys. Go play somewhere else if you aren't going to listen to the music." Josee shifted herself to another part of the blanket. Not a step forward, but Mack hadn't gotten ahead of him either.

Grinning into the mirror, Trinity decided a scruff didn't suit the Tony Curtis vibe and lathered up to shave after removing the shower cap. Yawning and stretching, Mack sauntered, completely naked, into the bathroom. His first move wasn't to use the toilet. His brother ripped Trin's towel from his waist and used it to snap his butt. That did smart, but he didn't flinch, always a mistake with bullies—and he'd had lots of experience in that area. Instead, he studied Mack's penis and remarked, "We're exactly the same length, and mine appears bigger because it isn't dwarfed by muscular thighs."

"No way!"

"We can settle this. Get a ruler."

"I will." Mack thudded into the bedroom on the far side of the shared bath.

Trin turned the privacy lock and hurried to do the same to the hall door and the one that led to his bedroom. Brains over brawn. Humming *Little Liza Jane*, he shaved while Mack pounded on the door demanding entrance.

"I swear I'll beat you with this ruler if you don't open up! I have wheelchair basketball with Teddy's group in an hour. I need to take a piss and shower."

"Threatening to beat me gives me no incentive to open that door. This house has plenty of bathrooms. Use one of those."

"Fine, I will—the one next to Josee's room."

"Okay, okay. Put the ruler away. I'm nearly finished in here." Big mistake.

Mack surged into the bathroom, a bull released into the arena, and wacked him on the arm with the ruler, mussed his hair too. Trin shoved him against the double sinks. "Stay away from Josee's room!"

A voice as lovely as the person who owned it

sounded from the hall. "Did someone mention my name?"

That jerk, Mack, opened the bathroom door wide and lined himself up next to Trin, both of them naked. He offered the ruler. "Who is longer, me or my brother?"

Josee held out a hand. "Give me the ruler because it seems like a tie."

Smirking, Mack handed it over—and Josee rapped his knuckles like an avenging nun. She caught Trinity with her backswing as disgust curled her perfect lips. "You figure it out. I'm going for breakfast. I hear we're having sausage." Back stiff, no sway to her hips, she moved toward the staircase.

Across the hall, T-Rex, their teen little brother, poked his head out of his room. "Can't a guy sleep for an extra hour?" He took in the sight of his two nude brothers and called to his twin sister, "Edie, don't come out here. The boys are out of control again."

Edie's muffled voice replied, "Not interested. I'm printing out today's schedules. Trin, you have camp newsletter interviews this afternoon and lifeguarding this morning. Better get moving." She sounded remarkably like their mother.

He did. "The bathroom is all yours, bro."

No sweat getting dressed. Trin pulled on the camp T-shirt and jeans over his swim trunks, adding flip-flops for his feet since he'd be poolside half the day. Taking a little extra time, he added a tad of gel to his curls and used the pick X had given him to lift them up again. He'd be having breakfast with Josee before Mack finished in the shower—if he could face her.

He took the stairs and angled toward the kitchen

where Corazon, their Hispanic housekeeper, cook, Xochi's mother-in-law, Knox Polk's wife, their everything, placed a large platter in the center of the long table that once served a family of fourteen for breakfast. The menu for today was as stated, pancakes and plump sausages. Coffee, help yourself, on the counter. Pitchers of orange juice and milk already sat next to the butter and syrup.

Trin took a place across from Josee who sipped coffee cloudy with milk. He took utensils from a basket and a plate from the stack, loaded it with a couple of large pancakes and a trio of sausages. Before he spread the butter and poured on the syrup, he made his apology to Josee who hadn't offered so much as a good morning. "I'm sorry for that scene upstairs. Mack has a locker room mentality. I challenged him, and he can't stand that."

Josee raised her brows at him. "As I said, seemed like a tie. I now know more about both of you than I wanted to know. However, since I have an older and younger brother and been out in the world among male models, nothing astonishes me anymore when it comes to men. So, apology accepted." She selected one of the smaller pancakes, adding the lightest skim of butter and a few drops of syrup, and began eating without further comment.

"No sausage?" Why did he say that?

"I no longer have an appetite for it." Josee did pour a large glass of juice to fill in her breakfast.

"You still going dancing with Mack tonight?"

"If he apologizes for his boorish behavior."

With his long ringlets still damp and still sexy, the boor entered the kitchen. He'd retained his manly scruff and stuffed himself into a T-shirt a size too small to show off his abs. Trin waited for him to make an ass of himself again, but even Mack, usually oblivious to the emotions of others, noticed the frigid atmosphere at the table. He filled his plate with a short stack and piled on the sausage, but ducked his head before saying, "Sorry, Josee, if I embarrassed you. Things between Trin and me got out of hand. Are we still on for tonight?"

With a hefty arm, Corazon whapped him with a wooden spoon on the back of the head. She had that privilege, having helped with the raising of all the Billodeaux children from Dean on down. "What you do to Miss Josee, bad boy?"

"We sort of exposed ourselves."

"We? He's the one who opened the door," Trin said, defending himself. He noticed the ruler lay next to Josee's plate and half expected her to wield it on his knuckles again. Corazon frowned at him. He knew the Billodeaux kids had helped put those deep grooves into her broad, brown face and probably the wide gray streaks in her black hair.

"You, Trinity, I ashamed of you."

"Yes, ma'am. I've already apologized." He finished his breakfast and rose to make his escape.

Corazon's brown eyes softened. "Always a good boy, always on the computer. Wait to go in the water for one hour."

"That's an old wives' tale, Corazon, but thanks for caring." He carried his plate and glasses to the sink and lingered a moment waiting for Josee's answer to Mack's question.

"Yes, we can go dancing, but when I want to see what you have to offer, I'll let you know." She blotted her lips on a napkin and also bused her dishes. "I have another makeup class this morning." She headed for the outer door.

Trin, right on her heels, said, "I'm going that way. See you later, Mack." He'd been forgiven. Good enough for now.

****

Trin climbed on the lifeguard stand and put the whistle claimed from the office around his neck. He'd chosen a sun visor instead of a hat to preserve his do. Although olive-complexioned like most of the Billodeauxs, he slathered on sunscreen. None of the college girls hired as aides for the summer offered to help the way they did Mack. Not that he cared. The only woman who mattered was laying out makeup in the pool house. He placed his sunglasses on his nose and motioned to one of the girls to open the gate.

Kids of all ages, sizes, and mobility surged inside. Some were the brothers and sisters of the sick children. A few of those cannonballed into the water. He blew his whistle. "No more cannonballs. The pool is too crowded." He'd say that over and over throughout the morning. One of the aides lowered a wheelchair bound boy into the water while another helped an unsteady child down the ramp. They'd stay near their charges as long as the kids wanted to be in the pool. Another ran a snack bar doling out free ice pops and bottles of water.

Time passed slowly, but he stayed vigilant, shifting his eyes from one end of the pool to the other, trying to see of anyone showed signs of distress. When Josee's class let out, he gave her a thumbs-up for her achievement and scanned the pool again. In that brief moment, a child had gone under. He saw the dark shadow in the bottom of the deep end and prayed the kid only held his breath, but no air bubbles escaped.

Throwing his visor and glasses aside, Trinity surged off the stand, and blowing his whistle to clear the way, dove into the pool, forcing himself to the bottom, feeling for the child. He cupped the boy's chin and brought him up and out of the water in classic lifeguard fashion and began CPR immediately. The kid came around quickly, spitting out some water and a breakfast that appeared to be Rice Krispies. When Trin glanced up, he found himself surrounded by a crowd, among them Josee with her arm around the frantic mother who'd been in her makeover class.

"I should have stayed out here. His sister was supposed to be watching him, but Trace always thinks he's stronger than he is. No deep water, I said. I should have kept an eye on him." She broke away from Josee and went to kneel by her son and Trinity. "Thank you, thank you."

Nurse Shammy, who staffed a first aid station in the pool house, pushed through the crowd, her white and very old-fashioned nurses' garb giving her authority. She'd been the triplets' baby nurse and had once taken a bullet for the Billodeauxs, which translated into a place at the ranch for however long she wanted to work. Semi-retired, she shared a small house just outside the gates with Brinsley, her husband. Though up in years, she squatted by the child fairly nimbly and applied a stethoscope around her neck to the thin chest. "Sounds good, but we'll send him to the hospital overnight to be sure. Good work, my baby."

It wasn't easy to cull a compliment from Nurse Shammy, as starchy as her uniform. Trin suspected that being the most critical of the triplets and needing the most care, he'd become her favorite, though Shammy would scarcely admit that. The "my baby" gave her away no matter how much it embarrassed him with Josee standing nearby, but his dream girl didn't laugh. Her pink lips parted. "My hero," she said before returning to the pool house to welcome her next class.

"And mine," the mother echoed, wiping away much of her makeup, destroyed by tears, on the edge of a towel someone had handed her.

"It's what we're trained to do," he answered modestly, though it was true. Tiny Edie could hoist a drowning full-sized male from the pool if need be. Before he went to climb the stand again, he announced, "Watch out for your buddies. Know where they are, okay?"

Josee ate lunch with him, no Mack around because his brother had moved from wheelchair basketball to the football toss and catch. Mack got to spend all morning with Dad, but Trinity would choose Josee's company any day. She didn't seem to notice the many curls dangling across his forehead since his dive into the pool.

The caterers had laid out huge trays of cold cuts, cheeses, toppings, and a variety of breads and rolls for do-it-yourself sandwiches. Plenty of fresh fruit and veggies were available, but the tray with giant chocolate chip cookies was emptying fast. Trin snagged two for himself and Josee who worked on making a chef's salad by piling ham, roast beef, turkey, and cheese on the top of a large plate of greens. She garnished it with olives, cherry tomatoes, tiny sweet pickles, and a dash of vinegar and oil. Trinity slapped together two sandwiches, ham and cheese on rye and roast beef on a Kaiser roll, threw a handful of baby carrots on his plate, done.

"Grab two Diet Cokes. I'll show you a quiet place to eat." He led the way around the house to a bench in the shade of a live oak not too far from the threshold of the porch.

"Oh, this is where you buried your dogs," Josee remembered, but two small markers helped her make the connection.

"Not my dogs, really. Macho belonged to Tom, and Titi came here with Stacy, but in the end, they belonged to all of us." He recalled X's advice. Ask about her. "Do you have a dog?"

"No, I've been traveling too much. You?"

"Always at work either for Hartz Technology or on my side hustle, so no."

"And what would that be?"

He found even the way she nibbled her food adorable. He took his eyes off her lips and said, "I'm developing a new game featuring football, but not just football. Each person playing can select an avatar and customize it. They'll have personal lives, too, can choose what position they'll play, what kind of car they drive, form teams with others, date starlets and models."

Josee stopped eating her salad leaf by leaf. "I think you should have female players if this is a fantasy."

"Well, Tom's wife kicks for the Sinners. I guess that could be allowed."

Josee wagged a sweet pickle in his face. "No, women should be able to create avatars any way they want, women quarterbacks and wide receivers, or maybe pretend they are men if they want."

"That's a thought." A startling thought—when had this conversation become all about him again?

"I could help by giving you a feminine perspective."

"You'd have the time for that?"

"I did tell you I'm retiring. I had a tutor traveling with me before I turned eighteen, along with my mom who wouldn't allow my modeling career otherwise. I insisted on going my own way once I finished high school classes. I've been taking business and computer courses online ever since. I must have enough credits to graduate twice from college by now."

"Well, ah, that would be great." Would it? Working close to Josee, great, but what if they argued over the game that had been all his up until now?

Josee finished her salad and eyed the chocolate chip cookies. "I'm retiring." She seized one and took a huge bite. "That is so good."

"Yep, no oatmeal or raisins or nuts. Corazon always baked our cookies, and Mom insisted they contain something healthy. She sometimes sneaked in carrots. But for Camp Love Letter, she says these kids need calories, so she isn't as strict."

"I love your mom. She's one of my role models."

Trin almost said he loved hers but remembered his earlier faux pas and stopped himself. "Yeah, Mom is great. She insisted we all learn CPR and lifesaving. I never had to use it before today."

"When you did, you never hesitated. I so admire that."

"Any of us can do the same. Edie towed Mack out by the hair for her test. Teddy with his upper body strength can do great CPR and probably drag someone to the edge of the pool if he doesn't have his braces on. I really didn't do anything extraordinary."

"You paid attention. Yesterday, I swore Mack spent more time chatting up the pretty aides than he did watching the pool. I'm glad the drowning didn't happen on his watch." She leaned in and gave him a kiss on the cheek, then used her thumb to rub away a trace of chocolate she'd left behind.

Stunned, he simply sat there until he blurted out, "Are you still going dancing with Mack tonight?"

"I told him I would. I always keep my word when I've made a promise. Sorry I'll miss the movie, but we are on for tomorrow night."

So, the kiss meant nothing personal, only a reward for a job well done. "It's Spaghetti Sunday. Bayou-side church service early for those who want to attend, a rodeo after lunch, then the movie after dinner."

"Sounds like fun."

"It is. We used to complain about having to help with the camp when we got into those teen years and wanted to do our own things, but Mom gave us the lecture about all we had and how fortunate we were to be healthy and wealthy, if not wise. Dad seconded that with a big *mais* yeah. No more grumbling, or we were given extra tasks and less free time."

"I'm sorry I went off to do my own thing around then and didn't help before. Say, I need to get to the pool house for my next class."

"I promised Edie I'd start interviewing the families for the newsletter. I'd better get to it."

"I'd begin with the boy you saved. No matter what you say, that was no small thing."

"Maybe. See you later." He didn't have it in him to wish her a good time with Mack.

****

Because hope springs eternal, Trinity saved a place in the home theater for Josee by placing his sun visor on the seat. He checked incessantly to see if she walked in and paid no attention to a side approach. A voice asked, "This seat taken? Because if you saving it for Josee, she done rode off in Mack's Jaguar some time ago."

"The seat is all yours, X. I hoped she'd change her mind, but it appears she always keeps her word." He removed the visor and hung it on the armrest.

"The girl got a mind of her own. Here, I brought you popcorn as a consolation prize." X handed over a striped cardboard container filled to the brim.

"And a brain. Besides being beautiful and kind, she's been studying business and computers. She offered to help with my game development. But I don't know. Up until now I haven't shown it to anyone. Anyhow, she's still way out of my league."

"Accept her offer, fool! Heard you was a hero today. Work with that." X dug into his popcorn.

"Doesn't seem right to exploit a child to get a woman to notice me. I should be taller."

"As my mama would say, you are as God made you. Do your best with what you got. You taking part in that rodeo tomorrow?"

"Hell, no! Being bucked off a bull or scrambling in the dirt to hogtie a calf isn't my idea of fun."

"Is Mack doing any of that stuff."

"Not likely. He has a clause in his contract to protect his legs from dangerous activities."

"Who is then? Your dad?"

"He'll do his comedy routine with Rascal, our trick horse, and Teddy will show how he can get on Rascal and ride. Dad contacted that retired bull rider, Bodey Landrum, who has a place up by Rainbow, to organize a small show for the kids."

X-avier snapped his buttery fingers. They made no sound. "I remember seeing pics of Landrum and his wife in *People*."

"You read *People*?"

"Who don't? I aspire to be their sexiest man alive one day. Anyhow, Landrum ain't no big guy, but his wife is a tall blonde. You know what makes up the difference? Cowboy boots wit' those high heels."

"Those heels keep your feet from slipping through the stirrups. If you get thrown, you won't get dragged. You can dig in with them, too, when you're roping, but they aren't great for walking. I guess cowboys always ride," he informed his buddy.

"You grew up on a ranch. I know y'all ride. Tell me you don't have pair of boots like that."

"They're probably still in the back of my closet here. I didn't take them to Lafayette when I moved."

"Find 'em and see what it like to look Josee in the eye when you're standing up."

The lights dimmed. Except for the crunching of popcorn, the auditorium grew quiet. Trin gave a shrug that X couldn't see in the dark. "Might as well give that a try."

The movie began, telling the tale of a young clown fish with a deformed fin who gets lost and is returned to his loving father with the help of friends he meets on the way.

Not a bad lesson for the kids in the audience. Not a bad lesson for himself either.

Chapter Five

Trin discovered Josee had attended the early bayou-side church service while he slept. Nice that Mack hadn't gotten up either, but he discovered his mistake at breakfast when Josee didn't show. "I guess she stayed out late with Mack," he told Corazon who shoveled eggs, bacon, and a dollop of grits onto his plate.

"Oh, no. Miss Josee is up early and go to church with only coffee and toast in her belly. I offer to make her eggs, but no, off she go." Disapproval of light breakfasts tinged her words.

"Mom and Dad?"

"Went to hear the Reverend Rev preach and X with his singing. X brought his mama to meet me. He is a good son. I feed them both before the service. Only Mack stays in bed so long." She checked her watch. "I be late meeting Xochi and Junior for eleven o'clock Mass. You should come with Mawmaw Nadine."

"Give my apologies to Mawmaw. I have to get ready for the rodeo."

"You already look like a cowboy. What more you need to do?"

He guessed he did, turned out in jeans, a chambray shirt tucked in with sleeves rolled up, and his well-worn boots hooked over a chair rung. He hadn't bothered with the hair gel since his Tony Curtis do would be hidden under a black Stetson with enough dust caught in the leather band to show its authenticity as a real working hat. Once he switched out his glasses for his shades, he'd be all X wanted him to be, and maybe Josee, too.

"Stuff, I have stuff to do. Look, you go to church. I'll clean up the kitchen and feed Mack if he shows up before noon." Which he doubted.

Corazon beamed upon him and pinched his cheek. "You a good boy." She untied her red apron and hung it on a peg, grabbed her keys, and was gone with a happy smile on her face. No doubt Xo and Junior would take her to On the Riverside for lunch, then back to their brightly painted Victorian home in Chapelle to play with her granddaughter for the rest of the day. Nothing Corazon liked better, and she deserved it.

Trin cleared his dishes, wiped down the table, and washed the pans soaking in the sink, familiar tasks since they had been the standard punishment for sassing Corazon or making extra work for the housekeeper. He'd never been mouthy, not like Mack, but he did have a tendency to leave his clothes on the floor and the bathroom a mess, simply because he forgot when his mind wandered to computer games. As he figured, Mack did not show, and he was free to find Josee somewhere on the large estate.

Trinity sashayed over to the barn and the large ring where the rodeo would be held after lunch. The rented bleachers had been delivered and set into place. A tarp provided enough shade to keep the seats from burning behinds. His dad sweated in the broiling sun, helping the King of the Bull Riders, Bodey Landrum, move a temporary chute into place to hold the bull currently chewing its cud in a livestock trailer. Another man as red-haired and freckled as his brother, Tom, assisted. Feeling manly, he offered another hand.

His dad wiped the surprise off his face fairly fast and made introductions all around. Bodey Landrum in his boots stood not much taller than Trinity. His body had grown stockier with age, his hair more salt than pepper, but stunning blue eyes shone out of his tanned face, and his smile still possessed a wicked gleam. The redhead turned out to be the famous rodeo clown, Ty Beck, somehow related to Landrum because his sister had married one of Bodey's boys. Even Trinity recognized the name, and he didn't follow rodeo. He firmed up his handshake and thanked the man for coming, risking his life in the ring with a wild animal.

"Oh, Black Water is old, but canny. He gets the job done, then waits for the gate to open so he can get back to his hay. He'll give a good show, but not much trouble. No blood on the ground today." The bullfighter offered a gap-toothed grin.

Trin could not imagine doing what he did for a living. His tender keyboarding fingers already felt grimy, and he thought he'd picked up a splinter. Imagine how he'd feel if a bull hit him broadside, hoisted him into the air, and left him in the dirt. Hey, that would make a great, visceral computer game. He'd give it some thought.

His father nodded toward the barbecue pavilion. "The caterers are laying out lunch. We have pulled-pork barbecue and burgers along with corn on the cob today. You want to eat before the show?"

Both Ty and Bodey shook their heads. "Not a great idea before a bull ride. You want to ride light, and if you are a bullfighter, run lighter," Landrum explained. "Ty needs to put his getup on. Maybe later, but my wife and granddaughter would appreciate it." He pointed them out, speaking to Mama Nell.

"Oh, Nell will see they get fed. Trin, we should wash up and eat."

Trinity didn't respond immediately. He studied the statuesque woman towering over Nell. Though Mrs. Landrum's hair had gone white early, she still owned a serene beauty. He guessed Josee would resemble her as she aged, and who should join them but the woman he desired. She stooped down to speak to the tiny, tow-headed granddaughter and made her smile.

"Trin? Lunch?" his dad repeated.

"Sure. I'll go over there and escort Mrs. Landrum and the little girl."

"Your mom will…"

Bodey Landrum elbowed Joe. "I think your son has his eye on another lady. Let him do the honors."

"Woo-eee, I recognize her, Josee Riley. I wonder if she likes a man who can make her laugh?" Ty Beck speculated. Good thing for Trinity, the clown didn't want lunch and had to get into costume.

Without waiting for more competition to pile up, he moved toward the cluster of women and tried to get his sashay on again. His mother eyed him up and down and smiled slightly, probably remembering how he'd chafed against helping with ranch work when younger, but she simply introduced Eve Landrum and little Addy Rose, a petite, blonde child who appeared to be around five but proudly asserted she was seven and going to perform in the rodeo. Glancing from her to Josee to Mrs. Landrum, he felt as if he gazed on his beloved in all three stages of her life, none of them bad.

He made his excuse for intruding on their group. "Dad says to get lunch early before the campers start lining up. Let me lead the way." As if his mom didn't know how to get there. Stupid thing to say, but the ladies went along with it.

They filled their plates according to their taste, pulled pork for the adults, a burger for Addy Rose, corn on the cob for everyone, fresh fruit and brownies for dessert. Josee revealed Eve Landrum as a well-known local artist and her youngest son an up-and-coming sculptor. She owned pieces by both of them—which made his collection of sci-fi movie posters and action figures seem pretty juvenile. He didn't mention them.

Joe Billodeaux joined them, dousing his pork sandwiches with his own hot sauce, and cooling it off with a heap of melon balls. "Say Trin, Bodey needs someone to spring the chute to release the bull, then run around to the other side of the arena and open the gate for the animal to exit. Soon as you do either, jump up on the fence and stay out of Black Water's way. How about it?"

Before he could digest what was asked of him and the potential level of danger, Mack loped up looking scruffier than usual and twice as handsome in his ripped jeans and tight tee. He tried to squeeze in next to Josee, but Trinity refused to budge, sending his brother to sit beside Joe. Of course, Mack had overheard and immediately offered to take the bull by its horns if need be.

His dad immediately said, "Don't you have a contract clause that forbids dangerous sports? Besides, you look a little rough this morning. Hard night?"

Josee speared a honeydew ball and remarked before popping it into her mouth, “He had too much to drink at Broussard’s Barn last evening. I took his keys and drove us back here.” Trinity rejoiced, except for the fact that he now knew she could drive a Jag too. His Tesla 3 required no special skills at all.

Joe handed Mack the hot sauce bottle. “Put some of that on your sandwich. Might clear your head. I think we’ll let Trinity do the job since he wasn’t out carousing.”

“Tell me bull riders don’t carouse,” Mack sulked. “It’s just opening a couple of gates, not like I’m riding.”

Eve Landrum offered a long-suffering smile. “I can verify that bull riders do carouse—but not before a rodeo if they are wise. Afterward. If you are done, Addy, we should get you dressed for your part. Wonderful meeting all of you, and Josee, stop by my studio anytime. It’s less than an hour away.”

“I’d love that. Maybe when I’m finished with camp. Just remembered I don’t have a car. My dad dropped me off.”

“I’ll take you.” Both Trin and Mack answered at once.

“Thanks for the offers. I’ve already ridden with Mack, so perhaps Trinity would oblige.”

“Sure,” Mack snorted. “His car is plugged in by the barn. I hope it has enough juice to get you there and back.”

“It’s a Tesla 3, an electric car that runs on clean, sustainable energy,” he explained almost apologetically. “It will get us to Rainbow and back, no problem.”

Josee smiled upon him. “I’m familiar with the

Tesla but haven't ridden in one. That could be fun. Maybe next Saturday afternoon, Eve."

"We'll expect you." Eve Landrum led her granddaughter away toward the motorhome the family brought along, as well as the bull and a horse in trailers.

"Mack, if you are up to it and want to be of some use, help T-Rex saddle the ponies. You can give rides to the kids after the rodeo," Joe stated.

"Is this some kind of punishment? Like you never got drunk."

"I did, but I never endangered my dates. You had precious cargo aboard." Joe flashed the smile that once made women swoon and sometimes still did at his namesake, Josee. He turned a frown on his unrepentant son. "The stalls need mucking too." With that, Joe Billodeaux let Mack know what he thought of men who drank and drove.

They went their own way, he and his father back to the arena, Josee and Nell to claim a seat in the shade, leaving Mack to stew over his late lunch.

****

Trinity leaned against the fence next to the bull chute where Black Water appeared to doze in the confined space. He'd seen his father's act dozens of times, but it still made him and the audience smile.

Riding long-legged, red Rascal, his father opened the show with the usual grand entry, a canter around the ring ending in the horse rearing up on his hind legs when given the cue. Dismounting, Joe announced the participants: the King of the Bull Riders, Bodey Landrum, famous bullfighter, Yippee-Ty-Yi-Yo Beck, barrel racer, Addy Rose Landrum, the 4-H roping team, and of course, Rascal, the wonder horse. Rascal took a bow before the audience, but as soon as Joe stepped in front of him, snatched the cowboy hat from the man's head. They went into their playful routine of Rascal running away with the hat, letting Joe catch up, the two of them tugging for possession, Joe pretending to be frustrated and shooting the stubborn animal with a gun formed from his fingers. "Bang!" At the signal, Rascal promptly fell on his side and played dead. Inevitably, some of the smaller children cried out.

Joe studied his finger. "I didn't know it was loaded. Wanna bet Rascal is faking it?"

"Yes, yes!"

"Stop playing around, Rascal. Get up and show the children what else you can do." Joe gave him the hand signal.

The horse arose, shook off some dust, and knelt down. Teddy approached on his crutches, handed them over to Joe, and mounted the animal. They raced around the arena, slowed down, and wove through the barrels set up for the demonstration to come. He polished off his ride with the same rearing as his father had done. Teddy gave hope to every kid in a wheelchair or braces lined up along the bottom of the bleachers that they might do the same one day. Trin noticed Jessie, with her baby and Lizzy dressed in red on her lap, proud as could be of her husband. As Teddy rode Rascal out of the ring, Joe announced pony rides to follow the rodeo to much applause.

"Now for a real demonstration of barrel racing, Addy Rose Landrum and her Appaloosa, Fancy Feet."

Her long, blonde hair now in a braid and a pink cowgirl hat on her head, the girl, looking mighty small on that big speckled horse, rode hell for leather around the three barrels weaving the cloverleaf pattern far faster than Teddy. She reversed the pattern and did it again. Pretty impressive. His dad invited everyone to meet Addy and Fancy Feet after the show.

The 4-H guys rolled the barrels out of the ring and drove a cluster of sturdy white calves from the ranch's Charolais herd into the arena. The calves formed a tight clump at one end of the corral. The boys mounted up and displayed the skills of the cutting horses they rode, each singling out a calf, isolating it, and holding the animal at the end of a rope while the riders jumped down to tie the calves' feet. Incentive to succeed ran high as each participant got to keep their calf to raise for their 4-H project.

Trinity had seen such demonstrations many times. His gaze roved to the stands where he sought Josee. There she sat on the top row—right next to Ty Beck in his clown getup, face painted white, big red lips, startled black eyebrows, and his trademark of a scarlet kiss stamped on his cheek. Wearing no hat, Beck had gelled his bright red hair into a mass of crazy spikes, no wig needed to be funny. He'd been working the crowd of children. With a burlap sack on his back, he handed out small stuffed toys of the kind a person might win in a claw machine and joked with the kids. Now, he searched his sack and found it empty and made his face tragically sad for Josee who seemed to be assuring him she didn't need a toy. Ty tapped the side of his head as if thinking deeply—and reached under his baggy, blue shirt spangled with stars, to withdraw a fuzzy unicorn. Whatever he said made Josee laugh. He thumped his hands over his heart and pointed to his cheek. Josee granted him the kiss. Shouldn't the clown be down here waiting for the bull ride to begin?

Bodey Landrum sidled up beside him. “About time for our act. I’m putting the cinch strap on Black Water now and will get my bull rope set. When I’m ready, I’ll shout, ‘Go,’ and you open the chute and get out of the way. The rides only last eight seconds at the most, so hustle to the other side of the ring and get that gate open to let the bull exit. Black Water knows the drill, but Ty will encourage him to move in the right direction away from me. Got it?”

“Easy. Doesn’t Ty need to get over here?”

“You rang?” While Trinity talked to Bodey, the bullfighter had made his way down the bleachers and joined them.

Up close, Trin could tell he wore a safety vest, just like Bodey, under his oversized shirt and had knee pads peeking out from beneath his long, red and white-striped shorts. No boots for Ty Beck. He had high-priced running shoes on his feet. Plucking a huge ten-gallon hat from his sack, he set it atop his spikes of hair. “All set.” He climbed over the fence and took up his position to one side.

Trin followed him and grasped the rope that would set the bull, irritated by the cinch strap, free. Bodey, aboard the beast’s back, pounded his bull rope into his gloved hand and settled a black hat with a battered silver concha band tighter on his head. Joe, from outside the ring, explained that the rider had to cling on the bull for eight seconds to win and not touch the animal with his free hand at all.

Trin heard the Go word, drew the gate back, and scrambled over the fence. He hot-footed to the other end of the arena as Black Water shot out with a series of high kicks and when that failed, went into a spin. Refusing to be drawn into the vortex, Bodey clung to the broad back as Joe counted off the seconds for the crowd. The bull straightened out again just as time ran out. Bodey released his rope and vaulted into the dust almost landing on his feet, but not quite. He stumbled. Black Water noticed and lowered his big head crowned with blunted horns to charge, but Ty rushed in front of him, swatting the bull on the nose with his big hat, taunting him with shouts of bully, bully, bully, drawing the animal away toward Trin and the exit gate.

For a second, Trinity froze as the clown and the beast headed his way, but he clambered over the fence and opened the gate. A flash of red caught his eye, a small child squeezed under the lower rail of the arena, crying, “Cow, here cow.” *Lizzy.* He knew he couldn’t cross the opening fast enough to snatch her, but he stepped out of the safety behind the gate and called out to Ty, “Get her!”

The bullfighter did, scooping up Lizzy as if she were part of the act, never slowing as the bull pounded behind him. “Trin, heads up.” He tossed her through the air across the gap. Trinity caught the solid little body of his niece and hoisted her over the fence as the animal bore down on Ty—who calmly stepped aside allowing Black Water’s momentum to carry him into the narrow holding pen on the other side. “Gate, Trin.” Both of them shoved it shut before the bull could change its mind and try to back out, but once inside, the animal calmed, totally losing interest. The crowd cheered over Joe’s narrative about wild rides and heroic bullfighters.

Trinity climbed out of the arena and found Lizzy already in a weeping Jessie’s arms. The baby in her sling added her howls. Teddy pegged his way toward his family as fast as he could.

Jessie wailed, "I couldn't stop her. She's so fast. Maybe I can't handle a toddler. She might have died. All my fault. We should have stayed home where I can keep her safe."

Her words reminded him of the mother of the boy who had nearly drowned. He put his arm around her shaking shoulders and said, "Jess, you and Teddy decided to live on the ranch because there are many hands to help you. Ty's hands and my hands were here to catch her. It's okay now."

Teddy arrived and leaned over on his crutches. Tears drying, Lizzy monkeyed onto his chest and, eyeing Trin, said, "Again?"

"Never again, Lizzy. Bulls are bad animals. You must stay away from them."

Bodey, still dusting himself off, joined them. "Bulls aren't bad. It's just their nature to want to throw a man and charge at him. I had to teach my boys real young to stay out of the bull pen. Want to touch the bull, Lizzy?"

The bold little girl nodded and transferred to Bodey's broad chest. He took her to the pen, let her help remove the cinch strap and touch the bull's flank. Bodey patted animal on its hump. "Good work, Black Water, we both still got it. But, Lizzy gal, you never go into a bull's pen because he'll chase you and maybe hurt you. Understand?"

She nodded and then wanted down to run to her mother. "I touch the bully. Don't go in bully's pen."

"Yes, that's right, Lizzy," Jessie said, still tear-choked, but at least the baby had calmed.

Having made a detour, Ty Beck showed up and held out his huge hat to Lizzy, a rare small child who had no fear of clowns or anything else, Trin thought. "Reach inside." Lizzy put her hand inside and drew out a plush bull toy often sold at rodeos. "Now that is the only kind of bull you play with, got it?"

"Yes, Mister Clown."

Over the speaker, Joe announced the start of the pony rides. Mack led two ponies, a pinto and a palomino toward the ring. T-Rex followed with a dainty, pure white animal given to the first granddaughter to be born, and a sturdy brown Welsh pony generally used by the eldest grandson. Neither were here today to object, and besides, they'd been taught to share as Mama Nell kept saying they couldn't get a pony for every grandchild, now multiplying at a rapid rate. Addy Rose stepped out, bringing Fancy Feet to meet his adoring public. The youngsters lined up, eager to get on the back of a horse no matter what their handicaps. Over the chatter of their excited voices, Joe announced free time until dinner at five-thirty, movie at seven for those who want to attend.

Trinity searched the nearly empty bleachers for Josee, but she'd gone. He didn't think to look behind him until Mack shouted, "Hey, Josee, want to ride my pony?"

There she stood almost eye to eye with him thanks to his high-heeled boots when he turned. Nothing witty or suggestive came to mind, but he could tell she hadn't liked Mack's by the tightness of her face and lack of reply. He settled for "Remember we're meeting for dinner tonight and the movie afterward."

She smiled like the Mona Lisa, mysterious,

enigmatic, unable to be understood by a guy like him. "Naturally I remember. I'm looking forward to sitting with the hero of the day—and yesterday."

He had to admit it. "Ty Beck was the real hero. I only caught Lizzy and shoved her over the fence. Just glad I didn't fumble her like every football ever thrown to me. I should have run in front of the bull to get her."

"That would have been damned stupid because you don't know shit about bucking bulls," said Ty Beck who approached wearing his huge hat again. He tipped it old-time cowboy style. "Miss Josee. Busy this evening? I would so enjoy the pleasure of your company. Promise I'll change my clothes. I'll put my good teeth in for you."

"Sorry, I am otherwise engaged. Maybe another time."

"I'll hold you to that. I figured you as a woman who likes to laugh." Ty tipped his hat again and sauntered off, a real cowboy, a true hero.

He had to give credit where it was due. "That man risks his life every time he goes into the arena—and he's funny and great with kids."

Josee emitted a wistful sigh. "Yes, but I suspect he's a rover with a girl in every rodeo town. He's on the road much of the year and living in that big motorhome. He's the type who will keep at his job until he gets too old or too injured to do it."

"Pretty much like football players," Trin pointed out.

"Exactly. Let's get a spot for spaghetti night."

"I should change and wash up before dinner."

"Do that. I'll save a place. But I do like your boots. They're authentic and have been well-used, the hat, too."

"I'll keep the boots on, but no hat in the movies. See you soon." Moving away, he tried to duplicate Ty Beck's saunter much as a woman might want to imitate Josee's model stride.

Chapter Six

X caught up with Trin again at the pool on Monday morning as he was lifeguarding. He leaned against the lifeguard stand, tall enough to carry on a conversation with his buddy. "So how did spaghetti night with Josee go? Heard you was a hero again, saved our little Lizzy girl. That must have scored you some points."

"I guess it did. She liked my boots. You were right about that. I ditched the western shirt for the evening but left them on. They pinched my toes a little, but I felt no pain with her nearby."

"Now you know what women go through for us when they wear those stiletto heels. You're doing great. I think Mack shot himself in the cojones by getting drunk when he took her out."

"Yeah, I believe so." He allowed himself a smug smile, but never took his eyes off the kids in the pool.

"I was way back in the movie. Did you get your arm around her?"

"Ah, no, but we shared a popcorn. Our fingertips touched."

"Oh, that is too girly a comment even for a sensitive guy like me." X biffed him in the leg just below his baggy swim trunks patterned in goldfish on a yellow background.

"I felt the electricity all the way to my own cojones." He blew his whistle and pointed a finger. "No dunking a smaller kid." Having been a smaller kid, some rules he made up as he went along.

"But did Josee feel the magic? You get a kiss at the end of the evening?"

"On the cheek again, along with a thanks for saving Lizzy." He blew the whistle. "No diving. Too crowded."

"See, you got to be that assertive with her. Next, time she does the cheek kiss, you turn your head and lock lips, understand?"

"Where were you when I needed this advice?"

"I took my mama out for Sunday dinner, then hung with Teddy, Jess, and the Liz. They still plenty shook about what happened. Besides, I didn't want to sit wit' you two in case my natural charm got in the way."

"Thanks for that, but I don't know what to do next."

"Why not take her dancing the same place as Mack, but don't get drunk?"

"First, it's kind of a dive. Second, I am the only one in this family with two left feet. I can push a girl around the floor in a slow dance but have absolutely no sense of rhythm. Tom is fairly bad the way he flails around like a mating whooping crane, but that doesn't stop him. All the other men can dance like my dad—except Teddy of course, but even he thrills a girl in his wheelchair when he takes one on his lap for a spin. I saw that at their wedding. So did you. Hey, hey, no running outside the pool."

X pondered that a moment, fluffed his fro in thought. "You know how long we worked on that first dance of theirs? Hours and hours. We even dressed up one of the kickers in a bridal gown to make sure he wouldn't snag her dress in the wheels. What you need is practice, like any good athlete."

"I'm not a good athlete."

"Anybody can learn, but of course there are those who believe us blacks are born with rhythm in our soul. Thought that might be true until I saw my Uncle Alonzo dance. Not all of us are blessed." X took a folded daily schedule from the pocket of his shorts. "Line dancing classes this afternoon in the pool house. Featuring the Electric Slide, Cotton Eye Joe, the Hokey Pokey, and the Chicken Dance taught by Miss Starr."

"Miss Star must be way over eighty!"

"Good, she'll go slow and probably start with those last two for the kids. Tell me you never did the Chicken Dance or the Hokey Pokey at a wedding."

"Sure, as a kid, but I'd feel pretty silly doing them now." Trin spotted a group racing into the pool area from the sandy palm grove. "Quit running! Wash those feet before you go into the pool."

"Relax, be a good sport, and you'll be scooting your boots in no time. Be sure to wear them."

****

Trinity didn't spot Josee at lunch, but at least knew she wasn't with Mack who entertained some of the camp counselors at his own private table. He glanced toward his brother and made a comment that drew some giggles, causing Trin to assess his clothes: boots, jeans, the camp T-shirt. Maybe he should have worn the chambray again, but no, too dusty and sweaty from yesterday. Too late now. He downed the last of his Diet Coke and headed for the pool house where elderly Miss Starr embraced him in her bony, yet graceful arms.

Miss Starr, a first-class hippie who never reneged

on her beliefs, still wore her hair in a long, silver braid. All of her wrinkles came from smiling. She'd breezed into Chapelle in the sixties and set up a dance school. The town had two already, one for white girls, one for blacks. She made it clear from the start that anyone could attend her classes, which would not be segregated. That made for a rough start, but it turned out white girls wanted to learn "colored" dancing and small black girls pined to become ballerinas. After a while, times changed, and no one cared.

Most Cajun kids learned to dance early from their parents who encouraged them to get out on the floor at weddings and other family events. When Mama Nell realized he simply wasn't catching on to an important part of the culture, she'd sent him to Miss Starr for dance remediation. It didn't take.

"Trinity Billodeaux, so glad you are back for another try."

"I think I'm your only failure, Miss Starr."

"Don't you believe that about yourself. You were at an awkward age and gave up way too soon. Now, we get a second chance."

"Anything I can do to help you set up?"

"Just clear the chairs and tables to the side for me. I have my music all ready to go. So good to see you again all grown up. You know I taught your boss, Jonathan Hartz, to dance. Now that was a challenge. We'll have you kicking your heels in no time at all."

Trim in skinny jeans, very flashy red boots, and garlands of Navajo turquoise jewelry hung over a peasant blouse, Miss Starr moved to the door to welcome her students as they filed in, some in wheelchairs as was a given at any Camp Love Letter activity. She positioned them in the first row with their pushers in the second. Several of the aides were girls who'd lunched with Mack. Lots of mother/daughter combos in the class, but Trinity remained the only guy by the time they got started.

The instructor did indeed begin with the Chicken Dance, where even the wheelchair bound could snap their beaks, flap their wings, wiggle their tailfeathers a bit, and clap their hands while laughing at the silliness. When it came to swinging around, those wheelchairs twirled. Trin caught one and spun it back into position. The girl assisting offered him a sweet smile. Maybe he could get into chicken dancing after all. The Hokey Pokey went well, too. He remembered his right foot from his left. Those in chairs just raised theirs if they could. He had no idea how they'd do the Electric Slide but felt sure Miss Starr would find a way.

She demonstrated the grapevine step, the one he always bungled, right, left, touch, back three steps, touch, scuff and turn. He did get confused, but in the midst of spinning wheelchairs and kids having fun, his awkwardness went largely unnoticed, or perhaps was appreciated as it showed the kids even a grownup could mess up a dance. By the time Miss Starr finished, he thought he had it nailed.

They took a break for lemonade and sugar cookies to replenish their energy. That's when Josee walked into the room. "Hope I'm in time for the last dance," she said, not exactly to him. Several of the girls had been in her makeup workshop and shouted a greeting, "Miss Josee, Miss Josee."

Miss Starr embraced her as she did most everyone. "Absolutely! So happy to have you join our group.

Next, we take on the Cotton Eye Joe which is actually a round dance but can be done in a line. Stomp, kick, triple step, scuffle step, repeat."

Not so easy for the ones in chairs, but they loved the stomp part if they could do it. They linked hands and moved from side to side. Josee latched onto him, and that same electricity shot up his arm, straight to his heart and down to his nether regions. Still no telling if she felt the same.

"Excellent, class! You all did your best. I hope you had fun today. Feel free to take some of those cookies with you. You earned them." Miss Starr turned to pack up her music.

Two tall black girls in the back row, possibly twins, though one wore a bright do-rag that signified a cancer victim, called out, "Miss Josee, you know the Catwalk?"

"Yes, I do, but maybe it's not appropriate for this group."

A chant of "Show us, show us!" rose to fill the room.

"We really don't have the music for it," Josee protested.

Miss Star thumbed through her musical selections. "Yes, we do, right here. The older girls always want this one. Usually, it's done in high heels which adds a delightful clicking sound, but we'll make do with our boots. I'll demonstrate with you."

She started the song, a pretty sexy tune, and a dance full of strutting and hip action that would have turned on any man. Miss Starr kept right up with the long-legged Josee. Trin bet the octogenarian was often requested to perform at the assisted living places where she'd definitely get any sluggish blood moving, maybe to inappropriate places. He knew where all his had gone watching Josee. They finished to huge applause. Josee's fans engulfed her.

Marveling again at her many talents, he simply stood to the side watching. The aide with the wheelchair patient who'd been dancing next to him paused as she passed. "Hi, I'm Jania. Your brother called you Super Geek, but you were so sweet to come here and clown for the kids. You really showed them anyone could attempt dancing. I think you're adorable."

"Um, thanks." Maybe he hadn't caught on as well as he'd thought, but he'd gladly accept the compliment offered by this pretty coed with big brown eyes, a jaunty blonde ponytail, and really perky breasts pushing against her T-shirt. Maybe he should think beyond Josee, the unattainable.

"Yes, he is adorable." A slim, long-fingered hand rested on his arm, possibly possessively. "Are we dining together again tonight?"

"Yeah, sure. I should have asked you last night. It's Mozzarella Monday, in other words, pizza, ziti, Italian stuff like that. You can make your own meatball sub from yesterday's leftovers and French bread if you want."

"Glad I got lots of exercise today to deserve a meal like that. We'll see you there, Jania."

Had Josee just given the attractive aide the old heave-ho? Whatever, Jania pushed her patient away while exclaiming, "Pizza, that sounds great" to the child.

Trin had to ask himself what would X do at this moment? The answer came to him. "Are we on for

Taco Tuesday too?"

"You bet." Josee's hand remained on his arm.

"I think there's a place near Bodey Landrum's ranch that has a line dancing night on Fridays." Well, he knew there was. He'd checked on his phone in case the lessons took. "Maybe we could visit Eve's studio, then catch some dinner and go there afterward."

"I'd like that." She did take her hand away, but they had to move out of the now vacant room sometime. Again, a flash of what they could do on the yoga mats piled in a corner passed through his mind. Nope. He swore he wouldn't be a jerk like Mack and screw this up.

Chapter Seven

Farewell Wednesday arrived with its traditional dragon boat races, an event Trinity had participated in since childhood and never won. Pigs and yams roasted in an earthen umu oven for the final feast. The leis given out were only paper, but a luau atmosphere prevailed. The female counselors, coached by Miss Starr, entertained by doing a hula with grass skirts tied over their bikinis. Josee joined in, good at the dance as she was at everything. X led songs accompanied by a ukulele. When the awards were given out for the boat races, Trin got nothing again. He'd been merely another rower among the parents, brothers, and sisters who manned the long, awkward boats with many oars down the bayou while the less able cheered them on.

Mack, of course, cherry-picked his crew, drafting the most likely to succeed. Still, he'd come in second to his dad who'd hoisted the very light Edie into the drummer's position, had a real knack for steering the awkward vessels, and a way of encouraging his team that Mack had not mastered. The prizes were incredibly cheap medals, but still, judging by his scowl, his brother wanted badly to win. As for himself, he didn't care because Josee again sat next to him at dinner and beside him on a blanket at the last bonfire. He'd gotten an arm around her and a thumbs-up from X-avier when Josee looked away.

Mack made his way toward them, dodging chairs and other blankets, ignoring those who called to him to sit with them. His brother might be an ass, but he was a handsome pro football ass and that overcame a lot. Mack sat down next to Josee and practically on Trinity's hand where it lay next to her thigh, forcing him to remove it.

"Hey, Josee, our week of servitude is ended. You want to blow this place Friday night and hit some of the clubs in Lafayette before I head back to Dallas?"

She inched a little closer to Trinity. "Sorry, I already have a date for Friday."

"I guess I could stay over Saturday and leave Sunday before Mawmaw Nadine tries to drag me off to church."

Josee shook her head. "Busy then, too. Don't let me keep you here."

How and who was she busy with on Saturday? Trinity wanted to know. But his brother had finally taken the hint.

"If this is about my getting drunk the other night, you need to give a guy a second chance.

"Not necessarily."

"Then, screw you!" Mack raised his body with the fluid grace of an athlete and stalked off.

Should he ask? "Sorry about that. Are you really busy on Saturday?"

"I am. My dad is coming to pick me up and take me back to Mandeville. He'll want to visit with your folks before we leave. We might have time for a horseback ride, maybe a picnic."

Had the fabulous Josee Riley just asked him out? Trinity managed a coherent answer. "Yeah, I'd like that."

****

Thursday morning, the guests departed, each family with a copy of the camp newsletter tucked under an arm. Trin or Edie had interviewed each group, written their story, and asked what they liked best about the camp. Mack, X-avier, and Josee rated mini-profiles as celebrities of the week. Much to Trinity's embarrassment, Edie had posted pictures obtained from some of the campers of him giving CPR to the drowned boy and catching Lizzy in midair. She ran them under the heading "Camp Hero" along with his own profile as a video game creator. Cringe worthy, he thought.

The cleaning crews came in, the caterers restocked the cabins, and the rest of the staff had a day off to lounge by the pool or play beach volleyball in the palm grove, whatever they wanted really. Trinity slept late and realized his mistake when he straggled down to breakfast and found Josee finishing her second cup of coffee and about to leave the table.

Corazon slipped half a large omelet onto his plate. "You finish this for Miss Josee. She say it too big, but full of cheese and vegetables." She added two pieces of whole-wheat toast on the side.

He poured his juice. Coffee later. Trinity cut a bite with his fork and immediately encountered broccoli and a mushroom, neither his favorite, but if Josee liked them, so did he. Not bad enrobed in cheese and hidden in eggs.

Josee asked before he could. "Any plans for today?"

"I thought I'd work on my video game since I have free time. Monday, I'm back at work." Josee snagged a triangle of his toast. He was happy to share.

"Me, too. I volunteered between assignments. Did you have to use vacation time to help with camp?"

"No, Mr. Hartz is a big believer in paying it forward. He feels he's been very lucky in life and likes his employees to feel the same. If we want a week to do charity work, we get it and are still paid. He knows about Camp Love Letter and that all the Billodeauxs give some time to it." He had her attention to himself for one glorious moment.

Mack entered, filling the quiet kitchen with his size and his hustle. A leather travel bag hung over one of his broad shoulders. He greeted no one, simply filled a stainless-steel travel mug with coffee and snapped on the lid. It figured his brother could steal the spotlight in a second without uttering one intelligent word—the gift of good looks, fame, and attitude. Josee watched his minimal performance.

"What you want for breakfast, Mack? An omelet like Trin and Josee?" Corazon stood, spatula poised to go into action.

"*Nada*, Corazon. I'll pick up something on the way back to Dallas. No sense hanging around here." He flicked a quick glance at Josee.

"Your mama like to see you longer."

Right on cue, their mom entered the room. "Not staying the weekend, Mack?"

"I have things to do in the big city. I'll be here for the Fourth of July celebration, if I can get away."

Mack moved toward the door. Mama Nell intercepted his brother for a hug and a kiss on the cheek. "You're always welcome here. We'd love to see you more often during the offseason."

"Yeah, I know. Bye." He pushed through the door to the outside as if he had to break through a line of opponents to escape.

Corazon sniffed her disapproval at his rudeness. His mom poured her coffee, sighed, and came to sit at the table. She offered Josee a warm smile. "Thank you so much for volunteering this week. Your makeup classes were very popular. You gave those girls hope they could be pretty again."

"I truly enjoyed doing it. They show such courage. If I had more time, I'd stay another week."

"Maybe next year." Nell contemplated the dark pool of her brew. "For a while, I thought you and Mack might hit it off. He needs a strong, independent woman so badly to keep him on track."

Josee studied her own coffee for a minute before meeting Nell's big, brown, and so very sincere eyes. "I don't think that's the type of woman he wants right now."

"He'll grow up someday, I hope."

Feeling invisible as the women discussed his wayward brother, Trinity cut into the conversation. "How about me? Don't I need a strong, independent woman?"

His mother's eyes crinkled at his obvious play for attention. "You'll be fine when you meet the right woman because your heart is true."

"You make me sound like a hero." He shook his head.

"You rescued two children in a week, Trin. That counts for something." He was very glad Josee said it and not his mom. Somehow, it meant more. He finished his breakfast, scraping up some melted cheese onto the last of his toast. “Guess I’ll get to work on my game.”

Josee also rose. “I’d love to take a look at it.”

“Might be boring for you since it’s still in development.”

“I don’t think so.”

“Well, sure, if you want. I usually work on the desktop in my room when I’m here, but if that would make you uncomfortable, I can load it on my laptop and set up in the dining room.”

“I’m not worried about being in *your* room.” She seemed to imply she might be if he were Mack.

He wished she didn’t see him as the true-hearted, nice guy. He’d like to be considered a little bit dangerous, but he’d take what he could get. “Okay, let’s get started.”

Strangely, Josee stayed by his side all morning and made insightful suggestions along the way. “I know Football Game is your working title, but this is more than football as it encompasses the lives of the players. Have you considered branding it with a Billodeaux association—like Joe’s World after your dad? He’s a true legend. I’m sure he’d let you have an endorsement.”

“I’d want to cut him in on it if I used his name, but I’m not sure it will take off.” Joking, he said, “I could call it Josee’s World.”

She swished her blonde ponytail. “That world would be about modeling and makeup.”

Trinity thought a moment. “We could develop that. I’ll bet it would sell.”

“That’s a thought for later, but let’s work on getting this one finished first.”

They kept at it, breaking for a lunch of barbecued

pork sandwiches and yam fries, the expected fare after the pig roast. Stocking up on cans of Diet Coke, they returned to Trin's bedroom and put in several more hours before dinner. He stood and stretched. Josee in the chair next to him did likewise with much more beauty and grace. He tried to keep his gaze from scanning the length of her body from her delicately arched feet encased in sandals, past the short shorts and tee knotted at her waist to that perfect face, but with no luck. He hoped she didn't notice. Fat chance.

"I could use some exercise. Why don't we walk to Teddy's house and chase Lizzy around for a while?" she suggested.

They set off along the oak-lined path, past the pool where a few of the counselors lounged, and through the meandering path in the palm grove, at last breaking through to the road that led to the new home. From a distance, they could hear X-avier's unmistakable voice singing the Lizzy song accompanied by a ukulele, perhaps not the best instrument for the words. Lizzy, sitting at his feet on the patio, cared less. As Trinity and Josee came around the house, she shouted, "Again!"

"Saved," X pronounced. "The last was number five. I'm running out of spit. Lizzy, look who's here."

"Unc Trin." She attacked his legs with a huge hug. Looking upward with her delighted blue eyes, the child said very solemnly, "Don't go in bull pen."

"I don't plan to do that ever again. Where is everybody?"

"Jessie and the baby are having a nap. Teddy is working on his book for boys. I said I'd watch the munchkin for a while. Man, she can wear you out. We went swimming and played tag in the palm grove. She's harder to catch than a loose chicken. Don't know how her parents do it. Coach Buck's two-a-days are easier. You been scarce."

"Josee and I worked on my game all day up in my room. She has some great ideas."

X made a hurt face. "I thought I was the only one you stole ideas from."

"I'm giving mine away for free," Josee said as the patio door slid open and Teddy walked out.

"I think X needs some relief. Anyone else want a cold drink or something stronger?" Far back in the house, the baby cried, awake and ready for her dinner.

"Parched," X croaked. "I won't say no to a beer."

"Trin?"

"Sounds good."

"Let me help with that," Josee offered and followed Teddy into the house. Lizzy dogged their steps like an excited puppy.

X-avier eyed his friend. "So, up in your room working on the video game. Is that code for something else?"

"Unfortunately, no."

"No progress to report at all?"

"She did give me a kiss—on the lips—last night when I walked her to her room. Kind of soft and sweet, not hot. She said I was a nice guy. Not what I wanted to hear." He threw himself into a chair, stretched out, and couldn't help noticing again how much shorter his legs were than X-avier's.

X drew his in and hunched over to dole out his thoughts. "I tell you, you gotta take it up a notch. Next time she kisses you, you raise that heat level. Your daddy had a big reputation with the ladies before he settled down. Didn't he give you any advice growing up?"

"He tried. When Teddy reached seventeen, I know he took him to a bordello in New Orleans and let the ladies there teach him the ropes."

"Oh, Trin, they weren't no ladies. That the way you learned?"

"Nope. I was so embarrassed I turned him down and said I could get my own girls."

"Did you?"

"Not for years, but geek girls do like sex it turns out. My dad left me with this advice, 'Let the lady go first and remember to wear your rubber raincoat.' I didn't figure out what he meant for a long time and hated to ask Mack who could get girls early on."

X thought for a moment. "I'm guessing orgasms and condoms."

"You guess right."

Their conversation came to an abrupt end as the patio door slid open again. As elegantly as Brinsley, Josee carried a tray with the beers and a plate of cheese, crackers, and sliced boudin sausage. With a stylish dip, she set it on a table and helped herself to one of the beverages. Just watching Josee put her lips to a longneck turned him on, and he suspected X wasn't immune either.

She turned toward his friend. "I've enjoyed your singing, both at the campfires and the church service last Sunday. You could have a whole new career when you're done playing."

"Who's waiting? I plan to cut an album way before that. Got to get my football creds down first is all. Fame sells." X-avier threw back his head and chugged half his bottle in a masculine display of thirst quenching. Trin attempted the same, choked on the third swallow, and received a slam on the back from X to clear his throat. "No rush, bro. You weren't singing to Lizzy for the last half hour."

"You all right, Trin?" Josee did seem concerned.

Mortified, he merely nodded.

She continued talking to X. "Yes, fame does help, or I wouldn't have a makeup line. Are you heading back to New Orleans soon?"

"Sunday afternoon. I plan to attend voluntary training activities. Can't let myself go soft during the offseason. You?"

"Back to my parents' place in Mandeville. I have a shoot in the city."

"Maybe we can get together for a drink at Mariah's Place one evening."

Trin wandered behind Josee as if enjoying the view of the bayou. He shook his head frantically at X who'd let his natural charm bubble over like the head on a beer. X caught himself. "You're coming to the Big Easy next weekend, right, Trin? We could all go out together."

He hadn't planned on it but would be there if Josee was. One of his sisters would put him up, or Xo and Junior might loan him their condo for a few days—and nights. His dad's old bachelor pad was another possibility—but too obvious? "Absolutely, I pop down to New Orleans all the time." A three and a half-hour drive to the Quarter one way, worth it for Josee's company.

"Or maybe you could join us tomorrow. We're going to Bodey Landrum's ranch to see some of his wife's art and then out for dinner and line dancing." Josee picked up a tidbit of cheese, mounted it on a cracker, and nibbled.

Again, Trin shook his head desperately as he watched his private time with Josee turn into a group date. X got the message. "Nice offer, but I promised my mama I'd spend the weekend with her."

"It's wonderful the way you treat her. So good with Lizzy and the other children, too. You are going to make a great husband one of these days."

Setting his fluffy fro waggling, X shook his head more violently than Trin. "Not ready to settle down yet—maybe Trinity is, but not me."

Not very subtle. Thank God, Teddy, Jessie, and their kids arrived at that moment. Lizzy sucked a juice box and baby May a tit. Teddy grabbed a beer while Jessie brought along a can of lemonade in her cup holder. The conversation turned away from marriage and children to his great relief.

Tired of camp food, he suggested they order from the Golden Dragon, Chapelle's only Chinese restaurant. They ate out of the cartons, sharing pot stickers and sweet and sour chicken. Lizzy polished off a mound of popcorn shrimp and ate some of the vegetables in order to earn a fortune cookie. She finally wound down and went to bed, allowing the adults to watch the sun set over the bayou in that brief, magical moment when the muddy waters turned golden.

As he escorted Josee back through the palm grove, rustling with an evening breeze and other activities some of the camp aides pursued in the deep shadows, she tripped over a fallen frond. He grabbed an elbow, stopped her fall.

She turned toward him and said, "My hero. Skinned knees would delay my photo shoot." Her lips came down on his.

X's words sounded in his brain. Raise the heat. He backed her toward one of the slanted trunks of a palm bordering the walk, cupped her face, and leaned in. Damn that he wasn't wearing his boots and had to rise up on the toes of his sneakers, but Josee rested against the sloping tree and suddenly their heights matched perfectly. He moistened her plush lips with his tongue, seeking entrance. She granted it. Tongues twined. If he grew any harder, he'd need to take her deeper into the grove and lay down in the sand.

Then, he remembered and broke off their embrace. "Sorry."

"Trin that wasn't the worst kiss I've ever had. Nothing to be sorry about."

"Relieved to hear that, but this isn't the best place for it. Knox Polk has security cameras in the grove."

"Should we warn the others?" Josee stood with the help of his hand on hers and nodded to the interior clumps of palms.

"I don't think so. I doubt if Knox is watching right now, but he might review them in the morning. Heck, it was just a kiss."

"Yes," Josee echoed. "Just a kiss."

Was her tone wistful? He couldn't decipher it but kept her hand all the way back to the big house. At her door, they kissed again, maybe not as good as the first time since a guy never knew when one of his siblings might intrude. She didn't invite him in. He could wait. Tomorrow she would be all his at last.

Chapter Eight

The electric Tesla hummed along the highway making less noise than the flap of an egret's wing. At one point, a semi that neither saw nor heard the Tesla almost swerved into their lane, but Trin, an ever-vigilant small car driver, hit the gas and got them past the big rig. Josee, his precious cargo, put a hand over her heart, most likely beating as hard as his after the close call.

"Good reflexes," she murmured.

Trying to be cool about it, Trinity said, "Just Louisiana defensive driving where most people drive an SUV or truck bent on wiping out the little guy. At least, it seems that way. We turn off here on the access road to get to the Landrum place."

Trin completed the maneuver and soon had them entering through the open wrought iron gates displaying the three golden bees of the Three B's Ranch. Passing pastures with grazing horses and several bull pens, each with its own fierce tenant, they arrived at a good-sized mansion that sat on the top of a hill above a pond. Beyond it lay the buildings that housed Bodey Landrum's Famous Bull Riding School. Eve said her studio sat behind the house by the pool and to simply walk around the side. She'd be waiting for them.

They followed her instructions and at least to Trin, found an unwelcome sight—Ty Beck, a straw cowboy hat covering his face instead of sunglasses, sunning his freckled body on a lounger by the pristine blue water. He wore a Speedo almost as well as Mack, though he ran to long, lean muscle, not bulk. Why wasn't the clown wearing big, baggy trunks similar to his own, Trinity wondered.

The bullfighter heard their approach and cocked his hat upward. "There y'all are. I thought you might get here before lunch and have time for a swim." He swung his legs to the side and sat up to greet them. A few interesting scars showed across his ribs. Trin envied those scars, signs of a real man. He had none, hadn't even broken an arm as a kid.

Trinity tried for cordial and hoped he succeeded. "Nope, we didn't show up for dinner at the ranch house last night, and Corazon insisted we eat the leftover carnitas before we got on the road. Lots of pork from the pig roast still in the fridge."

"Nothing better than good carnitas, except maybe the ribs at the Rainbow Café. Best place to work them off is the Longneck Saloon on line-dancing night."

"Yes. Those were the places I found on my phone. The café has excellent Yelp ratings and the Longneck is said to be very authentic." Trin felt compelled to show he'd done his research.

"Hell, Bodey and my parents were eatin' at the Rainbow Café before there was a Yelp. The Longneck gives dance lessons at six if you need 'em. The real fun starts at seven. I'll be happy to show y'all around."

"Don't you have to be moving on to another bullfighting gig?" Trinity asked, maybe too obviously.

"Nope. I work for Bodey's school until the professional bull riding season starts up again full force.

Got nothing else to do tonight but entertain you and Miss Josee. So happy to see you again, ma'am." Although largely unclothed, he tipped his hat her way. "I probably had enough sun for the day. I burn real easy, but I'm trying to get the rest of me to match my cowboy tan." The man's neck and arms were browned, hiding his freckles.

"I have a product in my makeup line that can help you with that. Being pale myself, I wanted a lotion with a high SPF but not so high that I couldn't get a glow to my skin," Josee offered. She dug in a purse about the size of a bucket but more stylish and handed Ty a small tube. "I carry some with me, but you can get it online."

"I surely will try this. Right now, I think a shower and some clothes are in order. Miss Eve is in the studio expecting you. We thought we'd hear you drive up."

"Not in a Tesla," Trin said.

"That's what you drive, huh? Interesting. Well, see you later. Enjoy your visit." Ty moved off with that saunter that still worked even in a very brief bathing suit and the flip-flops he shoved on his feet. How did he do it, Trinity pondered.

Alerted by the voices, Eve Landrum appeared in the doorway to her studio. She wore her long, white hair in a messy bun atop her head. A full black apron spotted with paint in every vibrant color covered her jeans and tee. "Ty is exactly like one of my own boys. I know his mama worries about his safety as much as I do. Anyhow, I enjoy having him around when mine are gone. But, come inside out of the heat. Let me show you what I'm working on, a commission."

"One of your famous landscapes seen through the branches of an iconic tree?" Josee guessed.

"Absolutely. Sometimes I get tired of painting them, but people are willing to pay my price no matter how high I raise it. This is a big one for a rancher in Texas, of course. You can see the hill country, his house, and the oil wells that made him wealthy, some cattle and bluebonnets to add interest and color beyond the oak." Eve and Josee paused to study the details of her work.

Trinity wandered around the room, taking in other smaller landscapes hung on the wall or stacked on the floor, mostly swamp scenes or portraits of the rolling hills around the town of Rainbow nearby. He overheard words like "unique perspective" and "low key colors" as he strolled. Josee knew a bunch about art. He'd have to learn more to keep up with her.

Coming to a stop before a shelf of small bronzes, he studied each one, turned them over, and widened his eyes at the prices. All were rodeo-themed: two bull riders standing shoulder to shoulder labeled "Brothers", some dynamic bucking bulls with and without riders, an older man peering out of a barrel entitled "The Barrel Man", and one of a clown so obviously Ty the viewer could imagine his flaming red hair. The conversational voices of the two women neared the place where he stood.

"Done by my youngest son, the only one who inherited my interest in art, his rodeo series. He always sends me his latest to add to the shelf."

Trinity found himself saying, "I'd like to buy one if they are for sale." He picked up a bull that had obviously just thrown its rider and had it hind quarters still lofted in the air. "This one reminds me of Black Water." No way would he dole out money for the studly bull riders or one of Ty Beck.

"That's exactly who it is—in his younger days. The others are my older sons, Ben and Shea, Ty of course, and the barrel man who inspired him, Snuffy Jones. I'd be happy to sell you one as I can always get another from Rick."

"Yeah, I'll take it to remind me and Lizzy never to mess with another bull. Credit card, bitcoin, or check?'

"A check would be fine since I'm not sure what a bitcoin is and usually let my gallery representatives take care of sales."

Eve's lovely, self-deprecating smile, eased the pain of writing out a check for three-hundred-fifty dollars, not that he couldn't afford it. He'd paid that much for vintage Star Trek memorabilia, and he'd done good as he could tell from Josee's nod of approval.

As Eve wrapped the small but masterful statue in bubble wrap, then placed it in a box padded with tissue, she said, "I should have mentioned before that you can get these online or at rodeos but made out of resin and much cheaper."

"It's okay. I like having the real thing, not a cheap substitute."

"You have fine taste in art, Trinity. Help me pick out a painting," Josee said, her hand on his arm guiding him back to the pictures on display.

"Um, that one." He pointed to a scene of the dark clouds of a thunderstorm racing across the flat landscape of a rice paddy, dousing the surface with a veil of rain. "It reminds me of squatting in a duck blind with my dad when he took us goose hunting on a wet day. I liked being out in nature but hated killing the geese. They mate for life, and I always worried I'd take down half of a pair. I don't hunt anymore. I guess that makes me a wimp."

Did Josee's blue eyes soften as she said, "That makes you a sensitive guy."

Eve nodded. "I've always liked that Bodey never took up hunting, though he does things way more dangerous. You don't have to kill something to prove your manhood."

Was it suddenly hot in the studio with the two women staring at him like a model for millennial men? He diverted them by saying, "This one is nice, colorful."

"Downtown Rainbow with its pastel cottages. There's the Rainbow Café where you'll want to eat tonight," Eve told them. "It's part of the local experience and far better than anything I could offer you for dinner."

"We're going to dance off the meal at a place called the Longneck Saloon that Ty recommended."

Eve's lips quirked into a humorous smile. "Used to be the Rainbow Express when my husband hung out there years ago, but the new owners worried it might be mistaken for a gay bar and changed the name."

Josee laughed. "I'll take this painting of Rainbow as a souvenir of our trip. Say, you and Bodey should come with us for an evening of dinner and dancing."

Turn her down, turn her down, turn her down, Trin repeated in his mind. If he had them along, he might as well be going out with his parents in tow.

But Eve Landrum didn't get his psychic message. "We haven't done that in quite some time. Bodey is wrapping up the last class in the bull riding school this afternoon. It will be a fun change of pace for us. We don't have Ben's twin boys staying with us right now, so no need for a babysitter." Her gray eyes warmed to the idea.

Nice lady, he couldn't rain on her parade. His glance returned to the painting of the rain-swept rice paddy. "Wrap that one up for me, too." What was another three thousand dollars to commemorate a day spent with Josee?

Eve checked her not-so-fancy watch, its big dial flecked with paint. "Time for a break." She used the statue of her two bull rider sons as a paperweight for the three-sizable checks almost absent-mindedly like a true artist more concerned with what she painted than how much it brought. Of course, as Bodey Landrum's wife, she'd never starve if she didn't sell a one, Trin guessed.

Eve shed her apron and sank her brushes into a jar of turpentine before leading her guests to the spacious great room of her home. The long saddle-leather sofa bore scars from the three boys she'd raised, and the entire area had a distinctly western air about it right down to Ty Beck lounging behind the rustic coffee table and all cleaned up for their night out with polished boots, fresh but worn jeans, a blue-checkered shirt Trinity knew he could never pull off, and hair combed back and tethered into place with gel. He'd opened a bottle of white wine, Leibfraumilch, which Trin had heard of but not tasted, and set out a basket of mixed crackers and a plate of assorted cheese cubes most likely shaken from a bag.

"I thought you'd be coming in soon for your break, Aunt Eve," the bullfighter said.

"How nice of you to get out some refreshments for

Josee and Trinity." Eve blessed him with another of her gentle smiles. "I'm not really his aunt but might as well be."

Josee examined the bottle. "One of my favorite German wines. Some people find it too fruity, but I love it."

Great, another thing he'd need to learn more about if Josee knew her vintages. Not that the Billodeauxs didn't drink, but they were more beer people, with champagne for special occasions. This left a gap in Trinity's social education he'd have to fill, but he offered, "Shall I pour?" He knew enough not to fill the glasses to the brim before handing them around. Just as he finished, Bodey joined them.

"I could use some of that, too." He took a seat next to Eve on the sofa, oblivious of the dust he'd dragged in, but then, it was his house. "We'll be giving out the certificates for the bull riding school in an hour, then I'll cut them loose. Only one or two has the grit to make it as a rider, and I doubt they'll want a life on the road all the time. Most of them just want the fancy paper to hang on their walls. Eve designed the diploma with an edging that looks like a corral and some bucking bulls in the corners." He gave his wife a sweaty, affectionate one-armed hug.

"Bodey, we're going over to the Café for dinner, then line dancing with Ty, Josee, and Trinity. Won't that be fun?" Eve stated rather than asked.

"Better put on my good dancin' boots, then." Bodey helped himself to a handful of cheese cubes and a couple of crackers. Trin noticed the tough bull rider didn't grumble one bit. For all her mildness, Eve Landrum had some authority, exactly like Josee.

Bodey tossed back his wine. “Better get showered and gussied up for my love. We need to leave directly after the diploma ceremony. Y’all can go ahead and get a table. We won’t be far behind. The guys have been eating Janae’s catering all week and are likely to head over to the Café for more as soon as we finish. The place will get crowded.”

Ty led them to the restaurant in one of the ranch pickup trucks with Three B’s branded on the side, and Trin and Josee following in the Tesla. Not that Trin needed or wanted the help. He could have found it using his GPS.

Chapter Nine

Though the Café had a forest of dangling ferns and a long salad bar offering three kinds of olives, the ribs did stand the test of time being based on Janae Plato's daddy's recipe, or so she told the newcomers, Josee and Trinity. Her mother had carried on the tradition after his death, and Janae after hers. Now, Mama Tyne watched over the establishment in the form of a large portrait of a hefty black woman wearing a righteously large wig and a big smile that trebled her chin. Trinity noted the lady was surrounded by pictures of celebrities who had eaten at the Rainbow Café, among them Bodey Landrum on a bucking bull, all of his sons, one of Ty in his clown outfit, and former Louisiana Governor Foster in his biking leathers, not to mention quite a few musicians and actors.

Trinity definitely felt welcomed by her smile as warm as her mother's, though Janae, an attractive, light-skinned woman as trim as her mom had been hefty and about the same age as Eve, with her hair straightened into a sleek, black bob, showed not a strand of gray nor her face a wrinkle of worry. Sometimes, he wondered if he had a thing for older women. Their strength and experience appealed to him just as Josee's did.

"We put slaw back on the menu because Bodey couldn't live without it," Janae claimed.

Bodey disagreed with their hostess. "It's made with green apples but still pretty good. She hasn't messed with the stuffed potatoes yet. Be sure to get one of those."

Janae countered that with, "Hang up your hat, Bodey. You're not in a barn." Ty quickly doffed his as well.

Trin knew he must have shown surprise at how she treated the famous cowboy, but Janae only laughed at his expression. "We're very old friends, Bodey and I. Josee, how about a picture with me for our wall of special guests?"

That out of the way, they ordered ribs, slaw, and stuffed potatoes all around with iced tea for the women and the first beers of the evening ordered from the impressive mirrored bar that spanned the restaurant. As they finished, Josee cleaned her fingers on a Wet Wipe and invited Eve to go with her to the Ladies Room to check their teeth for rib remnants before moving on to line dancing.

"Do you think we should do the same?" Trinity asked.

"Grin for me, boys," Bodey ordered. "Nope, you're both fine. How about me?"

"Good," Trinity answered. As soon as Josee and Eve returned, they headed for the Longneck Saloon.

The honkytonk lived up to its rep as being authentic. As soon as they entered, Trinity sniffed the atmosphere of beer vapor, sawdust on the floor, and the testosterone of men leaning against the bar and waiting for the women to finish the last line dance instruction being done to a country/western tape. As soon as it ended, a live band with just the right amount of twang took over, and the males surged forward to cut a female from the herd.

"Grab a table quick," Bodey commanded. "I'll get the drinks."

Trin dashed to a four-top surrounded by bent wood chairs. Ty claimed one from another table and made himself comfortable next to Josee even as Trinity held out a seat for her. Damned third wheel. He settled on her other side after offering Eve the same courtesy. Manners never hurt even in a dive like this. Bodey returned and distributed Lone Star longnecks for everyone. Ty took one swig and started to rise, but Trinity beat him to it.

"Josee, would you like to dance? It's the Electric Slide. I've got this one down."

Ty threw him a well-done grin and turned to ask a bouncy blonde at the table where he'd stolen a chair. Her two girlfriends got up and joined the line without male partners, but Ty assured them they were next on his dance card. To Trinity, the clown had the same ease with women as X. As for himself, he believed he did fairly well even if he repeated each move under his breath. Still, the dance seemed endless. Thankfully, the next was slow.

He kept Josee on the floor with him despite the fact with both of them wearing boots, he had no height advantage. That didn't appear to bother Bodey who twirled his taller wife with confidence. Trin pulled himself up and did the same, making Josee laugh happily. By the time they returned to the table after another slow one, he gave way to the need to chug the beer. Bodey took off to get them a second round.

"Next up, the Boot Scootin' Boogie," the band

leader announced. "I know y'all learned this one, ladies, so get up and show the world if there ain't enough cowboys to go around."

Ty had worked his way through the three girls at the adjoining table, but the last, a redhead who claimed they matched, though her hair obviously wasn't natural but just as bright, didn't drop his hand. "Let's go again." Ty shrugged at his companions and allowed himself to be towed into the line.

The blonde approached Josee. "Mind if I borrow your li'l man? He's so cute with those Buddy Holly glasses and those curls on his forehead."

Trin wanted to object that his glasses were more Clark Kent and he wasn't that li'l, but he found himself saying, "I don't know this one, and I'm not her…"

Josee cut him off. "Yes, you can borrow him. Just return him undamaged. His name is Trinity," she supplied since he hadn't.

"That's a great cowboy name. Yeah, I saw he had some trouble with the footwork, but he tries harder than most guys. That's simply adorable." The blonde's smile stretched wide, bright with red lipstick. "I'm Jilly by the way—and you remind me of someone too."

"Not Buddy Holly, I hope." Josee did not reveal her identity, and he certainly wasn't going to betray her. The way some of the men goggled at her, he suspected they knew a supermodel sat among them.

Jilly giggled and touched Josee's shoulder. "If he's not a virgin, I'll bring him back in one piece. If he is, then I can't guarantee it."

The joint was dim, hiding the blush Trin knew crawled up his neck under his olive-toned skin. He started to deny the charge, but let it go as Josee prompted, "Just have a good time. I'll still be here when you get back." She accepted another beer from Bodey who claimed his wife for the dance.

Trin stumbled through steps more complicated than the Electric Slide. Evidently, he should have worn a western hat to use for some of the parts as Ty and Bodey did and had to mime those motions. Every time he turned, he tried to keep an eye on Josee who had sparked a conversation with the girl left behind at the other table. She didn't need his help to get through an evening. Mercifully, the dance ended. He started back, but the band struck up Cotton Eye Joe, and he made the mistake of muttering, "At least, I know this one."

Jilly grasped his hand. "One of my favorites. Let's dance."

Trapped, again. When the song started, he saw trouble as big as a Texas tornado approaching Josee. A massive guy, who had six inches and a hundred pounds on him, shoved chairs out of the way to reach her. Judging by his drunken sway, he wanted to dance in a big way, whether capable or not.

Josee shook her head, gave him a pleasant smile, and returned to her conversation. The big dude grasped her slender wrist hard. Trin winced, knowing she'd bear bruises tomorrow. This jerk yanked Josee from her chair. Over the music, Trin heard him bellow, "I ain't good enough to dance with you when you show your near naked body on magazine covers."

Josee stomped his instep with her boot and pulled free. She lost her balance and struck the edge of the table. Empties crashed to the floor. Beer flowed from the full bottles into the sawdust. Trin shook loose of Jilly. "Sorry, gotta help her."

He dodged the dancers and followed the aisle the brute had carved between the chairs. Josee's assailant stooped and grasped a broken longneck, its edge jagged and sharp. "See if you're so pretty after I mess you up."

Trin grabbed his bulging arm and drew it back with all his strength. Flinging him off, the thug pivoted. "You want to fight me for her, you pansy geek?"

"Yeah, yeah, I do, asshole."

Vaguely, he heard Josee say, "No, Trin! Here come the bouncers."

Too late. The ass took him up on his offer and feinted at his face with the broken bottle. One advantage to being smaller, Knox Polk, the ranch bodyguard, always told him, was the ability to go under the guard of a bigger man. He lunged forward, but low, barely feeling the slice of the jagged edge across his forehead as he head-butted the enemy in a soft belly not steeled for the unexpected move. With an oomph, the giant fell amid shards scattered on the floor. Trin braced for another assault, but the ugly drunk stayed down with a boot topped-stitched with bucking broncos pressed hard against his Adam's apple. The boot belonged to Ty Beck.

Though he wished he could finish the fight alone, he knew better. "Thanks, man." He blinked his eyes a few times, but the right one remained blurry, one lens filmed with something and the other bearing a diagonal crack. He pushed the glasses into place and shook his head. That didn't help either, only made it worse.

Bodey Landrum appeared beside Ty. "Get the ladies out of here and see Trinity has medical help."

Ty nodded toward the door. Eve shooed both Trin and Josee before her and herded them into the parking lot as efficiently as a good roping horse. She went to her vehicle and took a first aid kit from the trunk. “Our boys were always getting banged up, and my grandsons are no better.” She taped a wad of gauze on Trin’s forehead and twisted a cold pack to release its iciness. “Hold this against the cut.”

“Cut?” Trin said as he accepted the packet. Red stained his hand.

“Yes, you’re bleeding. From my past experience, you’ll need stitches. Ty, would you lead them to the Urgent Care on the highway outside Opelousas. I’ll wait in the truck for Bodey and meet you there.”

“Keys,” Josee demanded, holding out her hand.

“Huh?”

“I’m driving. You could pass out.”

“No.” He shook his head. Waves of dizziness and nausea surged through his body. “Okay.” Great end to his date with Josee, being fussed over by two women and beholden to Ty Beck.

****

Since the hour was early and the Friday night casualties hadn’t piled up yet, Trin got an examination room immediately. Or maybe, attendants didn’t want blood splattered all over their carpet since it had seeped through the gauze and now ran down his cheek. He’d left his ID and insurance card from Hartz Technology at the desk. Josee sat beside him like a glamorous secretary, asking him questions and filling in the paperwork since his vision still wasn’t the best. “Diabetes, epilepsy, heart disease, STDs?” No, no, no, and no! She knew his whole medical history now, including that last one.

The nurse entered, cleaned his forehead, snipped

away the carefully cultivated, now blood-soaked curl, and placed the hair in a pan. The doctor arrived, administered a local, and sewed eight stitches into his forehead. "Scalp wounds always bleed a lot. You're slightly concussed." They'd done the eye thing, the holding up of fingers and following side to side. With the blood wiped from his broken glasses, Trin thought he'd done okay, but he admitted to a headache.

"Being a Billodeaux, you should know better than to head butt without a helmet." The doctor chuckled at his own humor. Eve must have filled him in on the brawl which accounted for the voices in the corridor prior to the doctor's appearance.

"The cut is a bit jagged but should heal okay. Being so close to your eyebrow, it won't be very noticeable. Lucky he missed your eyes. Take it easy for a few days. No strenuous exercise."

"Too bad that scar couldn't be a thunderbolt," Trin muttered. Josee got the joke and smiled, but the Harry Potter reference zinged right past the doctor.

"I'll give you some pills for the pain. Don't drive as they might make you sleepy."

"I'll see he gets home safely," Josee said.

Wonderful, she had to look out for him. He glanced up. Ty Beck lounged in the doorway, the grin on his freckled face only making it worse. Then, the bullfighter said, "Not bad for your first bar fight. Women love an interesting scar, believe me."

"How do you know it's my first bar fight?"

"'Cause playing computer games don't end in real injuries, but like I said, you done good, podnah. I'd want you on my side. You're scrappy."

Scrappy, huh. He'd take that as the compliment it

was. Did Josee consider him scrappy—or simply nuts for taking on a guy that size?

"Come on, Scrappy. Let me take you home and put you to bed." Josee offered her arm as if he couldn't walk by himself. Come to think of it, he did feel a little weak-kneed and leaned against the warmth of her side, up against her breast more heavily than necessary.

On the return drive to Lorena Ranch, he fell asleep. The painkiller provided him with a wonderful dream of being in bed with Josee and performing manfully despite his wound. She wasn't the person who woke him, took him to his room via the elevator, and tucked him under the covers after helping him out of the blood-stained clothes. Mom and Dad. The first placed a kiss carefully on his forehead. "I've left your spare pair of glasses on the night table."

The second handed him another painkiller and made sure he took it. "Me, I brawled some in my younger days. Son, you'll hurt in the morning."

****

He did hurt. The wound throbbed when the noises of Camp Love Letter in full swing roused him from some spectacular fantasies; Josee's lips pressed against his crotch for one. Nothing wrong with him below the waist, and his erection proved it.

The triangle rang announcing lunch. Trinity sat up a little too fast. He was supposed to be on a horseback ride, galloping along the bridal path with Josee, heading for the thick oak grove on the far side of the pastures where the counselors and kids rarely penetrated and the moss on the ground grew as thick as a mattress.

He'd asked Corazon to pack a special picnic basket filled with delicacies like bowfin caviar and pâtés to be spread on dainty crackers, red grapes, and slices of exotic melons with a good wine pairing, plus Belgian chocolate, the kind of food the rich and famous ate, not chips and baloney sandwiches. To which the housekeeper replied, “I got to go to Lafayette for that kind of stuff and don’t have time—but I do something nice for you and Josee.” She’d pinched his cheek with love.

He had to get dressed and downstairs in a hurry before Josee and her dad ate with the campers. Stumbling to his feet, he sniffed his armpit. Ugh, sweat, beer, and blood. His hair probably smelled the same. Couldn’t get the stitches wet, he remembered and ransacked the medicine cabinet for large bandages, slapped one on and then took the world’s fastest shower. Didn’t bother to shave. The stitches and the scruff lent him a rough, tough look Josee might appreciate.

He settled his backup glasses into place and noticed the artwork on his desk as he rummaged for clean jeans and a T-shirt that didn’t have a camp logo. The bucking bull anchored a note in front of the thunderstorm painting.

Dear Trinity,

I’ll take a raincheck on our ride and picnic. I don’t believe you will be up to it today. Leaving early. Get well soon. See you in New Orleans.

Yours, Josee

Damn, if only she were.

Chapter Ten

Sometimes, Trinity thought his parents tried to sabotage his pursuit of Josee Riley, maybe so he wouldn't get hurt. His mother insisted he stay at the ranch at least through Monday and rest. His dad, who should understand, backed her up by saying he couldn't drive under the influence of his meds, but if he could do without them by Monday he was free to go home. He considered rebelling but couldn't find his car keys, mysteriously not on the peg board where such items were kept. It would be easy enough to cadge the keys to any of the ranch vehicles, but shaking his head to talk himself out of it reminded him why he shouldn't drive.

The intense June sunlight bothered his eyes which crossed off lounging by the pool from the docket. He had no camp obligations to pass the time either as he'd done his stint. Instead, he retreated to his dim bedroom and worked on his video game, now entitled Joe's World. Josee had begun to develop female characters: girlfriends, cheerleaders, a female kicker like his sister-in-law Alix, and another she'd named Hulda who did have the size and brawn to play with the big boys. Trinity considered the last unlikely, but the game was a fantasy after all, so let Hulda play if anyone drafted her. Hoping Josee might work with him again, he wouldn't touch those.

The only other idea he could develop at the

moment took a simple phone call. He asked his sister, Xochi, if he could borrow the condo in New Orleans for a weekend or so since her husband, Junior, the massive cornerback, wasn't likely to participate in the voluntary training sessions in June.

Xo gave her permission with a warm chuckle. "Sure, you know Junior would rather be fooling around at the restaurant than sweating at the training center in Metairie. I keep telling him he'll have to work off any extra weight at camp in July, but he doesn't listen. Besides, with me expecting again, I'm not fond of going into the city with all those dark auras around. I'll bring you the keys sometime this weekend."

"You could just send them with Corazon after church since Mom has me grounded until Monday."

Again, his sister laughed, a sound often compared to vocal hot chocolate and Trinity agreed. "You were the baby she came nearest to losing. Someday, she might let you grow up. She wants me to lay my healing hands on your injury and do my woo-woo stuff as way too many in this family call it."

Trinity released a hefty sigh. "Figures. The Billodeaux billboard at work. If one of us knows, we all know. I guess Lorena in Australia got the word about my fight by now."

"Probably someone sent her a message. The more good thoughts sent to you, the better. Think of it that way."

"It's only a cut with a few stitches. I'll survive. You don't have to go to any trouble for me."

"It's no trouble. It's what I do. See you Sunday."

"Love you, Xo, and Junior and Pilar, too."

That settled, he returned to developing his own

characters: a wide receiver with long, golden hair like Josee's dad at one time, maybe another with an attitude like Mack, perhaps a fast, young rookie like X. He had lots of material to merge into his game.

****

Another Spaghetti Sunday arrived at Camp Love Letter bringing with it Xochi and her family. Trinity put himself into her care without a fuss. In the quiet of his room with no audience, she laid her fingertips on his wound and murmured some words in Cajun French that meant nothing to him. A small surge of warmth shot through him just as others said it did when Xo worked on them. He felt no difference in his stitches, but the headache dogging him all weekend vanished. He'd be able to ditch the pain pills and drive to New Orleans.

"Thanks, sis. That really did help."

"Anything else I can do for you?"

Of all his sisters, she was the easiest to confide in. He wondered if he should seek her advice about Josee. Although she practiced as a *traiteur*, a traditional Cajun healer, she did keep any consultations private, exactly like a doctor. The way she cocked her head and looked at him, he suspected she might be reading his aura right at this minute. He might as well fess up because she already knew he was in love.

"I have deep feelings for a woman, but I don't know if she returns them."

"Josee Riley." Xo stated it as a fact, not a question.

"You keep saying you don't read minds."

"I don't, but I've seen flashes of your affection for her, at Annie's wedding and other times we've been together. But, it's deeper now, not simply a boy's crush. I think this week you spent with her changed the way you think about her. She's not just a pretty face, but a real person with more depth than you knew."

"Yes! Does she feel the same about me?"

"I'd have to see her to tell. One thing I do know for sure is that you are braver and truer than you think. You may not show it on a football field like Dean and Junior, but you have the courage of the Sinners." Xochi grasped his hands, and her deep brown eyes gazed into his. "If Josee Riley can't appreciate those qualities, she isn't the right woman for you." She squeezed his fingers gently, and again he experienced that warmth course through him, giving him not healing, but confidence.

"Thanks, Xo. You are the best."

She dropped his hands. "Never thank a *traiteur*. I give my gifts freely to anyone who asks."

"Okay, let's just say you are the best sister a guy could have."

"Since you have five others to choose from, that's saying a lot." She pressed the keys to the condo into his hands. "Enjoy it. Now, let's get down to dinner before Pilar is covered head to toe in spaghetti sauce."

Really, Xochi was the best at more than being his sister.

Chapter Eleven

Trin put in a week of work he surely owed his boss but left directly from the Hartz Technology campus on Friday afternoon bound for New Orleans. He'd made two phone calls in advance, one to Josee and one to X. While Josee seemed pleased to hear his voice, she did say she'd have to work part of Saturday because they'd had rain delays all week that made the exterior shots impossible. The weekend promised to be clear, steamy but clear. They could spend the afternoon and evening and Sunday together if he wanted. Did he ever want it!

Next, he checked in with X. "You still at your mama's house?"

"Hey man, I only left the ranch so my sexual charisma didn't rub off on Josee, and you had a chance wit' her. I did spend Sunday with Mama, then headed back to my pad in the Big Easy. Went to the voluntary training exercises to stay sharp. Place is dead around here in June. How'd it go with tall, blonde, and luscious?"

"Would have been better if Ty Beck hadn't lurked around us. We bought some of Eve Landrum's art, went out to dinner at a great rib place, then line dancing."

"Now you just showing off your new moves."

"I think I held my own on the dance floor. Another woman asked me to partner her, and Josee insisted that I go do the Boot Scootin' Boogie with this Jilly. While I was obliging Jilly, some big dude tried to pick up Josee. He recognized her from her cover photo and got pretty ugly when she turned him down. I intercepted a broken bottle headed her way. Got cut on the forehead myself but head-butted the guy down. Then, Ty Beck held him off until the bouncers arrived. I ended up at an Urgent Care getting stitches, and she had to drive me home. Josee left early the next day because she didn't think I was up to riding. I'm not sure if our outing was a win-win, win-fail, or fail-fail."

X paused for a minute. "I'd say a win-win. Sounds like the first part of the day went okay. Eating ribs together should be considered an aphrodisiac, and you took a hit for her."

"But Ty Beck subdued the drunk." He'd have to remember cowboy boot to the throat as a means of defense if the occasion came up again.

"You bled for your woman. Counts more in the long run."

"Anyhow, I'm coming to the city for the weekend and staying alone at Junior's condo. Josee said we could spend some time together."

"Score!" X shouted into the phone.

"Well, maybe just a field goal. You want to meet us at Mariah's Place around seven Saturday night? Bring a date to soak up your excess sexual charisma—if you can find someone."

"X never has a hard time finding a date. See you there, bro."

Ah, to have the rampant confidence of X-avier Hopkins.

Trin took the easy route through the small towns and across the vast cypress swamp, entering the tedious traffic stream outside New Orleans and following it all the way to the *Vieux Carre*, the old quarter. Junior's condo sat just across Canal Street from the most famous portion of the city with its ancient buildings, famous restaurants, great music venues, and on the downside, nudie bars. He parked in the pay garage for the weekend. This part of town was better experienced on foot if a person could endure the steam rising from the streets all summer. He raised a sweat simply crossing the side street to get to the air-conditioned comfort of the apartment where the doorman immediately stopped him to inquire whom he sought.

He'd been here before visiting his brother Dean in his bachelor years, Tom and Alix, and Junior and Xo who still lived in the big brownstone building, but never with his Tony Curtis haircut now marred by a sinister line of stitches above his right eyebrow. Sure, he was among the least recognizable of the Billodeauxs, but really, his black-framed glasses should have given him away.

"Arturo, it's me, Trinity Billodeaux. I'm staying at Junior Polk's place for the weekend."

The stocky Hispanic man, who could have doubled as a bouncer but preferred his spiffy uniform and the genteel clientele who often led rather interesting lives, gave him the once over. Trin held his hands out at his sides and slowly twirled around.

The man's brown face split into broad grin. "Sure, sure, now I see you. New look? *Bueno.* Check in at the desk, then you can go right up."

"Thanks. Um, I might be having a lady friend visit, too."

He hadn't meant it as a brag, but Arturo took it that

way. The doorman had seen it all from Dean and Stacy's meltdown romance to Alix moving in as Tom's roommate. "Good for you, *mi amigo*." He nodded at the stitches. "Women, always trouble."

Trin declined to tell his story. "This one is worth it." He went toward the elevator and felt like whistling, then after an attempt or two, remembered he wasn't any good at it.

No matter. As soon as he entered Junior's brown leather and big chairs domain, now softened by bright, original art work on the walls and forgotten baby toys scattered about, he called Josee.

"Just got in. I know it's after eight, but would you want to do something tonight?"

"Not tonight. I was out all day in this humidity. I swear the makeup girl had to primp and powder me every five minutes. Tomorrow, we'll wrap up the photo shoot on the Riverwalk where at least there should be a breeze. I expect to be finished before noon, then the day is ours."

She did sound exhausted. He should have been more considerate. "No problem. Do you think I could watch you work?"

"We'll be at it early, certainly by seven, but we won't be hard to find. Come if you want. It's not as exciting as people think."

"If you are there, it is exciting. See you."

He hadn't stopped all the way to his destination. Famished, his next call went to a pizza place to order a large pepperoni pie, unfortunately for one.

****

Fortified by cold pizza and a bottle of apple juice he found in the nearly empty fridge, Trin set off toward the Riverwalk by seven. He strode down Canal Street to Canal Place and sought one of the staircases up to the Mississippi promenade also dubbed the Moonwalk for the former mayor, Moon Landrieu. Runners, so addicted to their exercise they'd persist in any weather, passed, soaked with sweat. The less athletic walked their dogs in shady areas. A preacher trying to drum up an audience offered him coffee and donuts if he'd consider pausing to hear the word of the Lord under a white tent. The back rows were already filled by the homeless dining on the free eats. He shook his head and continued on like a missile seeking its target.

In the distance, he saw the clump of people surrounding the Monument to the Immigrant erected by the Italian American Marching Club, New Orleans having offered a home to so many of their nationality. He'd walked past it often and paused once or twice to read its inspiring dedication. Now cordoned off, the curious were kept away from the marble immigrant family of four gazing toward the French Quarter while a muse with a graceful arm upraised wrapped them in her diaphanous gown as she stared toward the mighty river flowing just beyond her perch. There, he found his own muse.

The photographer shouted directions at Josee who posed on one step and attempted to duplicate the statue above her. Possessing skin as fair as the Carrara marble, she rose on one bare foot and held her arm skyward, but the long white gown she wore failed to float in the nonexistent breeze. "Someone bring up the fans. Josee take a break and get the shine off your face. You are supposed to be a muse. Muses don't perspire."

The man should talk. He sweated profusely in an

artsy black turtleneck. Rivulets ran from under a beret slanted on his shaved head down his florid cheeks and into a dark goatee. Who wanted to look like an artist so badly that he'd wear black on the Riverwalk in summer, Trin wondered? What an ass.

Josee relaxed, padded over to a huge industrial cooler of water, and filled a paper cone to the brim. As she sipped, a frantic woman dashed toward her with powder puffs and brushes in hand. Josee spotted him on the periphery of the crowd and waved. All in that area waved back, and she gifted them with her smile. A very young man that even Trin would have called puny ducked under the ropes and charged her way waving a bouquet of daises probably purchased in the nearby French Market. "I love you, Josee. Marry me!"

Before he reached his goal, the photographer screamed, "Security!" Two city cops standing nearby hoisted the guy by his armpits and marched him away, but not before he'd tossed the flowers at Josee's bare feet. Trin had to give the fellow credit for saying the words and bringing her flowers. He'd never done either. Josee didn't pick up the blossoms. The makeup woman cleaned them away. With a "Thanks, Janis," his dream girl returned to her station and assumed her position again now that two fans provided the wind to lift her long, blonde hair and sweep the dress made of many layers of nearly transparent white cotton tight against her body and flow out behind her like wings. He snapped a photo with his phone as did many others. The photographer walked around taking the picture from many angles before releasing his model from the torturous pose. "Get changed for the next shot," he directed.

Josee disappeared into a portable changing room. She reappeared still barefooted but now wearing a short gingham frock. A matching bandana secured her hair behind her neck. “Bring out the kids. Josee, hold the little girl. Boy, stand close to her,” were the new orders issued. Handed over by her mother, the black child about two wore a similar bandana barely containing her dandelion pouf of hair and a dress of the same fabric. The boy, Hispanic and maybe ten, sported a cap and had a sack slung over his shoulder like his counterpart on the statue. Obviously a pro, he held his position while the girl struggled to get down. Her stage mother called out, “Be still, Netta, or we won’t get a paycheck.” As far as he could tell, the kid didn’t care. Josee whispered in the child’s ear, and she settled down long enough to complete the picture. Setting the toddler down, Josee told the anxious mother that she owed her daughter a promised snow cone.

“Okay, that’s a rap. Let’s move to the Old Man River Statue before it gets any blasted hotter out here.” The photographer mopped his face with a damp cloth some assistant provided when he held out a hand. Trin watched the dog and pony show close down with amazing speed as Josee barely managed to change into what he’d call a swimsuit cover-up and sandals before her changing room rolled away. All the equipment, even the cooler, had wheels. The oglers dispersed almost as rapidly, most likely to places offering cold drinks.

A golf cart whizzed up. The photographer got in and offered, “Are you riding with me, Josee?” almost as an afterthought.

“No, I think I’ll walk.” No telling if she wanted to

stretch her legs or avoid riding with the man by the tone of her voice. He often had the same problem interpreting Josee.

Working his way to her, he was muscled back by security. “It’s okay. He’s a friend,” she told them. Good thing or he might have been hustled off to who knew where like the last guy who accosted her.

“May I walk along with you?”

“Sure, the statue is only a couple of blocks away. Frankly, I’ll be glad when this shoot is over.” The guards formed a phalanx around them as they marched to the next site.

“It did look like hard work, and the dude taking the pictures is kind of a tyrant.”

Josee shrugged. “They’re artists, demanding and temperamental, and nearly always men, but they can make a hag seem beautiful with the right light and angle.”

“I don’t think he has to work very hard to make you lovely.”

“Why Trinity Billodeaux, I think you have become a flatterer. Please don’t do that. I get enough empty compliments on my appearance.”

“Like the guy who threw flowers at you?”

“I have my share of fans and stalkers. Sometimes, it makes going out in public difficult. That’s why I enjoyed the ranch so much, private and everyone there so nice and kind and unconcerned about my face or long legs.”

“If you got it, flaunt it,” he said without thinking first.

“That’s what I’ve been doing and exactly why I don’t want to do it anymore. I’d like to be more than a pretty face. I'm sure that's all Mack saw in me. I hope you see beyond the surface."

"I do. I mean you know about art and wine and business and coding." He followed X's advice to be truthful. "You are beyond awesome." And way beyond a man like him.

"You were doing really well until that last part. I'm no more awesome than anyone else."

She set the pace, and a pretty smart one at that. Though he'd worn his prescription sunglasses, the glare off the water to their right still bedeviled his vision. Sweat ran into his stitches making them sting. "You'd think your employer would provide a limo with A/C," he mumbled.

Josee slowed down and took a good look at him. "Are you okay? Why don't you sit for a while and catch up later? I think that fight is still affecting you."

"No, no, I'm fine, just not in as good a shape as you are. That's all."

"I do work out nearly every day. Really, I have to for the profession."

He refrained from telling her he lifted five-pound weights while he worked on his computer. That did account for his better biceps and shoulders, but they were still nothing much to brag about. Arriving at Old Man River, he sank onto a nearby bench and studied the sculpture.

One of the stranger pieces of public art in the city, the massive nude male figure stood with arms upraised and legs akimbo. The rock-hard buttocks and sculpted chest didn't say "old" to Trin in any way. Oddly, it possessed no hands or feet. When Josee shed her cover-up and moved into position between the statue's legs, he felt glad that the Old Man had no genitals, just a rough patch for a crotch. Surely, the creature would have sprouted an erection when he eyed Josee.

She wore a turquoise bathing suit not as skimpy as those for the swimsuit issue, but still plenty revealing. Josee was no stick figure of a French runway model. He'd watched those full breasts bud and blossom as she grew up, pressed them close to his chest when he got a chance to dance with her. Entirely real, she'd inherited their size from her mother, along with the endless legs the photographer instructed her to spread in mimicry of the piece of art. "Arms up, Josee, arms up! Open those legs wide," the photographer shouted.

Then, she wasn't dewy enough to emulate the river that could be glimpsed beyond the vee of the giant's legs. The ever-hassled Janis came forward and sprayed her with water—which probably felt refreshing at this point. Finally satisfied, her boss dismissed her into the changing room for a switch into a scant golden bikini. Wearing various suits, Josee leaned, lounged, sat upon, and hugged the grotesque statue, beauty and the beast come alive. He hated every minute of it. Josee deserved so much more than to be ordered about by an egotist with a camera.

As the shoot ended and Josee again retreated to her room, a man in a light weight, elegantly cut gray summer suit approached with distress etching his face as if he were in severe pain. White artfully streaked his swept back black hair as if each strand had been perfectly placed. He accosted the photographer. "Adolphe, how could you abuse my beautiful Josee this way—out in this heat, her complexion possibly ruined by sunburn. She won't be able to work again for a week." Flailing his hands in the air only drew a Gallic shrug from his target.

"Marcello, the client wanted his designs framed by iconic New Orleans art. We began very early, and now we are done." The photographer again held out a hand to receive a damp cloth from an assistant and received it.

"Josee has gone above and beyond for you all week. I invoke the special charges clause in her contract." This time, Marcello leaned close into the man's face.

As he mopped his brow, Adolphe launched his own defense. "We had many rain delays, and consider the difficulty of filming in this humidity. Who knows what damage has been done to my equipment? Extra charges, *mon Dieu*! I should bill you for insisting the shoot be done in the summer."

"The designer demanded authenticity."

As the shouting match continued, the staff calmly packed the equipment and rolled it away to a waiting truck. Josee emerged makeup free from her enclosure and clad in white shorts, a red fitted tee, and sandals. She'd drawn her hair into the high ponytail she'd worn at the ranch. Plonking down a huge tote bag of the same lipstick red as her shirt, she went to sit on the bench with Trinity.

"Does this happen often?" he questioned.

"With Marcello, all the time. He's always trying to squeeze more money out of a contract. Of course, he takes a big chunk out of everything he gets, exactly like a sleazy lawyer."

Trin snapped his fingers, not a very crisp sound as his hands were sweating. "The same Marcello who created the Amberello Agency here in town and used to be…" Again, he caught himself before blurting out "one of your mother's lovers." He changed that to "a male model himself," and switched to offer a family anecdote. "Marcello once told my mom she was very gamine but unfortunately too old to be a model. I think she was like twenty-five."

"That's *the* Marcello, yes. He and Amber, the supermodel, formed the agency. They're still together as business partners but never married. Marriage, it is for peasants, no?" Josee said mimicking the man's slight Italian accent. "Still, they had two gorgeous daughters together, both models, but the oldest retired to marry a billionaire real estate man."

He took a chance. "Is that what you plan to do when you give this up?—marry some rich guy. Or do you think marriage is for peasants too?"

"Trin, I'm rich in my own right and not a peasant. I'll do what suits me."

Her blue eyes gazed into his shaded ones so intently, he wished he could read minds, or at least see auras like Xo. Then, he might understand her. Josee lightly traced the stiches on his forehead with her fingertips. He trembled beneath her touch. She noticed.

"You are still shaky from the fight. Did you have breakfast?"

Much as he loved her concern, he admitted, "Two slices of cold pizza and some juice. There's plenty leftover if you'd like to go over to Junior's place and have some."

Her full lips curved into an I-don't-think-so smile. "I was thinking of going to Tujague's. It's nearby on Decatur, and they serve brunch. I think you could use a second breakfast."

"My treat," Trin offered immediately.

Josee called out to the quarreling men, "We're going to Tujague's for breakfast. Want to come along?"

Marcello waved her away. "No, no, we are not finished here. Josee, she is like my own daughter. I will not see her cheated." He waved a beringed finger in Adolphe's face.

"Let's go. They might be here arguing until noon."

Trin had to admit he didn't mind entering the cool, dim interior of the restaurant with its simple, dark furnishings, and a long standup bar where many indulged in mimosas and bloody Mary's early in the day. They settled for ice water and a table away from the window. Josee ordered the famous shrimp remoulade in its spicy pink sauce. He went for Tujague's Benedict, poached eggs on a bed of pulled pork covered in Tasso sauce, no wimpy English muffin, and slice of Canadian bacon for him. "A side order of biscuits and honey too," he added.

As their menus were whisked away, Josee gave him another of those curious smiles he could never interpret. "You may not be a football player, but you certainly eat like one. I don't know where it goes as you certainly aren't fat."

"High metabolism, remember." Groping for another topic that didn't involve his eating habits since Josee hadn't been tempted by his cold pizza, he came up with a good one. "Over there is a picture of Julian Eltinge, an early twentieth century actor."

"Looks like a woman to me," Josee remarked.

"A noted cross-dresser. They took the photo down when doing renovations, but unhappy about being displaced, Julian showed up in a couple's selfie not too long ago."

Josee regarded the picture of the attractive woman wearing a large hat and a coy expression above a low-cut dress. "She certainly seems like the type of person not to be ignored. I don't know where you learn this stuff."

"A curious mind and a lot of ghost tours. Want to take a selfie and see if Julian appears in it?"

"Why not?"

Trim moved to her side of the table and snapped the shot. No ghost appeared, but now he had a picture of him and Josee to cherish. "Say, what are your plans for this afternoon? Are we still on for going to Mariah's tonight? X will be there."

"X is always fun. Maybe Mariah will ask him to sing. I'd enjoy that after taking a nap and getting a shower. I'm beat from the heat."

"He's bringing a date," Trin blurted. "But, yeah, X is always fun. You could nap and shower where I'm staying instead of going across the lake to your parents' house."

"Good idea. Like a turtle, I carry everything I need with me." She indicated the huge tote bag sitting on the terrazzo floor tiles. "Makeup kit, change of clothes and shoes. Let me call home and tell them I'll be out late." She did just that as the savory food came to the table and stopped most of their conversation. As they left, Marcello and Adolphe entered the restaurant like old friends, all their differences put behind them.

"Ah, Josee, our good friend would like to reshoot some of the French Quarter pictures. He will pay the extra charge." Marcello beamed upon his almost daughter as if he'd done her a great favor.

Josee sighed so hard her breasts lifted and the one nearest Trin grazed his arm coming back into position. He needed to walk far and fast immediately before she noticed the effect that produced on him.

"Text me with the dates, time, and location. I'll be there."

Trin took her arm and escorted her into the intense heat. He drew her quickly past the mule-drawn carriages lined up in front of Jackson Square awaiting tourists desiring a ride. Babbling like a tour guide, he told her about horses not being allowed as they didn't stand up to the high temperatures and pointed out the bags beneath the tails that caught their droppings to keep the streets clean as if Josee hadn't grown up in the area. Clutching her elbow, he helped her down curbs and up and across cracked pavement until they reached the straight away of Canal Street and took a direct route to the brownstone condo.

Into the elevator, out into the foyer, a quick unlatching of the door, and they stood in Junior's abode. Josee took it all in. "I kind of love the juxtaposition of fine art and baby toys mixed with giant furniture," she said. "That Japanese screen is exquisite."

"Yeah, pretty. If you want to rest, the guest room is down this hall." He continued to escort her right to the door which he threw open as if showing real estate. Gulp, he'd forgotten to make the bed. Dropping Josee's arm, he rushed to pull up the crumpled duvet and plump the pillows. "Sorry about that. Just make yourself at home. It's a California king because most of Junior's guests come in that size, so plenty of room. I'll just hang out in the living room, and let you alone to rest."

"Nonsense. You truly do look peaked from being out in the heat. This bed has enough room for a family of four. You know, we used to nap together as little kids, you and Mack in an upper bunk and Lorena and me on the bottom, when we visited the ranch."

"I don't recall that." He wasn't peaked from the heat. His nerves were shot from being near Josee and a bed.

"We were very young. My mom took pictures because we were so cute together."

"I'll bet."

"Why don't you lie down on one side and I'll lie down on the other. We'll rest up for tonight." When he hesitated, she added with an arch of her brows, "I promise I won't molest you."

If only she would. "Okay, great." He shucked off his sneakers, folded his glasses carefully on the night table, and laid down on top of the duvet with his arms tucked behind his head. Josee unstrapped her sandals and did the same. A heavy breakfast, a fast walk on a hot day, he could not believe he fell asleep before she did.

****

The rush of water in the shower next door woke him. Trin's hand strayed to the impression Josee's body made in the down cover, still warm from her heat. He'd missed the chance of a lifetime by not making love to her. Putting on his specs, he padded to the bathroom and knocked, got no answer, only the sound of the water pounding down in the glass box enclosure. Maybe she'd fallen. Maybe he just wanted an excuse to open that door. He tried the knob, not locked, and cracked the portal an eye's width.

Josee stood under the downpour with her head bent and her blonde hair darkened by the water hanging over her face as she rinsed lather from the strands. God, she resembled a water nymph, her breasts clearly exposed and peaked by pink nipples, her body, slender and supple as a reed on the edge of a pond. He had to step back, but she whipped her wet hair over her shoulders and turned her head his way. Caught!

She slid the shower door open. "Want to join me, Trinity? I'd like to experience how well you kiss underwater."

Had he heard right? He took a tentative step inside the room, the tiles cool against his feet, but steam filling the air. Two more steps toward the shower.

"I think you'd better take your clothes off first." Josee gave him the full-frontal view, no less lovely than her profile. He registered a bikini wax job between her legs leaving just enough fluff to add interest, all the rest of her sleek.

He peeled off his T-shirt, unzipped the jeans that held in an erection as good as anything Mack could produce—and he'd gone commando this morning. Like most of the Billodeaux men except Teddy, he possessed a thatch of black hair on his not so broad chest that thinned to an arrow below his waist pointing the way. Unlike Josee, he wasn't buffed to perfection, not waxed in any way. Glad he'd forgotten to take off his glasses or he would have missed a great deal, he laid them aside now.

Taking another step forward, he remembered his father's words: Always wear your rubber raincoat and let the lady go first. Retrieving his jeans, he groped the pocket to find the condom he carried there in hopes of—this.

She smiled through the mist. "I'm on the pill, but okay. You don't know where I've been."

With better men than him, most likely, but he'd do his very best for Josee. Sheathing himself, he stepped over the threshold into the downpour, into Josee's arms. He drew back, licking droplets from her lips, her neck, her breasts. His hand roved into that small patch between her legs, and his fingers parted her labia to gain access to her most sensitive spot with his thumb. A long finger, strong from keyboarding, went in search of the elusive G-spot internally. He'd read up on it. Penetrating deeply, he flicked his finger in a come-hither motion as the article suggested. By the way Josee grasped his head and brought his lips to hers to mime the motion of having sex with her tongue, he'd found it. She shuddered hard and fast. She'd come first, but his restraint began to fail.

There was the height difference, but maybe if he backed her against the tiles, he might persuade her to wrap her long legs around him. He could bear her weight, he knew he could. Josee needed no convincing. Her legs swung upward. She trusted him to catch her buttocks in his palms and hold her there as he drove into to her as deep as he could get. By the way she responded, he knew he'd found the spot again and exploited that with his thrusts. He wished he could have held out longer, but he exploded inside her with a force he didn't know he was capable of. She came again.

Slowly, her grip on his shoulders weakened. Her long legs slid down the length of his body and her head bent to rest upon his shoulder. Good thing, because he'd also learned having terrific sex with a woman you loved fell into the class of strenuous exercise after a concussion. Worth it—the throbbing head, the dizziness, the sudden weakness in the knees.

"We'd better get out of here, Trin," Josee whispered.

She turned off the taps with one hand and kept her arm around his waist. They tripped from the shower and indulged in drying off with Junior's jumbo towels. His head spun. Had to make it back to the bed no matter what. Josee helped him under the covers, slid in next to him. Her fingers combed his wet, black curls. A hand pressed a dry washcloth against his stitches.

"We shouldn't have gotten these wet. I shouldn't have enticed you. You aren't well yet."

"I'm fine," he lied and asked the age-old question. "Was it good for you?"

"Spectacular."

That's all he needed to know before passing out.

****

Trinity woke to the scent of an amazing aroma as if he visited an outstanding Italian bistro. His hand went out across the bed. No naked Josee lay there. Figured he'd only been dreaming. Yet when he touched his hair, it lay in damp curls. He sat up slowly. Well, one of them was naked. Finding his glasses on the night table and his clothes neatly laid out on a giant-sized chair, he found clean underwear, put on the rest, and went to seek the source of the tempting odor and the equally tempting Josee.

He found her in the dining room placing a deep casserole dish on top of two golden fleur-de-lis trivets like a Fifties vision of the perfect housewife, her hands in oven mitts, her golden hair waving softly over her shoulders, a welcoming smile upon her face. She'd put on light makeup and a lipstick as red as marinara sauce and equally delectable. "Look what I found in the freezer, labeled with heating instructions."

Trin reeled off the exact words used to describe Junior Polk's perfect lasagna. "Tender noodles layered with mozzarella and a heavy meat sauce, no ricotta, and topped with parmesan cream, seasoned with onions." He scanned the rest of the table and found a tall glass filled with bread sticks, salads chunky with garden vegetables centered on dinner plates, and a resting bottle of opened red wine. "Wow," he said. "I meant to take you out to dinner."

"Consider me a cheap date. I like to dine in most times. Fewer interruptions—but we are still on for dancing if you feel up to it."

"Never felt better." At this very second, he meant it.

"I'm not so sure about that. Maybe just slow dances."

"I'm good with that too." So very good as he'd be able to press Josee's supple body against his and feel every curve. The hell with line dancing.

"I found a bottle of Sangiovese in the wine closet. I hope Junior won't mind that I used it. I'll buy him another"

He must have looked blank because she added, "It's a type of chianti."

"Right, chianti. I've had chianti. Good stuff. Junior is one of the most generous guys I know. Don't worry about it. Besides, Xo is pregnant again, and he doesn't like to drink in front of her, so his stock of wine is outgrowing that closet. You're doing him a favor by using some of it."

"Pour a glass, while I get rid of these mitts. Feel free to dig into the salad. It's already tossed with vinaigrette. I confess I ran across the street and got it takeout. You were sleeping so heavily, I was afraid to be gone too long in case you needed me to wake you—because of the concussion."

"Nope, woke up all by myself when I smelled food. I'm starving." Should he say, "For you" and cross to where she stood to smear that red lipstick with a kiss?

Too late. She'd gone into the kitchen to leave the mitts and retrieve a large serving spoon to dish up the lasagna. She set the salad aside to give him a large portion. As she leaned near, he smelled the pleasant herbal scent of Xochi's homemade soap found in all the bathrooms of the condo. He took a fast sniff of his own fingers, same scent with a remainder of being deep inside Josee. Not a dream? What did a guy say at a time like this? "I love…Junior's lasagna."

"Then, let's eat."

They polished off the salads, two glasses of wine each, but barely put a dent in the huge casserole. "Junior is always afraid Xochi will starve when he's on the road or at training camp, funny but true," he informed Josee.

"That's why he's so dear. Men like that are hard to find."

He wanted to say he was dear, too. Weak or bragging? He let it pass. "Say, I'll clean up and do the dishes."

"Because you are also a dear man." She'd said it for him. "I remember how you escorted the pregnant bridesmaid at Annie's wedding. Most guys would be embarrassed to do that."

Now, he had to confess he wasn't that dear. "To be honest, I complained about it at first. Annie had to talk me into it"—by saying Josee might be impressed by his kindness. Turned out she had been, but he felt wrong taking credit for the good deed.

"You did it, and actions speak louder than words. I'll get dressed for our night out. Won't take me long." She was gone.

If he hadn't volunteered to wash dishes, he might have been in the bedroom watching Josee dress, which simply showed he didn't deserve the "dear" designation. Oh well. He cleared the table and ran hot, soapy water while he covered the leftover casserole with foil and put it in the fridge. He could have placed the dinnerware in the dishwasher, but there wasn't much of it, and he didn't want to be a bad guest by leaving behind unwashed plates and glasses. He'd had his share of experience cleaning the aftermath of much larger dinners, though the ranch had an industrial-sized washer to cope with serving fourteen people every day. Any child who sassed Corazon had to cope with the overflow, a rare thing for him to do, but Mack frequently ended up with dish duty. He and Lorena helped him out, part of being triplets. Sponging each plate and glass, he rinsed them in hot water and laid them out on a dish towel to dry. He'd put them up later. Maybe Josee still primped in the bedroom.

He hurried down the hall and tapped lightly on the closed door. "You decent?"

She opened the door a crack. "Depends on what you mean by decent."

What he could see of her smile seemed coy. "When

you're finished, I need to get in there to change my clothes."

Josee opened the door wide. There she stood in a classic black slip dress that rose well above her knees. Simple and held up by spaghetti straps, it did reveal the tops of her creamy breasts. A single but large black pearl accented by a small diamond hung on a gold chain around her neck, and she'd boosted her height with strappy ice pick heels. Every inch of her was perfect and ready to go. She'd been teasing him and continued to do so. "Mind if I watch you dress?"

"Uh, no, but it won't be much of a show." He'd hung a dress shirt and dark slacks in the closet hoping any wrinkles would fall out. Below them rested a pair of what his daddy would call dancing shoes, supple and shiny. Facing into the closet, he peeled off his T-shirt and dropped his jeans. Should have kicked off his sneakers first because now he had to toe them off under the jeans using an awkward one-legged stance. He didn't dare turn around as the thought of Josee watching him was enough to cause a commotion in his black boxer briefs.

Taking a cue from his brother, Dean, he buttoned up a pale green dress shirt, rolled the sleeves and left the top two buttons open, just enough to show a little chest hair but not enough to be sleazy. With the tails of the shirt hanging down to cover any embarrassment, he removed the pants from their hanger and sat on the bed next to Josee to pull them up, cinching them with the belt already in the loops. He leaned over to unroll the dark socks shoved into the good leather shoes, so seldom worn they'd maintained their shine. "There, done."

"So easy for men," Josee said. She added, "However, I hope you never have to earn your living as a stripper because that wasn't much of a show."

Teasing him again. Trin wished he'd made it sexier rather than functional. He scraped his hand over his chin. He had the five o'clock shadow common to dark-haired men. "I guess I should have shaved first."

Josee ran a polished fingernail down his cheek. "I enjoy a little scruff."

"Good, because I've got one." Nervous, he ran his fingers through his hair and realized it had reverted to its usual tight-curled mess. "I need to do something about this."

"Let me help you. Did you bring any gel?"

"In my shaving kit in the bathroom." The mention of the bathroom brought back all sorts of erotic dreams, but he got up and led the way.

Josee pulled a small stool from under the counter, placed there by the thoughtful Xochi for female guests. She pressed him into place and put out her hand to receive the tube of gel. He turned it over and watched in the mirror as she squeezed out a glob and worked it through the tangled strands, finishing up with a comb as handy as Ike, the barber. She touched the spot where his forehead curls used to be, severed by the nurse to allow for the stitches still giving him a dangerous air. The stubs wanted to stick straight up.

Josee subdued them with the gel. "I do miss those danglers."

"I promise to let them grow back."

"I think we're finished here."

Then, she bent and kissed his nape. His mom used to do that when he had a fever or felt low. What he felt now wasn't anything like that. The coolness of the pearl she wore pressed against his back, but her lips were warm, even hot. He should suggest they stay in tonight and enjoy each other.

Josee stood up to her full height. "Come on. Mariah's Place is waiting for the beautiful people to arrive."

"Half of us is beautiful." He rose, a full head shorter than Josee in her heels.

"Why Trinity Billodeaux, I never suspected you were so vain."

"Uh, no, I meant you were the beautiful one." Now, he saw the teasing smile again too late to come up with a wittier reply. "Let's just go."

Chapter Twelve

Mariah's Place never changed. Though he and Josee had gotten out of a cab in seven p.m. summer sunshine, they entered a world of air-conditioned twilight. A jazz combo already played on the small stage keeping the music low enough for conversation. The volume would increase as the night progressed. Most of the four tops with their bent wood chairs were occupied with tourists trying to get shots of the place that would turn out too dark to use. Singles sat at the bar hoping to hook up with other singles of either sex. Couples on the small checkerboard dance floor swayed against each other rather than showing off their best moves. That also came later when the liquor kicked in. Although the atmosphere ran heavy with the scent of bourbon and beer, no smoke filled the air. Mariah, who had lost much of her vocal range to cigarettes and had to huff oxygen before a brief nightly performance, banned smoking long before the city did.

A long arm waved to them from a dark corner as if encouraging Trin to throw him a pass. X had snagged a table early. Evidently, he and his date had eaten bar food for dinner since a half and half tray of chicken wings and stuffed potato skins still occupied a central place on its top. "We saved some for you."

"Thanks, we ate Junior's lasagna for dinner. Like lions after a kill, we won't need to eat again for days."

Trinity pulled out a chair for Josee and tucked her into place.

X's date, very black with a head full of cornrows cascading in a multitude of tiny braids studded with beads around her broad and beautiful face, said, "Now that's a gentleman."

"Baby, I didn't want to insult your independence as a woman. This is my bro, Trinity, and his friend, Josee. Meet Caressa."

Caressa's carefully plucked eyebrows rose. "I know who you are—celebrities. I do read *People* just like everyone else. Guess I'm the only one at this table not famous."

"For now. Wait until you hear her sing. We got a duet planned for later. Let me stand a round of drinks to get this party started." X stood and mimed a waiter taking an order. "Miss Josee?"

"Sauvignon blanc for me if they've got it."

"I'll take whatever beer Mariah has on draft. The next is on me." That settled, Trin picked up a potato skin stuffed with cheese, bacon, and topped with sour cream, nervous eating. Any time now, the band might play a real slow dance. He'd stand as tall as he could, lead Josee out onto the floor, and resist the urge to rest his head on her chest.

X returned with the white wine in its stemmed goblet and an iced mug of foaming beer. "Thought you weren't hungry, my man."

"Mariah's knows how to stuff a skin. I couldn't resist."

Caressa chuckled, low and throaty. "That sounds almost obscene."

"Sorry, wasn't meant to be." Trin chugged some of

his drink, while Josee with a coy smile on her lips, sipped her wine and left the high calorie snacks alone. "Here we go." He pointed toward the front of the club.

In heels too high for a woman of her age, Mariah mounted the stage wearing her outrageous white wig and a red-sequined dress with a slit up the front. Neither Cher nor Tina Turner had anything on her when it came to wigs and legs. Even Dolly Parton might be envious of the depth of Mariah's cleavage. She filled her lungs with oxygen and belted out her signature song, *Fever,* in a smoke-roughened voice before welcoming her guests for the evening and promising some surprise performances. That done, she retired to her private table with the chair always reserved for her long dead lover, Billy, and discreetly imbibed air from a small, portable machine sitting next to her.

"Nothing keeps Mariah down." Trin finished his beer and braced himself for the first slow dance.

It wasn't long in coming as the band leader announced *Prelude to a Kiss*. "Friends and lovers, get out of your chairs and enjoy a whirl to Duke Ellington's great jazz ballad. This could be your chance to go way beyond that kiss."

The musicians began the instrumental version of a lovely song of longing that suited Trinity perfectly fine. He took a breath, stood, and offered Josee his hand. On the dance floor, he held her snugly, but not too tight, and kept his eyes gazing on hers even if he had to raise them. At one point, she closed hers and leaned into him, letting him guide her around with complete trust. Next best thing to being in bed with her.

The song ended far too soon only to be replaced with a fast number that brought out X and Caressa. Like most things X, he knew how to jitterbug. His date's braids flailed, and her sulphur-yellow dress flared around her abundant hips. They soon cleared the floor as other dancers stepped aside to watch the performance. Flipping his partner over his forearm, and she was no light weight, X garnered applause.

Figured that he could show Trin up so easily. "X is great. You'd probably enjoy dancing with him more, Josee."

"Not in these shoes. I'm looking forward to our next slow dance."

That restored his confidence. Returning to the table, X passed behind him, and Caressa, dabbing her sweating face with a napkin, dropped into her seat. "I shouldn't have eaten those wings. We're on soon for our duet, and I need to clean up and calm down. Ladies' room, Josee?" The women left together to do whatever groups of women did in restrooms.

X eyed Trin across his beer. "Looks like you're doing just fine with Josee. You don't need my help."

"Our dance was nothing compared to yours."

"Not what I meant. You have that 'got me some' look about you and can hardly hold back bragging about it. You're also wearing a red lipstick mark on the back of your neck in the shape of her lips. She done put her mark on you, man."

Trin moved his hand to his nape but didn't touch the spot. "I don't guess I'll wipe that off for a long time."

"Damn right, sexier than a hickey and not as painful. I keep tellin' you that you don't need me as a wingman."

Another fast song ended as the ladies returned from

the restroom. Mariah signaled for a drum roll and pointed toward X and Caressa. She climbed the three steps to the stage with an effort and introduced, "One of my favorite Sinners, X-avier Hopkins, the running back better known as the Missile, and a newly discovered talent, Caressa Moore, performing *Unforgettable*. Let's give them some encouragement." With her long, red lacquered nails flashing in the stage lights, Mariah lead the applause.

"Break a leg," Josee told Caressa as the couple left their table.

"Same from me," Trin said belatedly, sure X was about to show him up again, because the man just couldn't help himself.

He had to admit both performed the classic Nat King Cole song well, giving it soul and meaning though X's voice wasn't as smooth. He made up for that by staring into Caressa's eyes and taking her hands at key moments in the duet. As for Caressa, her voice was as rich and dark as duck gumbo and equally as satisfying. Not a great beauty like Josee and a little hefty, her singing could make a man forget the physical and go for the transcendent. Trin wondered if X had met his match. With a spellbinding performance underway, no one got up to dance. As the last notes sounded, he moved his hand over Josee's and said, "You're unforgettable, too, Josee."

"And you are…"

He didn't get to hear the rest of her sentence. Was he unforgettable or simply full of bullshit? As X left the stage, Caressa launched into *Lovefool* and beckoned him to love her, love her.

A tall shadow fell over their table, and it didn't

belong to X. Josee's face froze over, harder than Trin had ever seen it.

"These seats taken, Josee?"

He turned in his chair to view the movie star handsome man towering over him. Not that the guy noticed him. With cold blue eyes and a sweep of blond hair Trin figured had to be dyed, the bladed nose and high cheekbones of a Viking, but a build more slender, he recognized the man as Josee's last boyfriend, Dirk Bryant. Oh, how he'd rejoiced when the tabloids reported their breakup after six months of a volatile relationship. The actor wasn't good enough for her, but who was?

"No, Dirk, they are occupied. Why don't you move along since the restraining order I have against you says you must remain three hundred feet away from me."

"Honey, is that true?" his companion, a svelte brunette with eyes of feline green, said. Her nails, painted emerald and accented with tiny crystals, dug into his biceps.

"After riding my coattails for six months, this slut jumped off and accused me of hitting her. One time, and she gets a restraining order."

Josee stood, but no quicker than Trinity who knocked over his chair in the hurry. He stood between them but might as well not have been there at all as their angry eyes flashed above him like lightning bolts thrown by ancient gods. "More like you were riding on the train of my gowns at all those openings and award shows, Dirk. Hit me once, and a man never gets another chance," Josee spat in his face.

"Bitch!" Her ex reached for her slender neck with his manicured hands. Trinity grabbed them and shoved him away, dislodging the brunette who fell into the lap of a guy at the next table. He turned to see if Josee approved of his quick action. He'd head butt another jerk for her even if it meant a worse headache. Probably wouldn't be necessary since he caught the gesture Mariah made to the muscular men in tight black tees who worked on the Sinners practice squad days and moonlighted as bouncers at night.

Dirk didn't back off. "Who is this dweeb, Josee? He must have money because he doesn't have fame or great looks. I see you've already marked him with your vampire lips."

"I've known this dweeb since childhood, and he has done more for me in two weeks than you did in six months. Get lost, Dirk."

"Who's gonna make me?"

"Trinity and me." X loomed up behind him, full of muscle and the threat of violence. "I'm his wingman. Watch out because this dweeb is scrappy."

Still, the ass didn't have the sense to leave. The two bouncers seized both arms and dragged him away, pausing at Mariah's table to see what she wanted them to do with him. "Hold him outside for the police. Didn't you hear Josee has a restraining order on this guy?"

"I doubt your dump is three hundred feet altogether. I'm Dirk Bryant. Remember the name when I'm a famous star who will buy you out and tear this place down." Struggling against two men in far better shape, he launched one last volley at Josee before they dragged him out the door. "This isn't over!"

Mariah made her way to their table. "You're always safe in Mariah's Place," she assured Josee. Her green eyes turned toward the brunette still ensconced in a stranger's lap. "Deary, Dirk is bad news. Let me get you a drink and call a cab."

Dirk's date asked Josee, "Did he really hit you?"

"Once and only once. I blacked the eye he claimed happened when he did a stunt for a movie. Oh, he's a liar, too. He can't get a movie contract because of his temper. You are well off without him."

"Good to know. I think I'll accept that drink, but I'd like to stay a while with my new friend if that's okay?" Since both seemed pleased by the arrangement, Mariah gave her consent with a nod.

Trin picked up his chair, held Josee's again and seated himself, glad shaking knees didn't show beneath the table, not that they would have stopped him if Dirk actually laid hands on her. The music had stopped in the midst of the scene. Mariah waved a hand. "From the top," she croaked, almost out of air again. Caressa took up the lyrics, begging X to fool her, fool her.

Sending a brilliant smile and a thumbs-up her way, X folded into his chair. "Close one. I thought we'd have another barroom brawl on the way, and your stitches from the last one ain't healed yet. You're getting to be one bad dude, Trinity Billodeaux."

"It's my fault. I attract men like Dirk, and I've fallen for them before. No more." Josee finished her wine with one swallow. "I could use a refill."

"My turn." Trinity rose. "What are you drinking, X? Should I get something for Caressa? She seems very, ah, attached to you."

"Part of the act, my man. She's going to be singing the rest of the night. I met her in church, and I do know talent when I hear it. Won't hurt her career for our names to be linked for a while, but X, he ain't ready to settle down so soon. Now you two are more mature, let's say."

The hint was broad enough to make Trin hope he wouldn't go red, or if so, be spared any notice in the murk of the club.

A few more drinks, a few more slow dances, and X said good-bye after giving Caressa a kiss on the cheek during her break. "My work here is done. Y'all are on your own. I think you can handle anything from here."

Trinity wasn't certain of that. He looked toward Josee for a clue.

"I'm ready to leave, too. I might even consider another shower."

Not a dream, then. Trinity rose to face reality with Josee Riley on his arm.

Chapter Thirteen

They didn't head for the shower, but went directly to the bedroom of the condo, no debate this time about who slept where. Josee shed her tall heels along the way. On the edge of the bed, Trin stripped her little black dress over her head and came back for the lacy, strapless bra and panties, hooking the last with his thumbs to draw them all the way down. He paused on the way to kiss that beckoning fluff between her legs and do some tongue work that had her opening and leaning back to accept him. He stayed longer than he intended teasing that little nub and exploring deep inside her. He was right there when she clenched and arched back on the spread. His research said women enjoyed this, and he did too, the very taste and essence of her. Tempted to linger, but needing to move along for his own sake. he disposed of the panties entirely, leaving nothing but her necklace, and rose to tear at his own clothes, very much in the way.

He laid his glasses aside, unbuttoned his shirt, ripping off a button in his haste, and took his briefs down over a very prominent erection. He really should have kicked off his shoes before lowering his slacks. Cursing under his breath, he had to sit to get out of his britches. Why did he always forget to shuck the shoes?

Now curled on the bed, Josee laughed gently, reached out, and pulled him down full length on the spread. She straddled his legs and leaned forward. “Seems I should return the favor.” Her lips descended and ringed him in her red lipstick. She licked the head of his penis, already slick with desire, and began to suck.

“Stop,” he gasped. “I can’t hold out. Get the rubber raincoat. I mean the condom in my pants. Quick.”

She did, smoothing it over him with firm strokes that made the situation more urgent. When he tried to pull himself over her, she resisted. “No, I want you to take it easy. Let me do the work this time. I know that concussion is still bothering you the way you slept after our shower together.”

“I honestly thought I’d dreamed that.”

Now her laughter covered him with warmth and joy. “Hardly. I guess men do dream of me, but I assure you I took an active part. That thing you did with your finger, amazing. Wherever did you learn that?”

“Research, not another woman, I swear. I saved it for you.”

“Oh, Trin, you truly are dear.” With a few quick hand strokes, she restored any rigidity lost to conversation and lowered herself over him.

He didn’t close his eyes, didn’t want to miss a second of it from her full breasts moving over his chest, the black pearl bobbing between them, to her loose hair forming a golden curtain over them, even if the sight was a little blurry. All the while, the pressure built between his legs. He couldn’t hold on, couldn’t hold on, but then her blue eyes darkened and her lids covered them as she came, and he went right along with her. Josee collapsed against his chest, and he smoothed her hair away from her cheek, bent to kiss the top of her head. “So good,” he murmured.

“Better than that.” Josee rolled to lie beside him. “I wish I’d saved it all for you, but no, as soon as I turned eighteen and got out from under my mother’s wing, I did exactly what she told me not to do—got involved with a photographer, the very first one to do a shoot with me after I escaped from being the innocent ingénue. He was happy to teach me all about sex and nothing about love. His next model was his next conquest. Mom also said no male models. Their egos are too big. Actually, a lot of them are gay and very sweet, at least to me, but I managed to find a straight one. I had to break every rule she tried to teach me. Later, she said that man was Marcello all over again. I’d followed in her footsteps.” She shivered as their bodies cooled off from hot sex.

Trin folded down the covers, drew the duvet and top sheet over them, and held her close. “It’s all right. I doubt we’d be so good together if neither of us knew what we were doing.”

“I swear there weren’t as many others as it seems. Mostly, I served as arm candy for rising stars thanks to Amberello’s active PR department, good for both of us they’d say. See and be seen. Make the tabloids. I rarely slept with any of them, and truthfully, some I suspected to be gay as well. Then, along came Dirk the Jerk, charming and handsome at first, good in the sack, then possessive, and finally, abusive. He slapped my face just once for dancing with another man earlier in the evening. I balled my fist, blacked his eye, and called the cops from a neighbor’s house. The police held him long enough for me to gather my things and get the restraining order. I haven’t seen him since before tonight. In fact, I've been avoiding L.A. to stay away from his hunting grounds."

Every depleted cell in Trinity's body begged him to go to sleep but listening—listening was important. They were having a moment. He rubbed her back in soothing circles. "I wonder what brought him here—unless he's stalking you." He stifled a yawn. He cared, he really did, and that kept him going.

"Marcello did mention that my old boyfriend had landed a multiple episode part with *NCIS: New Orleans* playing a villain. Dirk shouldn't have to study too hard for the role."

"I agree with you there. I don't think he'll try anything more, at least not at Mariah's. It's our safe place." He continued his gentle massage. She didn't answer, but slept with total trust, her head on his chest. He didn't want to disturb her and allowed himself to drift off just as they were.

****

Bells sounded from the Quarter on Sunday morning, probably from old St. Louis Cathedral on Jackson Square. If Xochi or his Mawmaw Nadine were nearby, they'd be hustling him off to church. In accordance with the Billodeaux family rules, the boys were raised Catholic, all except Teddy, a well-established Baptist when he joined the family, and escorted to church by their reluctant dad. The girls followed their mom to an Episcopal service, with the exception of Xo, baptized into the religion his mawmaw called the Holy Cat'lic Church. But Trinity had fallen away as soon as he escaped to college. Now, watching Josee sleeping beside him, lovely in the morning light filtering through the curtains, he thought he should give thanks for a miracle next time he passed the cathedral.

During the night Josee had shifted to her side. Her long hair drifted across his chest like the sunbeams that illuminated her perfect face. Trin put his hands behind his head and pondered, "What would a dear man do?" Definitely not wake her up for early morning sex. Tucking the covers around her, he found his glasses on the nightstand, left the bed, went to the closet, and recovered the jeans he'd left balled there on the floor. Drawing them up, he tiptoed from the bedroom and headed for the kitchen. Maybe breakfast in bed.

He scanned the shelves and the fridge. Still some leftover pizza which would not do at all. He wasn't much of a cook, and with no fresh groceries he couldn't rely on scrambled eggs, but to his amazement, he found a box of complete pancake mix, just add water. Must be Xochi's as surely Junior made everything from scratch. Other discoveries included a can of frozen orange juice, a bag of chopped pecans, and a jug of pure maple syrup. The spice rack held cinnamon along with a large selection of dried herbs he had no idea how to use.

Okay, just add water to the juice and the mix. He heated a skillet and doctored the plain batter with pecans and cinnamon. If nothing else, the pancakes smelled good as they hit the pan. Another container in the freezer yielded what he suspected to be some very good coffee. If the coffeemaker was a bit complicated, so what. He didn't excel in math for nothing. After starting the brew, he flipped his pancakes to find one side burnt, disposed of those, and started a new batch. This time, he'd watch them more carefully.

He concentrated so hard on getting both sides of

the flapjacks just the right golden color that he failed to hear the light patter of Josee's bare feet as she approached and wrapped her arms around his waist. He jumped as he transferred a pancake to a plate and sent it spinning to the tiled floor like an out of control frisbee.

"Sorry," Josee breathed in his ear. "I didn't mean to startle you. No half naked man has ever made breakfast for me."

"How about fully clothed men?" He stooped to retrieve the fallen flapjack and flung it into the sink. She stood there garbed in some sort of silky, white full-length robe, tied at the waist, caressing her breasts and hips, nothing else underneath it.

"None of them either. I'll set the table. Smells delicious."

Her other men most likely ordered expensive room service or had their cooks whip up something. Still, he'd done his best, and that counted with Josee.

He warmed the syrup because that seemed like something Junior would do and brought it to the table in a small pitcher he unearthed in a cupboard. Josee waited for him with the juice poured and empty plates ready to receive his effort at cooking. Hey, the pancakes turned out pretty good, at least according to Josee who ate two, probably twice her normal allotment.

"I'll have to get on the road to Lafayette after dinner, but how would you like to spend the afternoon—NOMA, the aquarium, strolling the Riverwalk, or the Quarter?" Let her decide.

Josee licked syrup from those beautifully formed lips. "I'd like to spend the day in bed and order in for dinner if that's all right with you."

Trinity tried to suppress a smile that might have cracked his face wide open. A hint of it escaped anyhow. “Exactly my idea of the best way to spend a Sunday afternoon.”

The most difficult part came when they said good-bye beside the car Josee had borrowed from her father’s collection. Unlike the daughter, it was nothing special, almost inconspicuous. Obviously, she had no desire to stand out and be followed by her fans. They shared a kiss that lingered on the lips and tongue before he made sure her seatbelt was fastened, and her doors locked for her trip across the causeway to Mandeville. He watched her drive away, then headed toward his Lafayette apartment, his job, his not extraordinary life.

Chapter Fourteen

How he managed to keep his mind on coding and game development, Trinity did not know. He lived for the evenings when he spoke with Josee. His conversation centered around new additions to Joe's World. Her more exciting life around the photo shoot and hanging out with those in her profession, in other words, the beautiful people. She described Adolphe's latest demands in the art museum's sculpture garden such as holding hands with the somewhat beefy statue of naked Venus Victrix and plastering herself against the super-manly and also nude Heroic Man.

Sometimes, his call reached her at a nightclub with a loud band pulsing in the background. She'd gone out with friends, wished he were there. He didn't. He wasn't the type of guy the guard at the door would move to the front of the line—unless he played on the Billodeaux name and slipped the man a fat tip. Clubs were not his scene. What they'd started was good, but would it last if he didn't fit into her more frenetic lifestyle?

On Thursday night, Josee seemed more subdued, almost hesitant to talk. Could she be tired of him already? Had he called too often? He tested his footing with her. "I'm really looking forward to seeing you tomorrow night. That is, if we are still on for the weekend."

"Can't wait. I'll meet you in the lobby of the condo. I'll feel safe there with Arturo on duty."

He jumped on her words. "Why don't you feel safe? Hasn't Adolphe been providing security?"

"He has, but when I go out people always photograph me and sometimes post where I am. Dirk keeps showing up. At the club the other night, I slipped out the second I saw him, but I know he was searching for me. I had to leave a restaurant when he walked in."

"Hey, it's supposed to be the other way around." He hated the tone of anxiety in her voice and suspected things had gotten worse.

"I didn't want a scene, but I got one this afternoon. We were finished with our shoot for the day. Some of the crew mentioned they were filming *NCIS: New Orleans* street scenes a couple of blocks away. They wanted to take a peek. I shouldn't have gone along with them. There Dirk sat in a director's chair waiting for his cue. As soon as he spotted me, he stood up and pointed, shouting, 'Get away from me, Josee Riley. There's a restraining order.' He made it seem as if he'd gotten one against me."

"I'm guessing you didn't let him get away with that." He knew her that well from childhood. She'd always stood up for herself if the boys tormented her in any way.

"No. I called back, 'I got that restraining order against you, Dirk the Jerk.' Some of the onlookers laughed. Others took pictures. The director gained control by telling him he was on in two minutes, to get into place for a race down an alley as Dirk turned red with anger over what I'd called him. I got out of there in a hurry, but Trin, it's all over the internet. You might as well do a search for it."

He did, and found a brief encounter, an exchange of words, just the kind of sensational stuff that fed the trends. The hatred on Dirk's face showed plainly as did the fear on Josee's, though her words were brave and defiant.

"We'll be together soon. I won't let him hurt you."

"You might not be able to stop him."

"I'm scrappy, remember." He got her to laugh, a good sound. "Don't worry. We'll stay in Friday night and do as we please on Saturday and Sunday, Dirk or no jerk."

Her laugh this time came across as stronger, but she had more to tell him. "Sorry to say we won't have Saturday morning. Rain is expected tomorrow, and the final day of the shoot was postponed until then. But, please be there. We'll be filming in front of the Banksy stencil of the girl with an umbrella on Kerlerec and North Rampart. Directly after, we can have the rest of the day to ourselves."

"You can count on me." Trin wanted to end the conversation with "I love you," but held it back and settled for "I want to see you again so badly. Bye."

His wasn't finished for the evening, however. Never in his life had he downloaded an app on his phone to track celebrities. Just had no interest in them and knew how intrusive such apps could be. He did so now, not intending to spy on Josee. She slept in the safety of her parents' home tonight.

Nope, he wanted to know every public move Dirk the Jerk made while in New Orleans. Right at the moment, the man dined at a popular restaurant with outdoor seating. Bryant sat at a table in clear view of the public, bathing in adulation as people who hardly knew his identity took his picture simply because he'd appeared on the app. He emoted bonhomie with a toothy grin. See me, I'm a great guy. Yeah, right. Trin shut down his phone. He'd keep an eye on Josee's ex as long as the man lingered in the Big Easy.

****

She'd waited for him in the lobby of the condominium building exactly as she'd promised. Josee didn't run to embrace him, but she rose and took his hand. Though the vigilant doorman stood on guard, not just for them but for other celebrities who lived in the building, they could be easily photographed through the glass doors. Sedately, they walked to the elevator, embraced once the doors closed, and frantically moved as far as Junior's long sofa before their clothes came off, and they grappled to be together. Better than he'd ever imagined with Josee on top once more, stroking him, setting the pace. He'd get his chance to be in the superior position later, but really didn't care. With Josee, it was all good. Once the urgency left them, they made it to the bedroom and slept well until her alarm went off early summoning her to the last photo shoot on the corner of Kerlerac and North Rampart.

He grabbed coffee and croissants for both of them at the nearby coffee shop. They ate in the car that had been sent to deliver Josee to her assignment. After that, he sat patiently out of the way while Janis, the makeup girl, and a dresser with a weight problem and a homely face that said she wanted to be in the fashion business no matter what, went to work painting the model's famous face and donning her in a red dress with an innocent white collar open at the neck and cap sleeves.

A locket on a thin chain hung in the gap. The hem floated just below her knees. Nothing sexy about it until Adolphe signaled one of the assistants to spray Josee with water from head to toe, making the fabric cling to her body, forcing her nipples to rise beneath the cloth. Ironically, she held an open black umbrella as a prop, her pale face and wet hair in stark contrast against it.

Trin had no fear she'd catch pneumonia. This early in the day, New Orleans already steamed and demanded he sip continuously from a bottle of water. However, he did object to her exploitation, but had no right to say so. He also figured Banksy, the mysterious street artist who spent some time in New Orleans back in 2008 spreading his creations randomly around town, wouldn't approve of the commercialization of his drawing, the little girl in a similar dress also drenched despite her protective umbrella. Many thought Banksy had created a poignant commentary on Hurricane Katrina in the figure.

For no explicable reason, the art work had been vandalized many times, once with red paint, again with black tar. Only a covering of Plexiglas saved her. She'd been carefully cleaned each time and also survived a robbery attempt, but the thieves found it difficult to transport a painting attached to a building. If they had succeeded, the piece might have brought a million dollars on the black market.

Unfortunately, the koi fish painted by another artist on the sidewalk nearby and meant to convey warmth and happiness hadn't fared as well. Trin asked himself the age-old question as Josee modeled, "Why did some people have the urge to destroy things both good and beautiful?" That made him think of Dirk who'd once marred Josee's face with a punch. He checked the celebrity app again. The asshat currently played his role at the studio. Good. He and Josee could go anywhere they wished after this ended.

Adolphe called an end to the shoot at last. Josee folded her umbrella, and the crowd began to disperse. Trin stayed put and sipped more of his water. He'd have a wait while Josee changed from her damp clothes.

A shambling man, unshaven and thin, one of the many street dwellers of the city, pushed forward instead of leaving. He slid through a gap in the barriers more quickly than anyone seeing his poor condition might have expected. Trin thought he must be making for the table of beverages and snacks laid out for the staff, but no. One grimy hand poking from a ragged Army jacket clutched an open white bottle by its neck. Booze? No, since he'd been living on his own, Trin had occasion to use the contents of a bottle like that—liquid drain opener. He flashed back to Brother Benedict's eleventh grade chemistry class lecture on the dangers of handling sulfuric acid, barely listened to but evidently absorbed for this very moment.

"A common ingredient of battery acid and drain cleaner, sulfuric acid is a very dangerous substance. Before we make our thunderstorm in a test tube, put your safety glasses in place and glove your hands. If any should get on your skin, wash it off at the sink immediately." He made the connection in a flash and pushed forward. Thank you, underappreciated Brother Benedict.

The bum rasped, "Josee Riley." She turned her lovely face full toward him. Trin shouted loud as a trumpet at a jazz funeral, "Over here, Josee!" Her head swung his way as her attacker splashed the acid and fled. The fluid hit the tender flesh of her cheek and neck turning it red, bubbling the skin. Josee screamed, agony in every octave.

Trinity vaulted the barriers and squeezed his water bottle on the damage. He issued his own orders with the same authority as the Christian Brother, "Spray her!" to the crew frozen in place. "Call an ambulance."

Josee fell to her knees. "It burns. It burns." She grabbed at the oval locket nestled in the hollow her neck. He shoved her hand away and took his chances, snapping the slender chain and allowing the water now showering both of them to reach the acid pooled beneath it. He held back her hair to allow the spray to better reach her cheek, but he could see some of the strands had been eaten away. He remembered Josee consoling the boy with cancer, telling him his hair would grow back and said the same to her, "It will grow back. Don't worry, my love."

He doubted she heard him as she panted to cope with the pain. Sirens sounded. Medics arrived and pried Josee from his arms. "We've got her now. Quick thinking with the water."

He stood, dripping. "Could you transport her to Ochsner? I have a sister who works there," he said as he ran alongside the gurney.

"If they can take us." No promises made. He wanted Josee to have the best of care and the protection of his fierce sister, Jude. "You a relative?"

"No, a friend." A man who wanted to be so much more to her. "Can I go with her?"

"Not our policy. Check with Ochsner in an hour.

See if she was admitted. But, again, nice work preventing more damage. We'll give her something for the pain."

The EMT slammed the doors to the ambulance in his face. He became aware of others around him. Josee's dresser handed him a towel intended for the model. Mopping his face, he noticed that the thin chain of the locket was still threaded through his fingers. He shoved it in a pocket. To his right, the security guards sat on the man who had flung the acid. They struggled to get the cuffs on him and finally knocked his head against the cement. Police brutality? He didn't think so.

Adolphe wrung his hands and cried, "Thank *le bon Dieu* that was our last shot. *Pauvre* Josee. But this will make her more famous, *c'est vrai,*" as if nothing else mattered. Trin wanted to shove the photographer's beret down his throat.

"Ignore him. Adolphe is a brilliant photographer but otherwise a real French douche," Janis said. "You'd better go home and change your clothes, hero. Might have been much worse without you here. I've worked with Josee before and known her for a while. Whether it's a bad boyfriend or a crappy assignment, she's resilient. You'll see. When she falls down, she gets up stronger. If she needs my help to cover up the damage, she only has to ask."

"Yeah, thanks. I'll tell her." He balled the towel and handed it over to the hovering dresser who perhaps feared he'd steal it and she'd be held accountable. Shoving a hand in his pocket, he withdrew the locket. He studied it for a moment, a simple piece of jewelry on a now broken chain, probably gold, with a light engraving he could barely make out as if it had been fingered often. "I guess this belongs to the designer." He held it out.

"No, that's Josee's. I've seen her wear it often lately. It seemed to accessorize the simple dress well, so we used it. Would you give it back to her with our best wishes?"

The guards wrangled the stunned attacker into a squad car. The police didn't need his statement. Plenty of witnesses around to tell what happened. He'd bet some had photographed the attack while he screamed for water. He'd ridden in the town car with Josee to get here, but no one offered him a lift, and he really didn't want one. Certainly, the press would descend at any moment, and he desired to be far away when they did.

Instead, he began walking. Tourists stared at his drenched condition and his squeaking, sodden sneakers, just another bizarre New Orleans character they certainly assumed. Full of anger, he strode along checking the celebrity app. No way did he believe that pathetic creature had decided to throw acid in Josee's face on his own.

He searched for Dirk Bryant, went back to last evening's sighting at the restaurant and followed him forward coming out of a drugstore with an opaque white bag. Dirk held it up and leered at his fans. "Condoms," he claimed, but the sack seemed weightier than that. Dirk must buy the large economy size if it were true. The wannabe star, still trailed by a few diehards, stopped along the way to his room and paused to drop some bills in a vagrant's cap. The dozing man, propped against a lamppost, awoke from his nest of rags, astounded by the generosity.

"Hey, fella, let me buy you a meal." Dirk offered

him a hand up. Despite the glare of the doorman, they entered a posh hotel and disappeared into a private elevator, all dutifully recorded by the person the doorman failed to spot. Trin recognized the army jacket, the tall, bony frame of the man who had thrown the acid. Didn't Dirk realize the e-world never slept and never forgot?

By the time he reached the condo, he'd dried off considerably in the heat. Changing his damp clothes for dry, he had one more place he wanted to go besides the hospital to see Josee. It wasn't that far. He walked to St. Louis Cathedral and followed the checkerboard marble main aisle beneath the flags fluttering as tourists opened and shut the doors to a side altar where he shoved some bills into the wooden box and selected two unlit votive candles. Holding a match to one already burning, he lit his own.

"Mother Mary, I thank you for allowing me to love a woman like Josee Riley."

For the second prayer, he gathered his thoughts, finally saying, "Please permit Josee to have a complete recovery, but if that is not possible, let her know that I love her anyway and will care for her always."

He took a seat in a pew and called Ochsner. Yes, Miss Riley had been checked in, but no more information was forthcoming. Next stop, the hospital no matter how long he had to wait to see her.

Chapter Fifteen

Trinity sat in the waiting room—waiting. A nurse he suspected of being an undercover agent from her suspicious demeanor told him only that Miss Riley had been moved to a private room. Her parents were with her now. He, as only a friend, must wait until summoned. He dubbed her Nurse Starchy no matter what her ID said.

Eyeing the half-filled coffeepot sitting on a table surrounded by paper cups, packets of sweeteners, and dry creamer, he decided against adding caffeine, being jittery enough. Exactly how badly had Josee been injured? Had he done enough to save her from major damage?

A small TV set mounted high to prevent tampering ran and reran news of the attack on an entertainment channel, complete with footage of the two of them being hosed down to dissipate the acid. Yes, someone always had a camera ready these days. Josee still looked sexy soaking wet and suffering. He merely appeared lame with his curls hanging down over his forehead and his glasses fogged over as he supported her in his arms. He wanted nothing to do with being dubbed a hero or drawing attention to the Billodeaux family. They'd had enough from Stacy's trial to Xochi's kidnapping, and most recently his sister Annie's conceiving a child out of wedlock with Matt

Keaton, a Sinners' running back. Never a dull moment among the Billodeauxs.

So, he'd called in the evidence against Dirk Bryant found on the celebrity tracker to an anonymous crime stopper line and hoped the police took immediate action. The man needed to be locked up. He paced, constantly checking the news on the phone, to see if Dirk had been arrested. Not so far.

When the golden couple entered the room, the eyes of all the occupants from a blanket-bundled granny in a wheelchair to a middle-aged woman who had confided she awaited word on the effects of her father's stroke, turned toward the doorway. Trin stopped twiddling with his phone. Connor and Stevie Riley seemed to bring light with them—and maybe vital information.

Connor, once a Sinners' wide receiver noted for the long, blond hair that hung from beneath his helmet and the tragic accident that broke his neck and almost ended his career, possessed long legs, broad shoulders, and a trim body even later in life. His famous locks had been shorn into a cut more appropriate for a renowned sports commentator and inspirational speaker. Trin regarded him as the nicest of his dad's friends.

Stephanie Dowd Riley, always called Stevie, stood beside him, nearly as tall and just as blond, though both showed some streaks of white. She'd hewed out a career as a sports photographer and remained a natural beauty, not one to wear much makeup or fuss about clothes. Though her blue eyes had crinkles in the corners and the laugh lines beside her mouth had deepened, he still saw her as the crush of the older Billodeaux boys in their teens. Of course, their fantasies had been egged on by the erotic pictures of a young

Stevie they'd found on the internet. Now, Josee had taken her place in his heart.

Connor strode forward to grasp his hand in a firm, masculine shake. "Thank you for being there to save Josee from greater harm," he said with apparently no animosity that Trin had slept with his daughter the last two weekends.

Stevie embraced him to her full, warm chest. "Really, without your fast action, the damage could have been so much worse."

"How is she?" That's all he wanted to know.

"In surgery right now. We'll wait here until she gets out. Sit with us." Stevie led him to a sofa big enough to hold the three of them. Good thing because his knees had turned to jelly at the mention of surgery.

"I wasn't fast enough to prevent it." All his second guesses came roaring back.

"No, not at all. That spot beneath the locket is a third-degree burn but didn't reach the muscle and voice box underneath. All the rest are first and second degree and should heal in a matter of weeks. The plastic surgeon felt covering the throat area with cadaver skin would aid in closing the wound. Later, she might need a small graft from her own body to prevent scarring. It's wonderful what they can do for her." Stevie squeezed his hand. Years ago, this woman sat beside Connor Riley for hours waiting to learn if he'd be paralyzed. Now, she exhibited the same determined confidence that her daughter would be completely healed again.

"Excuse me," the woman who had been quietly praying for her father said as she approached their group. "I'm so sorry about your beautiful daughter. I'll add her to my prayers—but could I bother you to write an encouraging note to my dad. He's such a big Sinners fan and knows your story well, Mr. Riley." She held out a small notebook tentatively as if Connor might slap it away.

It wasn't in the man's nature to do so. The recipe he'd donated to Joe Billodeaux in order to support Camp Love Letter had been dubbed Connor's Sweet and Mild Sauce. That said it all. Riley penned not simply his name but a paragraph that Trin read as he wrote. "You can overcome this setback with good care and the help and love of your family. Do your PT. Don't give up. Geaux Sinners! Connor Riley."

"Oh, thank you so much!"

The woman stepped away to be replaced by the old lady in the wheelchair. Trin had assumed she'd been incapable of moving on her own or perhaps speaking as she hadn't said a word previously. In her blue-veined hands, she held out a couple of napkins taken from the coffee counter.

"I need two autographs. One for my grandson. He's in ICU from a car crash. His parents are with him, and I'm told I must wait my turn. Imagine when he wakes up and I show him I met *the* Connor Riley. Make one out to Wes and the other to Selma." Evidently, the aged did not require good manners.

Trin noticed she hadn't mentioned Josee, but her troubles did appear greater. Connor wrote more briefly, "Wishing you a full and complete recovery, Wes" and "Great meeting you, Selma." Happy with that, Selma stowed the napkins in her sagging bra and patted her hand over her breast as if she imagined Connor doing the same. She wheeled her chair into a corner and settled down for a nap.

Hostile Nurse Starchy poked her head into the lounge. "Mr. and Mrs. Riley, your daughter is in recovery and will be in her room shortly if you wish to wait there in more privacy." Her glare encompassed Trin and the two women.

Stevie rose, taking her comforting warmth with her. "Thank you. We'll do that." Turning toward Trinity, she said, "Josee will want to see you. We'll send word as soon as possible." Josee's parents left, taking their optimism with them.

Almost noon, he hadn't eaten since that early morning croissant. He guessed he should put some fuel in his body but didn't want to leave the area for a trip to the cafeteria. He settled on a packet of peanuts, some cheese crackers, and a Diet Coke from the vending machines in the hall. The middle-aged woman left to seek out a better lunch. Selma snored on as the news at noon blared with more details of the attack on Josee.

The man arrested suffered from extreme PTSD and had a record of becoming belligerent with tourists he suspected of being enemy agents. In the past, this had not amounted to physical violence. However, he carried a large amount of cash for a street person and admitted he'd done a favor for a true friend. That friend, Dirk Bryant, an actor and Josee Riley's ex-boyfriend was also now in custody. Trin breathed easier and began to eat his snacks. His relief didn't last.

"We have also identified the young man who courageously aided Miss Riley and stayed by her side until help arrived. He is Trinity Billodeaux, son of Hall of Fame quarterback, Joe Billodeaux. Employed by Hartz Technology, his Facebook page identifies him as a computer genius. He certainly is a quick thinker."

Great. Where had they gotten his name? Maybe from well-meaning Janis or Adolphe who more or less ignored him like a dog turd in the gutter. He'd been joking when he created that profile. They'd used his super-geek photo from the site, too. Scrubbing his face with his hands, he glanced up to find Selma holding out another napkin. Amazing how she could sneak up on people. "You didn't tell me you were a celebrity, too, and a real life hero," she accused. "Sign right here."

"Truly not much of either."

She obviously wouldn't go away until she got what she wanted. He looked to Connor Riley for inspiration and wrote, "Nice meeting you, Selma" with a cheap pen taken from his shirt pocket, lacking Connor's fine writing instrument. Selma stashed it with her other treasures and drew out a couple of sweat-limp one-dollar bills from the same place.

"How about getting an old lady a fully-loaded Coke and some of those crackers, sonny? I can't chew peanuts so well anymore. My family left me here to starve."

He did as she asked. Age before beauty, he supposed. Beauty, Josee. When would he be allowed to see her?

The peanuts, crackers, and Coke were gone by the time his nemesis nurse appeared again. Her stern face softened as she addressed him. "Josee is asking to see you." The only explanation for the change—she must have watched the noon news. Now a hero, not a persistent nuisance. Regardless, she did not give him a room number. A glance toward the supposedly dozing Selma told him why.

They walked the halls together until reaching a

spacious corner room with a not so picturesque view of the tangle of the interstate highway in the distance. Bouquets wishing Josee well already filled the windowsills. Her golden hair twisted up and clipped on top of her head, she sat garbed in a hospital gown and propped by pillows. He dreaded looking at her face. How much damage had he been unable to prevent?

Instead, he stared at the loose white bandage around her throat and worked upward following the raw, red streak on her neck and on to her damaged, blistered cheek that glistened with ointment. Thank God, her assailant had missed the delicate shell of her ear, the full pink lips, the wide blue eyes. Those eyes regarded him now. Those lips curved into a smile. "Trin," she said and held out a hand still perfectly manicured and tipped with nails painted red to match the dress she'd been wearing. Her other hand lay pierced by an IV needle. He grasped the one she offered, top and bottom. They might have been the only two in the place, but her parents stood nearby, and the nurse lingered.

Stevie broke the silence. "Your folks sent the daisy bouquet, though they are my favorite flowers, not hers, but very thoughtful. Well, we've had our time with Josee. I guess we'll go find something to eat. Keep her company for us." Skillfully, she maneuvered the others out of the room.

"Are you in much pain?" he asked.

"Nope, good meds. They put them right in the IV bag."

Unable to maintain eye contact, he gazed at the flowers on the sill. "I guess the red roses are from Marcello. I should have brought you some."

“No, from Adolphe. The all-white arrangement is from Marcello, who calls me his pale princess, and the mixed bouquet from Janis and the crew. I guess there will be more as word spreads. I don’t really need flowers. I want your company. Am I so hard to look at now?

“No! I mean I keep thinking if I’d tackled the guy as soon as he went through the barriers, none of this would have happened.” He gestured toward her cheek.

Josee made the sign of the cross, though he knew she didn’t practice Catholicism. “Trinity Billodeaux, I absolve thee of not being able to see the future.”

How could she joke about this? “I thought he wanted the food laid out for the staff and kind of pitied him. Not anymore.”

“You should. It seems he is another of Dirk’s victims. He’ll do time, and Dirk will walk if he can afford a good enough lawyer.”

He consulted his phone again. “Shit, your ex is already out on bail. The police should be guarding your room.”

“I doubt he’ll try again. Too suspicious for now.” Her chest heaved with a sigh. “The doctors want to keep me here for a few days to make sure I stay hydrated and the wounds don’t become infected. After that, I can go to my parents’ place across the lake, stay out of the sun, and keep the antibiotic cream applied. By six weeks, I should be back to normal—except for the skin graft. Did my folks tell you about the cadaver skin?”

Trin nodded. What could he say that wouldn’t come out sounding gross?

“Yeah, creepy, I know. Maybe I’ll be offered a part

on *The Living Dead*." Her sudden smile surprised him. "You can help me decide where to take a piece of my skin when they do the final graft."

He tried to answer lightly, but anger surfaced. "I have your locket. I'd like to throw it into Lake Pontchartrain for what it did to you."

"Don't! It holds something I treasure. The locket belonged to my grandmother and used to contain pictures of my mother and aunt when they were children. I still have the one of my mom in there along with something else I want to keep. Grandma said she used to finger it and worry about my mom's rough lifestyle and all the bad choices she made with men. That's why the engraving is so worn. Gran finally got her wish when her daughter settled down with a nice man and had her own children. Wild as my mother once was, I know she wants the same outcome for me."

"I do—I mean, that's what I want for you if that's what you want." He skated on the proverbial thin ice, which melted very quickly in Louisiana. Hell, he'd marry her today if she said the word.

Change the topic. "Uh, how about if I come over here tomorrow and bring my laptop. We can work on Joe's World. Maybe create a sports photographer like your mom as one of our characters."

"I'm not sure wife and mother would be very interesting."

Until he caught her slight grin, he didn't realize she jested again. How was she able to do that? Resilience, Janis said. "Your mother will always be interesting, but no, the wild Stevie. You and I were supposed to spend the weekend together. I just didn't figure it would be in a hospital."

"Sounds like more fun than watching the cars go by on the highway. I said no visitors because you cannot trust anyone in the fashion business. The papers would pay a lot to see me like this. Then, I realized how bored I'd be without company."

"You don't consider me boring?"

"Not in the least."

He couldn't touch her lips, so close to that wound. Instead he kissed the hand not impaled by a needle. Summoning his best *Terminator* voice, he said, "I'll be baaack." What did Ty Beck say? Leave them laughing. She did.

Riding down in the elevator, he checked the time. Just enough left to get to Schifferman's Jewelry Store and ask for the fabled Leslie his brothers always talked about as having perfect taste—because they doubted their own. Same went for him.

The slight, graying, and rather prissy man with the dapper, well-groomed silver mustache considered Trin's request. "A gold chain for a locket, you say. Box chain, snake chain…"

"Whatever would be best."

"A box chain always lies flat and doesn't tangle. Sixteen-inch, eighteen-inch…"

"I should come to right about here." He pointed to just below his Adam's apple.

"For you, sir?"

"No, no. For a woman, a beautiful woman."

"Then you will want the twenty-four-carat gold."

"Right." He dug out his credit card. Not being a football player or a rapper, he'd never bought a gold chain in his life. More expensive than he figured, but he could afford it, no problem. "Wrap that up, Leslie."

"Certainly, sir. I trust you will remember Leslie at Schifferman's when the time comes to select an engagement ring for the beautiful woman."

Probably worked on commission, Trin guessed. Must have made a fortune on Billodeaux engagement rings by now. "If that day ever comes, I wouldn't go anywhere else. I'll be baaack."

Leslie didn't smile. He simply didn't get it. Josee did.

Chapter Sixteen

On Sunday, Trinity arrived at Ochsner directly after lunch. He checked in at the nurses' station and got the nod to proceed to Josee's room. Carrying his laptop and a tiny black bag that held his gift, he threaded his way through the corridors to his destination. When he opened the door, he became intensely happy that he hadn't brought flowers after all.

Connor and Stevie Riley appeared to be sitting in the midst of a flower show, arrangements of all kinds everywhere, arrayed along walls when shelf space ran out. The loveliest flower of them all, even in her damaged condition, sat wearing a much more becoming gown than the one provided by the hospital. The blue of it brought out the color of her eyes, and the touch of lace laying along her collarbone diverted the gaze from the bandage around her throat. Sadly, her hand still retained the IV needle shunting fluids into her body. The doctor took no chances with his famous client. That made him glad, as did the smile that greeted him. He'd saved that smile.

Josee's dad rose to shake his hand. "I think we'll go out for a leg stretch now that our daughter has more interesting company than her parents. I know you'll take good care of her while we're gone." He escorted his wife to the door, tiptoeing among the vases of white tulips and other floral offerings. Stevie gave him a benign smile before closing the door.

He took both as an endorsement of approval but tried not to read too much into it. Could it be they still thought of him as Josee's geeky childhood friend, not her lover? Perhaps, she hadn't told them where she'd stayed over in the city. Regardless, they trusted him to keep her amused and safe from prying eyes.

He took the nearest chair still warm from her mom's admirable behind. "I brought you a present." He held up the black bag.

"Something expensive. I know a Schifferman's bag when I see one. Really, you shouldn't have."

"I owed you this. Do you need help opening it?"

"No, Trin. I'm not weak or crippled."

Josee withdrew the box and slipped off the gold ribbon he'd struggled with earlier in the day, trying to insert the locket without ruining the bow. He thought he'd done a fairly good job, but added, "I put something else inside besides the gift."

She ripped away the paper and raised the lid. "My locket on a brand new and much better chain. How wonderful. Did you pick this out yourself?"

He started to lie but couldn't do it. "No, I had help from Leslie."

Her smile faded. "Another woman helped you choose the chain?"

Could the fabulous Josee Riley truly be jealous? Yippee, as Ty Beck might say. He held in his joy at the thought. "Leslie is a clerk at Schifferman's, a male clerk, possibly a gay clerk, but that doesn't matter. I now know more about gold chains than I thought possible. So many choices—but you do like it? After all, I ruined your other one by ripping it off. No time to find the clasp and a good thing it was flimsy, not like this one."

"That was the original chain, almost as worn as the locket. You saved me from more damage." Her radiant smile returned. "Yes, I love the new one. I wish I could put it on right now, but you know." She gestured toward the bandage at her throat, then turned coy on him. "Did you open the locket?"

This he could answer honestly without thinking. "I was tempted when you told me it contained something precious, but I had no right. I did clean it. Guaranteed acid-free now."

"Perhaps you did have a right since it's something I stole from you. Look inside."

"I'm not missing anything." Puzzled, he inserted his fingernail and pried the snug locket open. On one side, a picture of a little girl with tangled blond hair grinned at him. By the cock of her head and defiant air, he recognized the wild child, Stevie Dowd. The prim portrait on the other side must be her sister who offered a smile that hinted she'd been told to say "cheese" on command.

Wedged between the two lay a lock of hair, a single dark curl matted with some mysterious substance. "What the heck is this? Can't be from a family member. You're all so blond." Now, who was jealous?

Josee started to laugh, then stopped as if she might be stretching the stitches of her wound. He could kill Dirk just for that. "It's your Tony Curtis curl, the one the nurse cut off after the bar fight."

He poked the lock of hair. "This is my blood holding it together? I don't know about you, Josee. First cadaver skin, now this weird souvenir."

"The cadaver skin came second, and I didn't have much choice. The alternative was pig skin. The keepsake came first."

"Look, if this ever grows out, I'll cut off a fresh one for you." He fingered the short spike of hair that refused to lay down even when weighted with hair gel. As he lowered his hand, it passed over the slash newly free of stitches. He'd have a slight scar but didn't much care. He'd taken one for Josee.

"Trin, this hank has meaning for me. You shed your blood for me. No other man has done that."

"By head butting a drunk. The cut was accidental."

"Doesn't matter. You thought fast and took down a guy twice your size."

"Ty Beck finished him off."

Irritation showed in the narrowing of her eyes and the thinning of her lips. "Would you stop it! You are brave. You saved one child from a bull and another from drowning. You stood up to Dirk at Mariah's, too. Now you know how dangerous he is. When the acid hit my face, you showed no fear of getting it on yourself and issued orders as good as any quarterback to deal with the situation. Don't you see you are as unafraid and decisive as your brothers are on the playing field." From her tone, she meant every word.

"I don't know. Maybe. I'd take a bullet for you, Josee." What a stupid, trite thing to say, but he knew he would.

"I hope it never comes to that. Once I'm out of the public eye, I won't attract the crazies anymore. I've already told Marcello I needed a break after this assignment. I want to make that break permanent. I won't have to worry where they take the skin graft, probably from my hip, because I don't plan to model thong bikinis anymore." She pointed at her throat. "Same goes if I have a scar here. When I think of the kids at Camp Love Letter, this is nothing."

The atmosphere in the room had grown heavy with emotion that weighed on his shoulders and nearly made it hard for him to breathe. He wanted to ask if they had a future together, but hesitated a moment too long.

The door burst open. Josee clicked the locket shut. Trin leapt to stand at the foot of her bed, ready to block a paparazzi or an assailant.

Connor Riley biffed him on the arm. "Good defensive reflexes you got. Too bad you aren't as big as Junior Polk, or you could have played cornerback for the Sinners." He held up a greasy bag, and Stevie followed with a carrier of coffee cups from Café du Monde. "We drove to the French Quarter to get you some beignets and café au lait. Nothing better to cheer a person up."

Did Josee seem a trifle chagrined? She answered sweetly enough. "I don't need cheering up, but thanks. I hope they are still warm."

"The way your father drove there and back, they probably are. No parking as usual. He circled the block over and over while I stood in line. Let me pull your bed tray over. Try not to get powdered sugar on the sheets." Stevie passed out the coffee. They shared the treat of square donuts, though he and her husband ate the bulk of them.

"If they don't let me out of bed soon, I'll gain ten pounds. When they release me to go home, I'm not allowed to do any strenuous exercises, no running, no elliptical machines, only walking—in the shade, no sun. The doctor said two weeks until he does the graft from my hip, then six weeks more of inactivity to let it heal. I might go nuts by then." She explained her restrictions to him. He added mentally, no sex either.

"Come on," her mother said. "We can binge watch *Game of Thrones* or *Outlander* together. You always say you have no time to watch a series because you never know where your next assignment will be. Time to catch up on all you've missed."

"I suppose so. Since Trin is here, we're going to work on the new game he's developing. He needs some feminine input. You'll both be bored. Why don't the two of you go home and get some rest. Trin will stay with me until…"

He filled in the blank. "I should be going right after dinner. I have to work tomorrow."

"You can come back in the morning, or even the afternoon. I've been taking care of myself for years now. I'll be fine alone for a night." Josee urged her parents to leave.

Stevie seemed doubtful. "I know you've managed fine in business, but you've made my same regrettably poor choices in men, current company excepted." She gave her husband a loving squeeze on the arm and nodded in Trin's direction. "What if Dirk tries to attack you here?"

Her father's fair complexion reddened. "They shouldn't have let that bastard out on bail. Trin, if anyone tries to get in here, I expect you to be on guard."

"I will be, sir." He felt compelled to add the sir despite knowing the man as Uncle Connor all of his life. Now, they operated on a first name basis.

Reluctantly, Uncle Connor rose and shook his hand in farewell. It seemed much like a handoff of responsibility. He kissed the top of Josee's blonde head and stood aside to let his wife do the same. "Take good care of her, Trin," Stevie said.

"Enough. Go. We have work to do." Josee waved them out the door. As soon as it shut, she said, "Now let's get down to it. I already have a name for our tall, blonde, tough sports photographer—Billie Denver."

"Hmmm, you think your mom will notice the similarity to the former Stevie Dowd?"

"I doubt she plays video games, but I think she'll be flattered. If you plan on having models or movie stars for these players to date, they'd better be kickass great like Tom Brady's wife, Gisele Bündchen. Beauty and brains. Got it?"

"Absolutely. Tom is a lucky man." He should be so lucky one day.

They worked on Joe's World until dinner arrived on trays. He did the complex coding. Josee supplied the characteristics she wanted in the women who would populate the game, a team effort if there ever was one.

Dinner wasn't awful, merely bland for Louisiana: a baked chicken leg on rice, green beans, small salad, whole wheat roll, and a chocolate pudding cup fancied up with a dab of whipped cream and a cherry on top. Not the meal he'd wanted to share with her at a fine restaurant, but the company excelled.

Despite her denials, he could tell the intense collaboration had left her tired. Soon after the trays were taken away, he kissed her on her fair cheek and left her with a promise to be baaack next weekend.

Chapter Seventeen

Trinity Billodeaux counted this summer as the best of his life so far. Not so for Josee, he realized. She'd hardly think spending every weekend working on a video game with him as fun when she'd normally be on assignment somewhere, probably a beach during the day, and hanging out with the rich and glamorous, not some computer geek, in the evenings.

Enough time had passed for her first-degree burns to heal to the pink of new skin. The second-degree burns closed from the edges inward and showed every sign of being gone shortly. After a couple of weeks, the plastic surgeon recalled Josee to replace the cadaver skin, the blood vessels beneath it having rejuvenated to the point where the temporary covering could be removed and replaced with the graft from her hip.

When they talked on the phone after the procedure, she told him, "The doctor used silk thread and tiny stitches for the second graft, not staples. He thought that would produce the best result with the least scarring. If I do have scars, they can be removed by laser. My throat feels fine, but my rear is sore."

She'd tried to get a laugh out of him, but it came out forced. What had happened to her should not be taken lightly. Still, Josee did have a sense of humor. And compassion. While at the hospital, she'd visited the burn ward and counted herself fortunate she'd gotten off so lightly. Talk about intelligent, too. Her ideas for Joe's World enhanced the game to new levels.

Last weekend when he'd showed up at the Riley's home, she'd presented him with a logo, three simple green leaves, not four-leaf clovers, a fleur-de-lis, or the serrated edges of marijuana. In their center the gold lettering read Trinity Enterprises. "Think about it," Josee said. "I know you intend to sell Joe's World to your boss. Jonathan Hartz will surely offer you millions, but with your own company, this game is only a start."

He'd shaken his head. "Then, I'd have to have investors, a production company, a public relations firm to market it, a distribution center. Hartz has all that set up and ready to go. Besides, I'd be competing with my employer."

"I'd be willing to invest in Trinity Enterprises, my dad and yours too. We all believe in you. From working with my makeup line, I know a great deal about PR, and the other aspects of running a company from my business studies." Her enthusiasm showed in the pink rising in her undamaged cheek and the brightness of her blue eyes.

He tried to deflect her by saying, "Only if you'll be my full partner."

"Deal." She held out her hand, the nails still perfectly manicured though coated in a pearly sheen, not red.

Hesitating, he said something as lame as any statement ever made by a nerd. "Your nails are really nice."

"They ought to be. I have nothing much else to do when sunshine and exercise are forbidden."

Sex, too, drifted through his mind. He took her fingertips and started to seal the deal with a shake when Josee pulled her hand away. "Never make anyone a full partner. You keep fifty-one percent of the whole. See how I could have taken advantage of you."

"But I trust you."

"Business is business. You must protect yourself. For instance, I've learned that Adolphe and the designer of the dresses I wore for the shoot have gotten an offer from *the* best of the high fashion magazines to use them in a layout they want to call *The Last Photo Shoot*. Thanks to a clause in my contract, I receive one third of the payment for any secondary uses of my image. Of course, the Amberello Agency gets a share of that, but still big bucks. I've also negotiated the title to read *Josee Riley: Her Last Photo Shoot*." Josee plucked at the bandage covering the new graft. "If they want to exploit this, I'll get my share. Of course, I had to agree to an interview to go with the pictures, but that's no problem."

To think for over ten years, he'd worshiped her beauty and not much else about her. His own shallowness appalled him. Yet all he could think to say was, "You put Taylor Swift and Beyonce in the shade, Josee Riley."

"Hardly, but I admire them both greatly. The real question is can you handle a strong woman, Trin?"

He flexed his hands and went for comedy. "I think I already have. The places these keyboarding fingers have been."

At that point, Stevie Riley, bearing a tray of coffee mugs and a plate of sugar cookies still so warm they steamed, backed into the room where they worked, a lightly used home office. She did her work in the photography studio her husband built on the grounds, and he went on the road so often dust gathered here. The maid had given it a thorough cleaning before turning the place over to Trinity and Josee.

Not known for her domesticity and admitting it, Stevie confessed, “They’re the slice and bake kind, but still good. I thought you could use a break.” She set the tray on the desk next to Trin’s laptop but didn’t leave. “Now what’s this about a photographer called Billie that strongly resembles me. Can I get a peek at her, perhaps give you some pointers?” The fact that the tray held three large cups indicated she planned to stay a while.

“Mom, we were discussing business,” Josee said a little sharply.

“No, that’s fine. Let me bring up Billie and see if you approve.” Trin’s fingers went to work while Josee’s question turned over and over in his mind like a pebble in a fast running stream. Could he handle a woman as strong as Josee turned out to be? He’d learned of her kindness at Camp Love Letter and knew she possessed a sophistication he had no hope of attaining, but this steely woman of business was another being all together.

“Here she is, Billie Denver.” He angled the screen in Stevie’s direction.

Josee’s mom nibbled a warm sugar cookie and scanned the character’s profile. “I like that she can hold her own in a bar fight. So can you, evidently.”

Trin fingered that scar above the thick rim of his glasses, a gesture getting to be a habit. “Only once.”

“In defense of my daughter—not that I haven’t

taught her what to do in a brawl." Stevie considered her avatar on the screen. "Nice work. Billie is sexier than I was at any time in my life. Are those double-Ds?"

The warmth of a blush crept up his neck. Josee's chagrin at her mother's presence changed to amusement right before his eyes. "We can reduce the size if you want, but I think you were—um, are—just as sexy as Billie. I've seen those pic…never mind."

Stevie laughed, low and throaty, so like her daughter. "Nope, I've had three children and one too many sugar cookies. I guess I'll never live down posing mostly covered with sand. I warned Josee not to do that either, but she seemed determined to repeat every mistake I made. I think that era is coming to an end for her."

The need to defend Josee rose up inside of him. "Once she recovers, she'll be as beautiful as she was before."

Stevie ruffled his hair as if she really was a matronly aunt, not a woman fairly hot for her age. "Good boy, coming to her defense like that, but not what I meant. I think my daughter is all grown up now and knows what she does and doesn't want. This is a fantasy game so let those melons be. It should be fun."

She gathered the mugs but left the remaining cookies. "There's more coffee in the kitchen if you want it. Feel free to stay for dinner before you go. Eula Mae learned to cook from her mother and always leaves something good in the refrigerator for Sundays when she's off. I think we have shrimp stew, and even I can make rice and a salad."

"Sounds great, but I should be on my way. All those boaters and weekend campers will be on the road soon. Thanks for letting me stay overnight here when I visit, Aunt Stevie." Both women would notice he'd cut his visit short this time.

Her brows arched as did her smile. "I think we've both reached an age when you can drop the aunt, Trinity. See you next weekend, I hope."

"I plan to be here," he'd said—if he had enough courage to take on a strong woman.

Chapter Eighteen

Trinity expected the phone call, his mom checking in with her children about their plans for the Fourth of July. Independence Day fell on a Friday this year creating a four-day weekend for many. Attendance at the massive barbeque his dad hosted every year was nearly mandatory. Only Lorena, in Australia, had an excuse good enough to skip the event. Not that he disliked the big party with its pig roast, dragon boat races, bouncy houses, and pony rides for the kids, all culminating in an evening fireworks display that rivaled any the town of Chapelle could afford. Camp Love Letter closed down for a few days. The grounds filled with relatives and friends. Since the cabins stood empty, they were available for those who'd traveled a long distance or overindulged, providing a practically perfect holiday.

He'd told Josee and her mom he'd return, no joking about coming baaack, but knew he had an easy out. They wouldn't expect him to pass up the big family get-together to travel to Mandeville and spend time quietly with them. The Rileys were always invited, making it some years and sometimes not. This time, he doubted they would attend because of Josee's condition.

His mother grew impatient waiting for his answer. "Are you coming or not, Trin?"

"Did the Rileys accept the invitation?"

"I called them personally to see if they would, but Stevie turned me down. She said Josee isn't ready to be seen in public yet and still needs to heal. I can understand that. How about you?"

"If it's okay, I thought I'd spend the Fourth with them. Josee needs the company. She doesn't trust people not to photograph her."

"Son, you don't need to ask me if it is okay. You're a grown man with a very good reason to be absent." That was his mom for you. She always understood, maybe more than he wanted.

"What about Dad?"

"I think we both know why you want to be with Josee."

Did they really? Did they see he'd gone beyond mere friendship or having a crush on a beautiful woman to a love so deep he feared he'd never be worthy of her?

He could envision his mother's smile when she said, "We guessed you wouldn't attend and told Mawmaw Nadine not to expect you and why since you know how she can be. Family is everything to her. She wants you to stop by to pick up a special pan of her bread pudding to take to the Rileys."

"I will. I'll do that on my way to Mandeville."

That settled it. He'd brave four days with Josee and see if he could handle a strong woman. Simply showing up was part of that.

On the day of, he swung by the ranch early and used his fob to open the gate. He caught no one off guard. Undoubtedly, Knox Polk watched him from the control room. In the kitchen, Mawmaw Nadine sat with her arthritic hands clamped around a mug of the dark roast Community Coffee his mother kept on hand for her mother-in-law as she pronounced all other brands swill. His dad, evading the de-caf his mom usually served, had joined her prior to digging out the umu pit to roast the pigs as he did every Fourth. In the wet Louisiana weather, the sides tended to collapse between uses. He'd open it up and stock it with fresh lava rocks before he lowered the pigs wrapped in banana leaves into the earth oven.

Physically more feeble as the years passed, her iron gray hair turned to white, Mawmaw still possessed a mind and a tongue sharp as the pinchers on a blue crab. "Gimme some sugar," she demanded, offering Trin a wrinkled cheek. He could only obey, not that he minded.

"Now you take that girl of yours the small pan of bread pudding in the ice box. I want my carrier back, and don't forget the rum sauce in the oleo container. That will put a smile on her face."

Trin removed a Tupperware container with handles so old he doubted if they were sold anymore and topped it with the margarine tub. "She'll enjoy it, but I wouldn't call her my girl."

"Why? She t'ink she too good for a grandson of mine?" Like his father, Mawmaw sometimes dropped an "h" when riled.

"More the other way around. What would she want with a geek like me?"

"That's not how a winner thinks, Trin," his father butted in. "You are more than good enough. You are strong and brave and bright as a new dime. Fight for her. Besides, you know how many times your mother rejected me? So many, I lost count. You don't give up on something you really want."

He had an inkling those words were similar to the ones he'd heard in the incubator when he struggled for life as the smallest of the premature triplets. Dad claimed prayer and pep talks accounted for this son's survival.

"You tell 'im, Joe Dean," Mawmaw agreed. "If Josee don't see that, she not wor't my good bread pudding."

"She does deserve this. Many thanks." He grasped the handles of the ancient piece of plastic, prayed they didn't give way, and made his escape, infused with new confidence from their harangue.

His dad called out as he left, "Be sure to stop by the barbecue pavilion and say hello to your mother. She's out there setting up with Corazon."

"I will." If Mawmaw held court in the kitchen, he knew his mom would be elsewhere as often as possible. Sometimes, he wondered if part of her resistance to his father's charms hadn't been a reluctance to take on Nadine as a mother-in-law, but the two women had scraped along well over the years. One thing his grandmother never faulted Nell on was the size of her family. The more Billodeauxs, the better.

He found not only his mom and Corazon cleaning the tables and shaking out tablecloths, but also Knox Polk apparently doing nothing but watching them. Holding up the container of bread pudding, he said, "Mission accomplished. Y'all have a great Fourth." He kissed the females and nodded toward Knox, but the man stepped toward him.

"I'll walk you to your car, Trin."

"I don't think I need a bodyguard, but sure. Happy to have your company." Knox rarely did anything without a purpose. He'd married Corazon for her courage in defending the Billodeaux babies from kidnapping long before Trinity entered the world, and maybe for her warmth which offset his coldness. That they'd had a son together came as an unexpected bonus.

He and Knox had barely taken two steps when Corazon rushed after them holding out a package wrapped in what appeared to be paper intended for Valentine's Day judging by all the imprinted hearts. "You two, you go too quick. Here, I crochet an afghan for Miss Josee to keep her warm until she well again."

"I know she'll love it. Thanks." He didn't have the heart to tell her that Josee wasn't bedridden but out and about the house wearing jeans and tees and sneakers, and complaining about her exile from sun and exercise. Nor did she need a cover in a perfectly climate-controlled house. Didn't matter. The way Corazon cared and fussed over those she loved scored high points with him and probably her husband whose thin lips wore the slightest of smiles.

The men reached his Tesla shortly. As Trin stowed the bread pudding on the floorboard and the package on the seat next to him, Knox said, "I got another present for you. You still remember how to use one of these?" He took the pistol, a blocky, black Glock, from the buttoned-down holster he wore.

"I wasn't your best student, but considering I had a great teacher, yes, I do. You know I'm not much of a gun fan. Besides, I don't have a concealed carry permit."

"I doubt Josee's ex has a permit at all. This one is legal, licensed to me. Just keep it handy. Any asshole who plots to scar a woman with acid will come at her again. Be ready. It's loaded with a seventeen-round magazine and ready to go. Got that?"

"Yes. You always look out for us." Trin offered his hand, shook firmly, and headed off to Mandeville with the unlikely cargo of bread pudding, a hand-knit afghan, and now a pistol in the glove compartment.

With the police out in force for the holiday weekend, one cluster of patrol cars idling at the westbound ramp off the Atchafalaya Basin causeway and another group covering the eastbound lane exit, that last item he transported made him nervous. He stayed on the interstate, veering off on I-12 in Baton Rouge, still light on traffic this early. No sense in dealing with small town speed traps and the always busy highways around New Orleans to reach Josee when he could take this route and travel along her side of Lake Pontchartrain. Easy off at the Mandeville exit. He wound through the narrow side streets toward the water's edge.

As he approached the gate of the Riley estate, it opened before him like the entry to a magical castle. In other words, Josee had been watching for him. No need to beg entrance on the intercom. A long driveway with pine trees and huge azaleas growing thick along the borders of the property provided some privacy, though the rear of the rambling one-story home faced the openness of the lake. Dressed in skinny blue jeans and a star-spangled, body-hugging red top, she waited for him just outside the front door. A huge straw hat sheltered her face. He could barely see her welcoming smile because of the shade it cast. As soon as he parked, Josee came to meet him.

"Why don't we take our morning walk before the

sun gets too hot." She linked her arm in his.

He held up the carrier of bread pudding. "Got to get this in the fridge. We don't want to waste Mawmaw Nadine's bread pudding made especially for you, *cher.* There's a present from Corazon on the front seat too." He failed to mention the weapon laying as black and dangerous as a coiled cottonmouth in the glove box.

Stevie came down the two front steps and claimed the dessert. "I'll take care of that. Take my daughter for some exercise. She gets crabby without it. Glad you came, Trin. I know you're missing out on a big party."

"There's nowhere else I want to be more than here."

Josee let out a happy squeal that had nothing to do with his words if she heard them at all. She'd opened the package and held up an afghan, pure white and so airy it might have been made of lace. "It's lovely."

"Corazon seems to think you are a total invalid in need of blankets. I didn't tell her otherwise."

"Good. No need to hurt her feelings, and I will treasure it."

Stevie claimed the throw, draping it over one arm. "I'll put it on your bed. Now walk before the sun gets too high." Josee's mom watched them start off along the drive before she went inside the house like a chaperone who approved of a suitor, and that's what he was, right?

He peered under the brim of the floppy hat. "Each time I see you, you look better and better. You're healing fast."

"Not fast enough," Josee grumbled. "The new graft itches, and I am forbidden to touch it. This inactivity is driving me crazy." She flung out her arms as if the beautiful surroundings were a cage in a nicely landscaped zoo.

"Let's walk it off," he suggested like a high school track coach.

He escorted her twice around the huge yard, past the mounds of azaleas and tree-like camellias, neither in bloom in the summer heat. As they approached Connor's multicar garage the second time, he took note that Josee had raised a sweat on her brow. "We'd better get you in the shade."

"Let's duck in here. My parents and Eula Mae hover over me, handing me drinks to stay hydrated and reminding me to put on antibiotic cream when I'm in the house. We can sit in one of the cars and take a break." She didn't bother to turn on the lights as they entered the small side door, simply allowed the shafts of sunlight penetrating the small, high windows to light their way.

"Sounds good to me." He hadn't roamed around Connor's collection of cars in some time. The accumulation had started with a truck, an Escalade, and a motorcycle, but now included the Porsche his own father drove in his wildest years and sold to Riley when he settled down and needed a place for baby seats instead of hot dates. When they visited, his dad sometimes took it out for spin with his mom by his side for old times' sake. They passed a vintage Mustang convertible of deep burgundy red that reminded Trin of his brother Dean's newer favored vehicle, now moth-balled in favor of a family car. All sat parked in humidity-controlled air conditioning, a relief from outside.

As they neared a silver Mercedes Benz, Josee

slowed. "This one. It has wide leather seats in the back, comfortable as a bed." She opened the door and motioned him inside.

"Shouldn't your dad keep them locked?"

"Oh, he says we have plenty of security around the house and grounds. If one gets stolen, they are after all only cars, mere possessions, not what counts in life. Yeah, I know. Sounds like one of his inspirational lectures, but he is right. What matters is your loved ones and how you treat others." She raised his arm and snuggled against him. Her good cheek rested on his shoulder. Her lips nibbled on his neck.

"Josee, I feel like I'm trying to seduce a cheerleader in the back of my daddy's car."

"Other way around. I'm trying to seduce you."

"Ah, great as that sounds, you aren't supposed to strain yourself." Yet, the very idea had him hardening.

"I need some relief. Couldn't you just do the finger thing? I promise to lie very still and won't scream when I come. It will be like exquisite torture."

"For me, too. I don't think we should…"

"That's right, don't think, simply do. I'll see you get your release too."

"No need for that," he said, knowing he lied.

She'd already pushed her jeans and panties down, swung her long legs across the seat, and nestled her hips in his lap. "Please."

Josee guided his hand into that bit of light fluff she didn't wax away. His fingers found her already wet and waiting for him. He thumbed her clit and inserted one long finger inside the damp heat of her core. He searched for the G Spot, found it, judging by the tightening of her body and the extra pressure she exerted on his crotch, but no sound strained her neck, only one extended sigh of pleasure. "Enough," she said and laid there, eyes closed, allowing her heartbeat to return to normal.

She sat up slowly, restored her clothes, and withdrew an entirely feminine handkerchief from her hip pocket. So delicate he could nearly see through the fabric, he noted an edging of embroidered shamrocks. "Now it's your turn. Sorry I can't use my mouth."

"Just so you know, I'm about to go off like a rocket if you touch me."

Her lips curved. "Well, it is the Fourth of July."

She unsnapped his jeans and drew down the zipper, setting him free. Swathing his penis in the thin linen, Josee stroked, one, two, three times until he kept his promise to be really fast. Resting his head against the cool leather, waiting for his breathing to normalize, he said, "I think I need to say thank you, not you shouldn't have. You came more prepared than I did."

"Oh, I got this hankie in Ireland. I wanted to show you the shamrocks, a sign of the trinity. Maybe you'd like it better for your logo than the plain leaves." She'd balled the soaked cloth in her hand but pulled on a corner to reveal the design. "It did come in handy. No mess to clean up."

"True. I'm not sure St. Patrick would approve of the use you made of it, but that's his problem. I'm not complaining."

"Good. Better tuck in. I think I hear the mom siren."

Faintly, he heard Stevie calling, "Lunch is ready. Come out, come out wherever you are."

Josee scooted to the car door. "Try to act normal."

"I don't know if that is possible for me, but I'll see what I can do. I kind of got the feeling you might have hidden out here before with a guy." He willed her to deny that. She did.

"Not me, my brothers. They'd sneak their girlfriends in here. Figured it was my turn."

"And what a turn it was. My brothers favored the hay loft and the back of their pickup trucks. Country boys. No Benz's on the ranch. Too bad in high school I didn't have anyone to practice my technique."

Her smile blossomed, and again he was grateful he'd saved it from harm. "I think you've caught up with them."

They emerged from the side door of the garage, waved to Stevie, and promised to be right there. Trin hoped guilt didn't shine all over his face along with satisfaction. They detoured to a bathroom to wash their hands, nothing suspicious in that. Josee tossed the hankie into a laundry hamper.

They went to the kitchen and assembled do-it-yourself sandwiches, helped themselves to tall glasses of lemonade to restore their fluids. The bread pudding, warmed along with the rum sauce, waited to be their dessert.

"I know this is nothing like the spread you'd have at the ranch, but we're going to boil crabs and shrimp for dinner with the usual corn and potatoes. Watermelon and Eula May's lemonade cake for dessert, then we'll watch the fireworks over the lake from our deck."

"Sounds great to me."

Stevie remarked, "That walk did Josee a world of good. She's much more relaxed."

"Yes, ma'am."

Connor glanced up from a French bread roll already slathered in mustard and filled with ham and cheese. "You look pretty relaxed yourself, Trin." He offered a knowing grin as he grabbed a handful of chips from a bowl.

"Ah, yes. Nothing like a nice walk and a tour of your automobile collection." Trinity turned his back and concentrated on stuffing a pumpernickel bun with salami, swiss, and lettuce.

Josee had already slapped together a BLT on whole wheat and added a dill pickle to her plate. She carved out a square of bread pudding, deposited it on a paper plate, and dribbled on the alcoholic sauce. Balancing the two dishes, she said, "If it's okay with you, we're going to the office to work on Joe's World."

"By all means, go. Don't let your characters do anything we wouldn't do." Josee's dad punctuated that with a chuckle.

Josee was already down the hall. Trin turned back to get a Diet Coke and caught the tail end of a conversation.

"Stop teasing the boy, Connor."

"Hey, we used to do it in the hot tub, and you know about our sons and the garage. Let them have some fun."

They broke it off when he appeared in the doorway. "Forgot my drink. I can't code without a Diet Coke."

"Help yourself to anything we've got," Connor said with a deep, short laugh.

"Thanks."

Trin left wondering what it would be like to have

Connor and Stevie as in-laws as he took one baby step closer to proposing to Josee.

Chapter Nineteen

Careful not to let the cracked crab carapaces, the papery shells of the boiled shrimp, and the buttery corn cobs escape, Connor Riley rolled up the newspaper that covered the picnic table and deposited it in a black trash bag. Stevie added the paper plates emptied of lemonade cake and a few beer bottles.

"Want me to take that to the trash can for you?" Trin offered, not really wanting to leave his space on the free-standing cypress swing where he sat with one arm around Josee's slender shoulders. The hot tub denied to her burnt skin burbled like a fountain. Peeper frogs began a chorus of love songs in the trees as the sun set over the lake. Yep, no place else he'd rather be, certainly not amid the happy chaos of the ranch with dozens of eyes watching them.

"No, we need the exercise more than you do." Josee's parents set off together, though they hardly needed two pairs of hands to complete the errand, giving the couple some time alone.

"I think they are on to us," Josee said.

"Oh, I know they are," he agreed.

From the deck, the panorama of the lake opened before them edged by the lights of New Orleans on the far shore. Connor's sailboat and bass boat bobbed by the dock on small waves as other watercraft jockeyed for a good place to watch the upcoming fireworks. The air, warm as the rum sauce they'd had earlier in the day, cooled slightly in a light breeze. Trin kissed Josee's unmarred cheek and worked his way down her long neck almost to the edge of the white bandage that warned him to go no farther. He sat back again. "Sweet as Mawmaw's bread pudding."

"Just wait until I'm fully healed, and you'll find I can be as spicy as your daddy's barbecue sauce."

"I think I already know that, but then, daddy's sauce is mighty hot. I'll have to see." He removed a hand that gently caressed her breast as the parental sandals sounded on the wood of the deck.

"That took longer than we expected. I noticed a light on in the garage. Someone left the back door of the Benz open. I hope the battery isn't run down," Connor explained.

"We did not!" Josee denied, and then had to endure her father's gotcha grin.

Stevie elbowed her husband. "Leave them alone and sit down."

The couple stretched their long lengths out on a pair of side-by-side loungers facing the water. The breeze kicked up some more, making tiny white caps froth the water. A sleek speedboat sped by going at an unsafe rate so close to the dock, Connor sat up and shouted, "Slow down, dumbass!"

Josee shivered against Trin's arm. "Cold?" he asked.

"A little. A storm must be coming in from the Gulf, but mostly that guy reminded me of the way Dirk used to drive his boat, recklessly, without any care for others."

"Why don't I get Corazon's throw for you?"

"That would be nice. Don't be long or you'll miss the start of the show."

The lights lining the deck had been turned down as night deepened for better enjoyment of the spectacle, but Trin had no trouble finding his way into the house and even less getting to Josee' bedroom right next to his where the afghan decorated the bottom of her bed. As he threw it over his arm, the first pops of the fireworks began.

Someone always died in New Orleans where guns were often fired in celebration and bullets went astray, the shots masked by the skyrockets exploding. His mind made a swift connection, insisting he return to his room and retrieve the pistol he'd stowed in the night table drawer when he brought his weekend bag inside. He had no intention of firing it but stuck the weapon into the small of his back beneath the loose tropical shirt he'd donned to look festive—or maybe ridiculous. Josee said she admired his bold choice and hadn't laughed. He'd probably sit down and shoot himself in the ass, but that comment about Dirk circled round and round in his gray matter and refused to exit.

Feeling foolish posing as some kind of *Hawaii 5-O* super-cop, he moved toward the back door. A thud rattled the window panes. He peered outside, glad he hadn't turned on any lights to destroy his night vision. He cracked the door open an inch or so. The speedboat had come around and barged into the dock. A tall man jumped ashore. Josee and the Rileys leapt to their feet. Connor started toward the invader of their privacy. "What are you, drunk? Get back in your boat and shove off before I call the cops."

Trin saw the gun rise up from where it hung in the

man's right hand. "Not what, who. No memory of me, Mr. Riley? But then, we met only once and didn't hit it off."

"Dirk, don't shoot him, please," Josee's voice pleaded.

"I didn't like him either, but I've come for you."

Connor sidestepped, placing himself in front of his daughter. Stevie joined him to make a protective wall of their bodies. Dirk waved the gun. "Get over here, bitch, before I plug both of your parents."

Fireworks arched above illuminating four blond heads. For once glad to be slight, dark-haired, and olive-complexioned, Trin ditched the pure white throw, sidled out the door and into the deepest shadows on the lawn. He freed the weapon he'd never expected to use and moved closer. He thought he had a clear shot if he could convince himself to take it, but then, Josee darted out from behind her parents and offered herself to her ex.

"I'll go with you. Let them alone."

Dirk's gym-toned, muscular arm snaked out and pulled her close to his body. The barrel of the gun went beneath her chin and the butt dug into the white gauze around her throat. Dim as it was, Trin saw her flinch in pain. Bastard, he'd kill him if only Josee weren't in jeopardy. Waiting for an opening, he two-handed the Glock as Knox had taught him.

"Don't hurt her," Stevie cried.

"Hurt her? Do you know how she hurt me? My big chance for a recurring role on a top show, and they wrote me out, killed me off, because someone tipped the cops that I passed that bum a few bucks to mess her up. It's her turn to pay. When I'm done with Josee

Riley she'll never work again either."

Connor elbowed his wife aside as if to make a move. Trin caught the tiny dip of Josee's head. They were about to try something desperate that might get them all killed. He called out, "Over here, Dirk the Jerk. I've got you covered."

The gun left Josee's chin and swung his way, but Dirk throttled her throat harder with his other hand, making her body a shield. Josee's elbow slammed back sharply into his stomach. She dove forward as the grip on her throat loosened. Trin squeezed off his single shot, not wanting to hit anyone but his target. As Dirk's body jerked, the man let loose a spray of bullets from his semi-automatic that hopped and pocked across the grass.

Trin hit the ground as he'd been taught in drills by the Billodeaux bodyguard. Watching with the eyes of a former wide receiver waiting to make a move, Connor dove forward hitting Dirk so hard he toppled off the dock and into the boat that had shifted with the wind. Instead of landing inside, the actor's head hit hard on the rim with a sound like an over ripe watermelon splitting. His body sank into the water. Stevie stood on the verge with a boat hook in her hand, whether to fish him out or shove him under again, Trin could not tell from his view on the ground.

He pushed up, started forward, and found one of his legs reluctant to move. It dragged along the grass and finally collapsed as he neared the deck. Didn't matter. Josee stood over him. A trickle of blood ran down her throat, but otherwise she seemed fine. Ha! He'd actually taken a bullet for her, no lie. Josee's face drew nearer, haloed by bursts of silver and gold in the sky. Beautiful, he thought as she leaned over him, went fuzzy, and disappeared.

Chapter Twenty

No need to ask where he lay when he came to. Trin recognized the antiseptic smell, the sound of medical carts rattling in the corridor, and the faint beep of monitors from his visits to Josee in the hospital. This time the monitors were attached to *him* and an IV needle pierced the back of his hand. He felt no pain. That bag of fluids obviously contained something to keep it at bay. His gaze roamed farther.

There she sat, coming into focus again, but still somewhat fuzzy without his glasses. Josee stood near the foot of his bed like an angel come to call him home. She wore a silky blue robe, not the usual angel or sick person couture. A heavier bandage ringed her throat. He tapped the side of his bed. “What are you doing way down there?” His voice came out dry and croaky.

She smiled as if he’d made a tremendous joke. “Change of shift a minute ago. Your parents were here all morning. They brought Xochi, and your sister Jude has been buzzing in and out making sure you get the best care, exactly as she did for me. I finally got my turn.” Josee sat beside him and smoothed away the curls rampant across his forehead with nothing to tame them but her gentle hand. Felt so good when she lightly traced the scar above his brow.

“You really did take a bullet for me, Trinity Billodeaux.” Her words were hoarse, but she offered him water from a cup with the bent straw rather than drinking herself. "You lost some blood and need to keep your fluids up."

He sipped. The water tasted like the best brew he'd ever imbibed. "What happened after I lost consciousness?"

"My dad whipped off his belt and put a tourniquet on your leg. He told me to get something to press against the wound. First thing I saw was Corazon's afghan. I'm afraid it's ruined. Mom is going to try soaking it in saltwater, but I doubt if that will work."

"You aren't going to put it in a plastic bag and preserve it forever like the curl, are you?"

"No, that would be freaky—but someone would pay big bucks for it on E-bay, I bet. Anyhow, my mom got the ambulance and police ASAP. You had emergency surgery and here you are two days later. Probably going to need some rehab on that leg once you're well."

"Great, I'll have more in common with my brothers. They're always rehabbing some part of their bodies during the offseason. Dirk the Jerk, did I get him?" He wanted to continue talking, but drowsiness threatened to smother him like a down pillow.

"Yes, you hit him."

"I hope I killed him," he muttered, never expecting to say those words outside a video game.

"We don't know. My dad plays golf with the coroner and has some pull. When they fished Dirk out of the water, he wasn't breathing but had some water in his lungs. Still alive when he went under, but he could have bled out from the chest wound or died from splitting his head open when he went under. I think cause of death will be multiple injuries."

"Good, good. He's out of your life." Damn this fuzzy feeling. "You, how are you? I saw blood on your throat."

She touched her bandage lightly with her fingertips. "This is nothing compared to what happened to you. Dirk tore out my stitches on one side of the graft. Since my plastic surgeon is in Florida on a deep-sea fishing trip, the resident on duty did his best to repair the damage. I might need a second graft if it doesn't take. They're keeping me for a few days, too. Whatever, I'll be fine."

"Thass what matters." Was he slurring his words? His lids grew heavy and closed.

A sharper voice than Josee's intruded. "You were supposed to notify us immediately if he woke. Too much talk has exhausted him. Leave and let him rest." Nurse Starchy must be on duty—or maybe they were all like Nurse Starchy.

Trin shook his head against the pillows. "Stay, Josee, stay. I might be sleeping, but I'll know you're here."

"Fine, if she doesn't talk and keep you awake." The nurse checked his vital signs, as if anyone could sleep though that, measured the fluid flowing into a catheter bag dangling off the side of the bed, and adjusted his meds. The last he heard was the clink of his chart knocking against the metal rail of the bed.

****

The warmth surged up his leg into his groin and dispersed throughout his body, a sensation not sexual, but rather strengthening. Without opening his eyes, Trin said, "Xochi, thanks for coming." He took care not to thank her for her healing touch as she would reject that in the manner of all *traiteurs*.

"If I hadn't volunteered, Mom would have dragged me here by my hair." Her chuckle was as warm as her touch.

He opened his eyes. She sat close, her hands still resting on his injury but as lightly as a butterfly on a log. In the month since he'd seen her, the baby in her belly had grown bigger. "You sure this isn't bad for the kid?"

"He seems to enjoy it. Kicks up a storm afterward. See, there he goes. Settle down, Knox Polk the Third." She patted her bump lovingly.

Trin observed the bulges moving beneath her skin covered by a light summer maternity dress. Made him feel a little queasy, but it didn't bother Xo at all. "He'll have to have a nickname. We're getting a lot of Knox Polks in the family. Say, did you see Josee and do the same for her?"

"Absolutely, but she didn't need much of a boost. Josee, her aura burns with a bright yellow flame. She is successful, creative, smart, and wise, very strong."

"And in love with me?"

Xo evaded his question. "That is for her to say."

What if she didn't?

He knew his sister sometimes scoped out the men involved with his sisters. Why wouldn't she tell him? Maybe the news was bad, and she didn't want to upset him while ill. Trin sighed slightly. Nope. Because he was the guy and should speak first. When he got out of this place, was allowed to drive, and could take a knee again, he'd head directly back to Leslie at Schifferman's and buy the best ring he could afford.

When he presented it, he'd have the answer to his question. No need to press Xochi.

Chapter Twenty-One

They were fighting over him—in a friendly sort of way. Trinity awaited the appearance of his doctor to gain his release into the world again. A male nurse practitioner had been in earlier piling instructions on him. His mom held the stack of papers in a tight grasp. In the warm hospital room, her fingers made moist indents on the pages outlining restrictions and rehab.

Just his luck he'd been shot in the right leg. Just his luck the doctor said that the bullet Dirk used had exploded into his muscle tissue, chipped a bone, but missed the artery. No driving for six weeks in case he undid the surgeon's work if he braked for a dog or random squirrel in the road. That meant he'd need someone to drive him to physical therapy and anywhere else he wanted to go like a certain jewelry store in New Orleans.

For now, he'd ride out of the hospital in a wheelchair but transfer to a walker when he reached his destination. Within two weeks, he'd be off the walker and using a cane. That, too, could be abandoned once his therapist gave the word. Six weeks seemed infinitely long, especially if they took him back to the ranch to be coddled by Corazon and fretted over by his mother, miles from Josee.

The Rileys stood on one side of his bed, the Billodeauxs on the other as if they were lining up to make a major play against each other. Connor made his offer again. “Look, we’ll be happy to see he gets to PT. New Orleans is just across the causeway. Since Rev Bullock’s son is an orthopedic surgeon at Ochsner, we can call on him if we need a second opinion. I wish he’d been on duty when they brought Trin in for treatment.”

His dad winced. “He was at our Fourth of July party. If I could see the future, I wouldn’t have invited him, but he did check in on our son from time to time.”

“If any of us could see the future, Dirk wouldn’t have gotten the jump on us. We’d like to repay Trinity for saving our lives by taking care of him.” Connor continued the argument.

“The ranch has its own gym and a pool if the therapist thinks that will help. We’ll have the PT guy come to our place. We have an elevator to get him up and down from his room. Plenty of folks around all the time if he needs help using the pot or anything else. Nurse Shammy could bathe him.”

Trin cringed, shoulders hunching. The thought of the elderly nurse, once a nun, giving him a sponge bath was, well, unthinkable, not to mention assisting him to use the bathroom. His dad meant well, but, jeez, Josee stood right there holding his hand. She, however, had a small, arched smile on her face at his embarrassment.

The bandage had been removed from her neck, revealing a thick crescent-shaped scab marring her perfect skin. The rest of her injuries had healed without a trace. Damn Dirk the Jerk for what he’d done to her. Not that a scar mattered to him. Josee would always be his dream girl, no matter what. He bet she’d be as lovely in old age as her mother or Eve Landrum, not that they were ancient exactly. He wanted them all to leave so he could tell her that, but fat chance they'd go until this was settled.

"Another point," Stevie Riley said. "Our place is quiet. No dogs jumping around or commotion from Camp Love Letter still in full swing for four more weeks."

"You're still on for the photography class, right?" Joe added, covering all his bases. "You can check up on Trinity when you visit, stay in the house with us. Connor is welcome too. We can always use him to toss the old pigskin around with the kids. He can be celebrity of the week."

Josee spoke up in a soft voice with just a hint of pleading. "If Trin stays with us, we could work on his video game together to pass the time."

"Yeah, I really, really appreciate her input," he said, hoping to sway his parents in the right direction.

"She'd be welcome to stay at the ranch, of course," his stubborn father continued.

His mom's elbow nudged his dad's ribs. She loosened her hold on the instructions and handed them over to Stevie. "I think Trin wants to stay with you. It's certainly true he won't have people bothering him like Edie, wanting help with the newsletter or one of the dogs jumping on his bed and causing some harm. Joe, I believe we can count on Connor to make sure our son follows orders and Josee to keep him from being bored. He might even finish that game he's been working on forever."

"You wouldn't believe all the progress I've made with Josee's help." Fine if he showed all his eagerness to ditch his parents for the woman he loved and would eventually get around to telling her he meant forever.

His father's broad chest heaved. "Okay. I trust Connor and Stevie to take care of him." Outnumbered and overwhelmed, sometimes all a quarterback could do was throw away the ball and drop to the ground, his surrender indicated.

"Mom, I promise I'll call every day or maybe night since you'll be out and about with the Camp Love Letter crowd. Dad, I'll be well before you miss me."

Lab coat flying, his doctor came through the door, scribbled his signature on the release forms and inquired if his assistant had gone over all the post-op instructions. "Anything else you need to know?"

Trin wasn't about to ask anything that would hold up his freedom. "No, I'm good."

"Great. Checkup in six weeks. See you then. Feel free to call if you have any problems." Like a very busy man, his surgeon was gone

The wait for the wheelchair seemed interminable, but it came at last with a large, black woman to push it. His dad offered to take over, but she shook her head setting numerous short braids quivering like Medusa's snakes. "Hospital policy. He got to ride. I got to push him out the door. After that, he all yours. Come on, skinny boy, let's roll."

Trin, wearing soft, loose sweat pants, slippers, and a black tee he thought defined what muscles he had, slid from the bed to the chair. His leg muscles twinged a little, but he refused to show any discomfort that might result in being kept in the hospital yet another week. Josee took a second to tie a silk scarf streaked with blue that matched her eyes around her neck. Then, she walked beside him with his elders bringing up the rear behind the sizeable rump of his pusher like some bizarre wedding procession. They toted vases of flowers sent by admirers and his boss, balloon bouquets starting to deflate, and a sack full of teddy bears and other stuffed toys.

Some bore cards with the names and addresses of women who'd like to meet him when he got well. Now, that had never before happened in his life. The tabloids had done their work pumping up his part in the drama. They all wanted to date a hero, one who would take a bullet for them. He'd posted a generic thanks on social media but declined to answer individually. Reading some of the notes brought color to Josee's pale cheeks, so they'd served a purpose.

Connor had chosen a vehicle from his fleet, a sensible Lexus, easy to board and with a trunk big enough to stow the walker, but the way was clogged by paparazzi some underpaid hospital worker had tipped off. Before the former football players could run interference, his wheelchair pusher guided him over a couple of feet. Bump, bump and a yowl of pain. "Make way for Big Edna and her patient!" She blocked the car door with the chair until Trin made the transfer easily to the front seat pushed way back to allow him to stretch out his bum leg.

"Thanks, Edna. You're great at your job. Mom, Dad why don't you take the flowers and balloons and all those stuffed animals to Camp Love Letter for the kids and their families."

"You're a good boy," Edna remarked, backing up into the crowd and further pushing them away with her bodacious behind. "You get well soon, you hear?"

Reporters called out to Josee, "Are you two a

couple now? When's the wedding?"

Coolly, Josee swung her long legs, model style, into the backseat and slid over to make room for her equally tall mother. "Take off the scarf, Josee. Show the world what Dirk Bryant did to you," the press implored. Big Edna slammed their doors. His mom and dad followed in Teddy's van tricked out for the handicapped. Nice of Teddy to lend it, but really.

They proceeded back to Mandeville and unloaded him like a total invalid. The only good part was Josee supporting his uninjured side snug against her and Connor heaving him up the couple of steps into the one-story home. He leaned into his walker and returned to the room where he'd been staying before the attack. His mom suggested he should stretch out and rest if he didn't need to use the bathroom. His parents seemed to be as obsessed with his production of urine as Nurse Starchy. Was he hungry? Eula Mae would make up a tray. No and no. He'd taken his meals on a tray for days and days. He only wanted to sit outside in the shade and breathe the fresh air off the lake after weeks of smelling disinfectant.

Bright as the sunshine, Josee suggested they all have lunch outside. It might have been the scene of the crime, but also a backyard filled with memories of time together and the site of her parents' wedding. He assented to that as he would to anything she suggested, even if it had been climbing into an oak tree to have a tea party as she'd sometimes insisted when a child visiting the ranch.

Wheeling out to the deck, jarring his leg as the walker passed over the door jam, he took a teak chair with sturdy arms at the end of a table. He'd already learned that such a chair made getting up and down easier. Josee sat beside him on a bench across from her mother. Connor occupied the daddy seat at the other end with the parents on the right and left.

No sooner had they settled than Eula Mae emerged from the kitchen with a platter of chicken salad sandwiches on white or wheat bread cut into little triangles, as if they truly were having a tea party. She balanced a bowl of potato salad studded with cherry tomatoes in the crook of her arm. That dish would have some nip to it as Eula Mae liberally used cayenne. His mouth watered for something other than bland.

"If'n you want soup instead, I'll go warm some for you, baby," Eula Mae said, tousling his curls out of his face after she'd set her burdens down.

"No, ma'am. This looks fine to me. I dreamed about your potato salad." Not quite a lie, but his dreams featured Josee far more often than good cooking. "How about a cold beer to go with it?"

Evidently, Stevie had read over the post-op material in the car because she vetoed that as quickly as his mom sitting beside her. "No alcohol as long as you are on painkillers. We'll have ginger ale." A groan issued from his father's mouth.

"Let the men have a beer. The ladies, too, if they want. Not everyone has to suffer because of me," Trin said.

Still, the women stuck to ginger ale to keep him company. When Eula Mae returned with the drinks, she announced, "I gots a nice chocolate mousse for dessert with whipped cream and cherries on top. It's a family favorite," she said, slyly eyeing her employers. "But you eat it here at the table. It's hard to get out of bed sheets. Besides, chocolate heals, so I'm told." He wasn't sure if she referred to her dark brown face or the mousse to come. It didn't matter which really. He'd do anything, eat anything to get well for Josee.

A breeze kept their lunch pleasant, but the heat of the day rose and brought along a dose of sticky humidity like an unwanted medicine. His parents declared they needed to head back to the ranch for Fish Fry Friday. The whole gang saw him into his bedroom where he hated to admit, he now wanted to nap, damn those painkillers his mother had forced on him because they were to be taken with food.

Mom kissed his forehead. His dad hugged his shoulders, and they were ready for the long drive home. Stevie and Connor followed them to the door to see them off.

Josee lingered by his side and whispered in his ear. "Not yet, but when you are ready, I can be on top for a while."

Trinity dozed off with a smile on his lips. Now that was truly an incentive to get well soon.

Chapter Twenty-Two

Trin hadn't realized how much ten minutes riding slowly on a stationary bike could hurt, even with a painkiller taken before his PT sessions. Holding his bad leg a few inches off the exercise table, no easy thing. Bending his knee back as far as he could—excruciating. But he progressed, not as fast as he wanted of course, with Josee's promise always on his mind. The walker gave way to a three-toed old man's cane, and that to a regular cane. Stevie generally drove him to the therapy sessions as Josee attracted too much attention wherever she went. Vile people offered to pay good money for a photo of the raised, red crescent-shaped scar she hid under her scarves.

After lunch, he tended to fall asleep for a few hours, and Josee always sat by his bed when he awoke. She didn't ask the question if he were ready, but he read it in her eyes. On days without PT, they put in hours on the new game. It began to shape up. They did trial runs with him posing as a quarterback and Josee selecting to be a female kicker like his sister-in-law. The characters started a romance, slept together in a discreet sort of way under the sheets. They didn't want to get an X rating on Joe's World. Games were won and lost by a touchdown or field goal. Though this was a fantasy, they tried to keep it as real as possible. A little more fine tuning, and he wouldn't be ashamed to show the end product to his boss.

The day came when he felt well enough to take up Josee's offer. Stevie worked in her darkroom outside the house. Connor played golf with his buddies in the morning despite the debilitating August heat. Eula Mae had gone for groceries. Alone at last, he placed her hand on his arousal, stirred up by a scene they'd been acting out on the screen. "I've saved the place on top for you." It sounded good, but he feared his healing thigh wouldn't hold up yet.

Josee fingered her scar thoughtfully, a gesture becoming familiar to him just as was touching his above his glasses. "If you are sure I won't hurt you. I'd never want to do that."

"I don't believe I will feel a bit of pain." On computer days, he skipped the meds that dulled his senses and made him drowsy but was fairly confident he'd be too distracted to notice any discomfort.

He led the way out of the computer room without a thought for the help of a cane to his bed, laid his glasses aside, and turned down the covers. Standing, they disrobed each other piece by piece. Not that it took long before flesh met flesh dressed as they were in tees and jeans, barefooted as they'd worked. The T-shirts sailed across the room. Josee's underwired bra, after a brief struggle, followed. His jeans slid down easily as he'd lost weight despite Eula Mae's every attempt to fatten him up and his briefs went with them. Hers, tighter, took longer, but removing the scrap of lace she called panties, covering the patch of golden fluff, was a pure pleasure. They tumbled into bed as close as twins who could not be separated.

She took the upright position immediately,

preparing herself by rubbing her labia up and down his shaft until he became bathed in silky slickness. He breathed deeply to hold back until she was good and ready for penetration. Then, she mounted and took him all the way in on the first stroke, no teasing. It had been too long for both of them to be subtle. His hips rose to meet her, but she pushed his shoulders to the pillow. "Lie still!"

He tried, oh, how he tried. His breaths came in pants now as the pressure built and built between his legs. Women panted to keep pain at bay in childbirth. He did it to delay ecstasy. His nails dug into the mattress. How he wanted to allow her to go first but couldn't hold on much longer. His release came like an explosion that rocked his body and left him uninjured but emptied. Josee still pumped over him, her pink-tipped breasts a blur before his face. "Soon," she murmured. "Soon." He felt the clench when she reached climax, kept going for a short time as if she descended from a high altitude before resting on his chest and slowly turning into his embrace. Her eyelids fluttered against his pecs and closed.

He held her until the position became uncomfortable, then shifted that beautiful face onto a pillow. After groping for his glasses, he studied himself in the mirror opposite bed. How had he gotten so lucky as to possess this woman? Lying slightly on her side with her golden hair fanned across his arm, the scar on her neck did not show at all. To him, she was still perfect.

He owned just as much chest hair as his athletic brothers and a dong at least as long as Mack's, but he'd always be slighter and shorter. His curls had taken over again, dangling over his forehead, around his ears and encroaching on his neck. Maybe the facial scar did make him look a little bit dangerous, but most people would assume he'd tripped over some cabling and bashed his head on a computer desk. As for the scar on his leg, he counted it every bit as manly as any his athletic brothers had.

Josee stirred and raised herself on one elbow. "Sorry about that. I'm as bad as a man, falling sleep right after sex."

"You did all the work and deserved the rest."

She sat up beside him without bothering to cover her breasts and took in the mirror view. "Hey, we're the same height sitting side by side."

"Sure, height is all the legs. You take after your mother and I take after mine, unfortunately."

"It doesn't matter to me." She touched her scar. "Does this bother you? I'm debating whether to have it removed or not. I won't be modeling much anymore, and it could be air-brushed out if I did. I think I should keep it to remind me beauty is not forever. Love and courage are."

"Whichever you want to do. I think we are a little more equal now that you aren't completely perfect."

"Trin, I never was. I've been buffed and air-brushed in my pictures, and I'm certainly not perfect on the inside either. How can you believe you're not equal to me?"

"Look at us. I'm still a dweeb, and you are still a supermodel even with that ugly mark on your neck."

"If you find it that ugly, then I've misjudged you."

"Come on, Josee. Before me, you dated handsome, talented men. Now, this is what you've got." He pointed at his image in the mirror—and watched her swing her legs over the side of the bed, leaving him. She gathered her clothes but didn't put them on.

"I told you I was window dressing to most of those men, and I repeated my mother's mistakes because I didn't listen to her. You, Trinity Billodeaux, are brilliant at what you do. Three times you stood between me and danger—and you still believe you are inferior? You know what? Perhaps I've grown up, and you are still stuck a the past where Mack lorded it over you and being tall and handsome is all that mattered to some women. When are you going to gain confidence in yourself? Or grow a pair, as Mack would say. Maybe until then, we aren't right for each other."

Josee stomped off, still naked, breasts jiggling, buttocks pumping, toward her room. Oh, God, he'd lost her.

Chapter Twenty-Three

Trin did what he always did when perplexed and discouraged. He retreated into his game, into Joe's World, where, sure, a guy could still be dumped by a gorgeous woman, but another waited only a click away. He immersed himself, accepted a turkey sandwich on a tray with a Diet Coke from Eula Mae for lunch and turned down her potato salad. Connor poked his fair head, still wet from the shower post golf game, into the room.

"Not joining us for lunch. You're really going at it today. Josee isn't helping you?"

"Nope."

"Where is she then?"

"Don't know." Trin kept his eyes on the screen.

"I'll check the garage. You can always tell what mood she's in by which car she takes. The Lexus, she's probably shopping. The Mustang convertible, she's in a mood. Heaven forbid if it's the Porsche."

"Don't know." He yearned to add, don't care either, but that would have been a lie. He heard Stevie's voice next and had to turn around and face her.

She stood behind her husband, her chin resting on his shoulder, her arms wrapped around his waist. "Our darling daughter took the Porsche. I heard her roar out of here a while ago. Don't worry about it. A Spanish Formula One driver taught her how to handle a sports car."

"He was Eurotrash," Connor asserted. "Not a decent guy like you."

"She'll be okay after she gets over her mad. Did you have a spat, Trinity?" Stevie asked in a way that reminded him of his mom.

It was one thing to answer another dude with short phrases that hinted, "Don't bother me," no matter how much he respected Connor, but Stevie had been his chauffeur for weeks, mothering him and always asking when he finished PT sessions if he needed to go anywhere else. Frankly, he'd just wanted to return to Josee and do nothing more than take a nap, but maybe he should have asked to get a haircut—or stopped by a certain jeweler for a special purchase before now.

"You might say that. Look, I'm done with PT tomorrow and see the doctor the next day. I'm good to go, and you've put up with me long enough. I'll call my parents and ask them to come get me on Friday. I'm glad Josee had a racecar driver in her past. I wouldn't want her to be injured over anything I said." Actually, the words were hers, and she'd hurt him deeply in a way far more than physical, but he'd take the blame. He didn't mean what he said about being glad over the racecar driver though.

Stevie slipped under her husband's arm. "Once Connor and I had a terrible fight that almost ended us. I ran away when I should have stayed and worked it out. Don't do what I did."

"Fact is, your daughter ended it."

"Like mother, like daughter, I'm afraid. Let her cool off and try again."

How long did it take to grow a pair? "For now, I

think I should give her some space." It seemed like the right answer.

"Don't wait too long," Stevie cautioned.

****

Trouble was Josee didn't come home for lunch or dinner or that night. As Trinity put on his sweats for his last PT session, he heard the roar of the Porsche, the slam of the front door, the raised voices in the hallway.

"I'm well over twenty-one, Mom, and can stay out all night if I like. And, Dad, there isn't a scratch on the Porsche. God, I need some sleep."

"You could have called. We worried, all three of us."

"I'm sorry, okay. I went to a few clubs, then stayed with a friend. We talked for hours. Big deal."

Was talking all she'd done with this friend? Trin couldn't help if that entered his mind right on the tail of the relief that she hadn't wrapped the Porsche around a tree or driven it into Lake Pontchartrain.

"You're being childish, Josee." Stevie issued the reprimand.

"Well, I still live with my parents. Maybe that should change."

Connor, always the more conciliatory, said, "We're happy you're home safely. Why don't you get that sleep? We can talk later." He called out, "Trin, you ready for your last PT session? You'll be too late if you don't get out here."

Forced to emerge, he headed bravely into the whirlwind. Josee brushed by him like the west edge of a hurricane. She wore tight ripped jeans, a clingy crimson top with a low neckline and a flounce that showed off her breasts, plus scarlet high heels that stabbed at the floor as she passed. Amazing she didn't draw blood from the stone. Her hair flowed loose and wild around her shoulders. Her pale skin showed both dark circles under her tired, blue eyes and the red scar on her neck very clearly. He stared after her. She kicked her door shut.

He'd never seen Josee in a temper like this. Even as a child, she'd seemed more mature than him or Mack, as most girls were. Where had the cool and collected supermodel, the businesswoman, the kind-hearted person, who helped a boy who wanted eyebrows, gone? "Is she often like this?"

"Never, that's what's so frightening," Stevie answered. "Even when we quarreled at length about her becoming a model, she simply kept coming at us with business plans and time lines for her career to prove she'd thought it out. But Connor is right, we need to get on the road. Maybe we can talk about your argument."

"I don't think so, but thanks." How did you tell a beautiful woman like Stevie that you had no balls?

Relieved when she dropped him at the therapy center and left him to his physical torture, he pulled out his phone as he did leg lifts now with weights on his ankles, searching quickly for Josee Riley on the celebrity search app. He found her, lashing her hair around to a hard rock beat as a colored strobe light turned it blue and pink and orange. Apparently, she danced with two men, who by their bemused expressions couldn't believe they'd attracted the attention of a famous model. Her neck wasn't concealed. More than a few took close-up pictures of it, as well as they could in the dark atmosphere of the club. Still more beautiful than any around her and more gutsy, she'd chosen to expose the damage to the world.

"Hey, Billodeaux, no phones in here. You know the rules. Give me twenty more of those lifts, then the weight machine," his trainer ordered.

The phone lay warm and tempting in the pouch of his gray hoodie as he pressed his foot against the pedal that raised an eighty-pound weight fairly easily now. He needed more information. Who had she gone home with last night? His mind stayed on that subject as his trainer did his exit interview, checking off the boxes, showing how far he'd come since his first session. "Ah, thanks. You did a great job," he managed and headed toward the exit that offered some shade under the drive-up canopy. Maybe Stevie would be late, though she rarely was.

He opened his phone again. Who? Who? Who? She left on the arm of a black man. X-avier? Would X-avier do this to him? No, too bulky. Junior, Junior Polk, his always mellow brother-in-law. Cheating on Xochi with Josee? Not possible. Only one thing to do. He called the man. It went to voice mail. Next, he tried Xo and got her immediately.

"Trin, I expected I'd hear from you, though you seemed to forget all about your family while staying with the Rileys." As usual, her voice sounded rich and warm, now slightly amused.

"I tried Junior first."

"Are you living in a bubble? He's in training. The Sinners have their last pre-season game this weekend. Haven't you been watching? Won two, lost the last one."

"Mostly I've been working on my video game. Pre-season doesn't matter anyhow."

"Ah, imaginary football, the kind that doesn't require any sweat. Your girlfriend called here last night wanting someone to pick her up because she'd been drinking—but she didn't want to go home. Junior wouldn't let me go, even in a cab, and she needed someone to take care of her dad's Porsche, so he rousted Dean out, too. Do you know what time those men had to get up this morning to train?"

"I'm sorry." There, he'd taken the blame again for something he didn't do.

"For what? You didn't call in the middle of the night."

"It's sort of my fault. We broke up, and she took off by herself."

"Actually, Josee said she broke up with you."

"You're going to take her side."

He detected a drop in the temperature of his sister's voice. "You should know I don't do that, but I can say her aura is a mess, brilliant yellow flares, then dying down to nothing like a sun going nova. She's seriously out of kilter, but only said you didn't do anything but put yourself down, and that was the problem. Fortunately, this baby is keeping me up the way he kicks, so I had the time to listen. I wanted to give her some valerian tea with honey, but it doesn't mix well with alcohol, so I sat there until she got it all out and dozed off on the sofa. Not that she made complete sense. I would have let her sleep in today, but Pilar was up like a bird with the sunrise and woke her. She said she had to go home and face the consequences, but she definitely needed get a place of her own, maybe in our building. You know, Trin, the scar really isn't all that ugly."

People always spilled their guts to Xochi. She'd make a cup of valerian tea and simply listen. Trin suspected the listening helped more than the tea. He'd like to dump his woes on her but again that balls issue. He needed a guy who knew his way around women.

"A poor choice of words. I kept thinking if I'd shot Dirk sooner, she wouldn't have that mark on her neck."

"Putting yourself down again, Trin, when you took a bullet for her and probably saved her life, and Connor and Stevie, too. Give yourself some credit for a change. You don't have to brag about it, just acknowledge to yourself you did all you could."

Maybe his sister was giving him advice after all. He'd ponder it. "Thanks for taking care of her, Xo. I hope you get some rest."

"When Pilar goes down, so do I. Have to take it when I can. This big boy is coming in a few months."

"Love you, sis. Take care."

A gentle tap on a horn got his attention. Stevie waited, parked nearby. He went to the car and got in, no hitch in his stride, no pain in his leg, cured of all but heart sickness. As usual, she asked, "Need to go anywhere else?'

"No, back to the house, I guess. I should pack. I can have my folks pick me up at the doctor's office tomorrow. No need for you to make an extra trip."

"You've been no trouble at all. I hate to think what might have happened if you hadn't stayed for the Fourth." She eyed his face before pulling out into traffic. "Corazon is going to think we didn't feed you."

"It's the PT, the painkillers, and my hummingbird metabolism. PT is over, and I'm ditching the painkillers. I haven't used them lately. Can't do anything about how I burn up the calories."

"Every woman envies you. We should be so lucky."

"At least, I've got one thing going for me. I'll never be fat."

"And a great deal more—brains and talent and courage."

The ability to satisfy a woman, he would have liked to add, but not to Stevie. He wasn't sure about the courage since each time he'd acted without thought, but yeah to the rest. It wasn't enough for Josee. She wanted something he couldn't define. Maybe X could, but he'd be in training, too, and not available until evening. Matt Keaton had told him Dean's advice on getting his sister, Annie, to marry him—groveling and a big honking ring. With his income, he could afford big, but maybe not honking size. As for groveling, that appeared to be the last thing Josee desired. But what *did* she want? Women, always a mystery.

Chapter Twenty-Four

Back at the Riley's house, Trinity began packing, not that it amounted to much. He shoved the multiple pairs of sweats that Eula Mae had kept sweet-smelling into his duffle and topped those off with clean underwear, socks, tees, and the jeans he'd begun wearing again when his leg ceased hurting. He threw in a dress shirt still in its wrappings and pushed on him by his mother in case he needed something less casual to be seen with Josee. Didn't need it anymore.

Eula Mae announced lunch in an hour. He took a shower for the sake of the others who would be at the table and again regretted not asking Stevie to take him to a barber on the way home. Like he wanted Josee to remember him as a shaggy dog with sad, dark eyes nearly obscured by curls. Too late now, too late for everything.

He called his folks. No Camp Love Letter chaos in the background since the children had gone back to school and left the cabins empty. His dad answered and didn't question his desire to be picked up at the doctor's office tomorrow.

"Glad you are coming home, son. We've shared you with the Rileys long enough." If his mother had gotten the phone first, she'd have asked what was wrong.

He said he'd stay a few days at the ranch, then go

back to his apartment in Lafayette, and return to work on Monday. He'd like to show him the completed Joe's World game, too.

"I tell you, I'm willing to invest in this if you don't want to sell it to Hartz."

"Take a look first before you decide. I'm not sure I want to go it alone now that Josee is out." He'd let that slip in a way even his often oblivious father couldn't ignore.

"How so?"

"She really deserves a share, but we've broken up. It would be awkward to work together now."

"Want to tell me what happened? You did follow my advice about keeping a woman happy, *n'est pas*?"

"Oh, yeah. That part worked great. It's other things." Again, he couldn't discuss having no balls with his dad who had great big ones, no one could deny.

"Maybe your mother…"

"I'll see when I get home."

"Son, you really shouldn't let yourself lose yardage. You got to keep going at her like I did your mom."

"Thanks for the opinion." Which wouldn't do him one bit of good. "They're calling me for lunch. See you soon. Love you, Dad."

He dragged himself into the kitchen where Josee already sat picking at a salad at the far end of the table, her scar on display on her vulnerable, naked neck. Eula Mae had placed a plate heaped high with leftover potato salad right next to her. Two quarters of a muffuletta oozing olive salad from its layers of cold cuts sat beside the mound, and a can of Diet Coke awaited pouring into an ice-filled glass. The Riley's maid had left no doubt about which seat was reserved for him.

"Now, you eat that up, Mister Trin. I drove across the causeway to Central Grocery and back for those sandwiches because they don't make 'em right in Cajun country. I don't want Corazon thinking I starved you none."

If he had any thought of fleeing, he soon found himself boxed in by Connor and Stevie. He would have described the conversation as strained, to put it mildly. Plans for the afternoon dominated. Stevie volunteered that she'd be in the darkroom again. Connor planned to take the sailboat out if Trin wanted to come along to catch the breeze on the lake. He declined the invitation.

"I'm going to put the finishing touches on Joe's World. It's almost set to go. Otherwise, I called my parents to pick me up tomorrow at the doctor's office. I'm all packed." He thought he heard Josee breathe the word, "Coward," disguised by taking a sip of unsweetened ice tea. She wanted him to stay? She wanted him to go? Which?

Josee also turned down the chance to sail. "I'm going to look at apartments. It's time I found a place of my own. I might shop for a car, too, but in the meantime, may I borrow the Lexus?" Her parents seemed relieved she hadn't asked for the Mustang or Porsche, as they clasped hands across the table.

"Why don't you forget about the darkroom and come with me, Stevie, my love? We'll sail away and leave all cares behind," Connor wheedled.

"I think I might take you up on that offer, dearest. Eula Mae, please pack up what's left of the sandwiches and add a bottle of wine to the basket. We'll be gone all afternoon," she said pointedly, glancing from Josee to

Trinity. Though devoted to each other, the Rileys were seldom so mushy. Another ploy to show how couples got along, Trinity wondered. Josee, however, did not cancel her plans.

Eula Mae tried again to help. "Yes, ma'am. Gonna be leaving soon myself. Left a chocolate mousse in the icebox for Mr. Trin's going away dinner in case anyone wants to know."

Someday, he'd figure out what exactly chocolate mousse meant in this family. It appeared to be a synonym for sex, but he couldn't ask any of them. Regardless, he'd have the house to himself because Josee shoved the remains of her salad aside, rose, and said, "I'll see y'all later."

He wanted to stand and shout the same word she'd whispered to him as her high swishing ponytail and rigid back moved away from him. Coward! She didn't want to be alone with him.

Stevie sighed ever so slightly. Connor squeezed her hand. "At least, *we'll* have a good time."

"I hope you do," Trin said. "Sorry I couldn't finish all this food, Eula Mae. Why don't you pack it with the rest? I need to get to work."

Honestly, he had little left to do, a tweak here and there that no one but himself would notice. He did want to add one detail, a dedication. The words were already engraved in his heart.

"To Joe Dean Billodeaux, the greatest quarterback, Jonathan Hartz, wizard-in-chief, and Josee Riley, forever my dream girl."

Chapter Twenty-Five

With Eula Mae gone and the Rileys out enjoying their boat, only Trin remained to answer the phone at five p.m. “It’s Josee,” she said, as if he wouldn’t recognize her voice anywhere at any time. “Are my parents around?”

“No, still out on the boat.”

“Okay, then please tell them I’m staying over with Xochi tonight and looking at apartments again tomorrow. A shotgun unit is open here: living room, dining area, kitchen, bedroom, bath, all in a row, spacious but only one window facing Camp Street. I don’t really need anything more.”

Great, if she took out a lease there, he’d have to avoid seeing her when he wanted to visit Xochi or Tom. He steadied his voice. “Sounds better than my place which is basically square, same stuff but economy size. It’s got a little balcony where I keep the hibachi.”

“You’ve never shown it to me.”

Now he wouldn’t, not his computer setup or his king-sized bed or all the magazines featuring Josee stacked under it. His digs hardly compared to the homes of movie stars and celebrities. “Nothing to see really.”

“If you say so. I didn’t want to make my folks worry like I did the other night. That was childish.”

He didn’t need to agree and make matters worse, yet how to keep her talking since this might be their last conversation for a long, long time until both had gotten over the breakup. "Joe's World is complete. I plan to show it to my boss on Monday and see what he'll offer for it."

"Hey, I've already offered to help you set up your own company. What about that?" He sensed challenge in her voice.

"I thought you wouldn't be interested anymore."

"I'm a business woman. Of course, I'm still interested in Joe's World and want to see Josee's World developed if you break with Hartz. Trinity Enterprises has a great future if you let it happen."

Her voice gave him a surge of confidence, at least about his gaming skills. "I owe it to Hartz to let him take a look at it, but I'm glad we talked before I did."

"Never assume anything about me unless I tell you directly."

"I think you already did. I guess I won't see you tomorrow. Goodbye—coward."

He disconnected before she hit him with a backlash. He'd gotten the last word but didn't feel any better about it.

Sails furled, the boat motored into the dock minutes later. He went to the rear door to greet the Rileys and see if they needed any help. Stevie's laughter floated toward him like bird song. Connor squeezed his wife's shoulder and earned an "Ouch, ouch, ouch" from her. As they drew nearer, he observed they'd both gotten too much sun, and Stevie's burn appeared to continue beneath the V-neck of her white cotton tee and across her covered shoulders. The sailboat had a small cabin, but he suspected they'd done it outside without sunscreen, carried away by the moment like young kids. How wonderful it would be at their age to still have such enthusiasm for each other.

Connor carried the basket with the empty wine bottle rolling up against some tight-wrapped packets in the bottom. “Fresh redfish to grill. We bought it right off the fisherman’s boat. All we need for dinner is a salad and garlic bread. That chocolate mousse for dessert. I’ve heard it’s good for sunburn when applied directly to the skin.”

Stevie giggled, and Trin knew for sure she wasn’t a giggler. Again, he envied them their playful love. “Oh, Josee called and said she wouldn’t be home tonight. She’s staying at Xo’s and still looking at apartments.”

“Too bad—but more mousse for us. I’ll clean the fish and heat the grill. You do the salad and bread, honey.”

“I’ll help her,” Trin volunteered. Cleaning fish, though manly, ranked way down on his list of favorite activities.

They put together their simple meal. Trin chopped vegetables: celery, green peppers, carrots, and fresh mushrooms. Stevie smeared a split French loaf with butter and sprinkled on garlic salt, parm, and a bit of parsley. She opened another bottle of wine. “We probably don’t need this, though it may act as an analgesic. I hope I don’t blister in embarrassing places tomorrow.”

This couple, so like his parents, Trin thought, their actions once a cause to blush in his teens, now the kind of long-term passion he desired with Josee and no one else. He dumped the vegetables over a bowl of romaine and iceberg lettuce and used the tongs to toss them together.

"This is nice," Stevie commented as she poured herself a glass of white. "You're like family, Trinity. We don't want to lose you. Did you and Josee talk when she called?"

"Some. She's still interested in backing Joe's World and developing Josee's World of modeling. I guess we can still be business partners, but that might be hard on both of us."

"Stick with it, Trin. Women change their minds about a lot of things."

"You'll always be my favorite honorary aunt, Stevie, even if we're never related." She bestowed a smile on him as beautiful as her daughter's.

They carried the food out to the deck and set up in the shade near the grill where the fish cooked quickly and practically flipped themselves onto the plates, they were that fresh. Weeks ago, blood had been spilled here, but they were erasing that awful memory and writing over it with a new and happy one. If only Josee were here.

He accepted a small portion of mousse for dessert to take to his room. "I've got a call to make, but I won't get any on the sheets."

"Hmmm, I think we'll do the same," Connor said with a glint in his eye for his wife who was too sunburnt to show a blush.

Trinity left them to it and went to make a call to the one person who might have some insight into what women wanted from men, someone not his dad or brothers. "Hey, X, you got a minute?"

"All the time in the world, but I gotta let you know Coach still has us doing drills outside to toughen us up, he say. If I doze off on you, just hang up."

"You're in the city then?"

"Hell, yeah. We playing football, bro, while you bask in the love of a supermodel."

"We, ah, broke up. I need the advice of my wingman to get her back."

"I thought you had her cold, man."

"I said something that set her off—that her scar was ugly."

"Dumb move."

"Tell me about it. Then, she said I should grow a pair and stomped out."

"Wait a minute here, you saved a drowning child, faced down a bull, confronted a drunk and a bully for her, and finally, you took a bullet for Josee, and she say you got no balls? That woman is whack. I wouldn't do half those things for any female except my mama, maybe the drunk and the bully, but count me out with bulls and bullets."

"You're a football player. You don't have to prove yourself."

"Gotta be more to it, Trin."

"Well, I guess I said we were more equal now that she has that scar, maybe."

He heard X's feet hit the floor and begin to pace. "No maybe about it. You admitted you weren't good enough for her. You're always putting yourself down."

"I'm not good enough for her."

"See, there you go. Look here, women like men with confidence. It's the only thing you don't have going for you—if the sex is good and you treat her right."

"The sex is great." He did voice that with some pride. "And I'd never hurt her in any way."

"Then you tell me this. Why isn't she wearing your ring by now, huh?"

"I was going to get one as soon as I regained my feet, but now it's no use."

"The hell it ain't. You get that ring. You ask her to marry you, and none of this shit about not being good enough, neither. Just like your daddy said about sex, make it about her. See if that don't work."

"I will!"

"Damn right you will. Who's gonna marry a supermodel?"

"I am!" Trin recognized a locker room pep talk when he heard one, not dissimilar to the essence of the words his dad whispered to him in the incubator—that he was strong and a winner.

"Good. Now let me get some rest. Good luck wit' that."

"You're the best, X."

"Sure, I am. Now you tell Josee you are, too. Night."

One more call to make. "Could you bring my car down with you tomorrow? I have some things to take care of around the city and don't want to hold you up."

"If your mother will drive the Tesla. It gives me leg cramps," his dad complained.

"Certainly, I'll drive it, though we could visit with the Rileys if you want to use ours," his mom offered on speakerphone.

"No, I'd rather have mine." No sense in letting both sets of parents connive to bring their offspring together again. He had to do it himself.

Trin finished his mousse, still wondering about its meaning, despite the noise from the bedroom down the hall giving him a big hint. Tomorrow, he'd buy that ring.

Chapter Twenty-Six

Trin ditched his parents as soon as possible, though they'd insisted on having lunch at the Acme Oyster House very near Xochi's place. However, they didn't invite her. No, they wanted to pry at him, trying to get at his soft insides like an oyster in its shell, to find out what had gone wrong with Josee. Only he could fix it no matter their good intentions.

To keep him longer, they'd ordered appetizers, chargrilled oysters, and the famous Boo Fries slathered with cheese and gravy before getting their Peace Maker po-boys stuffed with shrimp and yet more oysters on a bed of spicy mayo. Usually, his mom vetoed so much fried food, but she made a point of saying that sometimes you had to let your spouse have their way. He got the point, but letting Josee have her way wasn't the problem. He always deferred to her.

Naturally, he'd splattered gravy on his front and dribbled spicy mayo on a cuff of the dress shirt he'd worn to bolster his confidence for what came next. Too hot for long sleeves, he added sweat stains to the mix. Maybe he should buy a fresh shirt once he'd sent his parents on their way. Finally, the tab came along with his mother's sandwich, boxed to go as she'd dined mainly on the chargrilled seafood. He kissed her cheek lovingly, shook hands with his dad manfully, and prompted both not to worry about him. He'd see them tonight.

Yes, he'd buy a shirt after getting a haircut at his honorary Uncle Brian's favorite salon featuring mostly gay stylists, who were the best in the city according to Bri. When he told the hairdresser he wanted a young Tony Curtis look, the guy knew exactly what he meant, and spent extra time training and getting the curl dangling on his forehead exactly right. "Yes, yes, I can see this is the perfect style for you. We don't want to obscure that sexy scar, now do we."

Three hundred dollars plus an ample tip—but he doubted any other place would have barbers who recalled young Tony Curtis. He reminded himself he could afford the cut, the most expensive of his life. He also received advice as to where to get a dress shirt nearby and found himself clothed shortly in a slightly fitted outfit of pale yellow, so good with his olive complexion after he'd turned down lavender and pink. The clerk advised he wear the collar open and down two buttons. Trin compromised on one. Ah-ha, the perfect shirt had French cuffs and also required cufflinks. He settled on onyx rather than gold which went well with his dark trousers and dress shoes, or so he was told.

Two ordeals out of the way, he took on Leslie at Schifferman's Jewelry and began to sweat again. He stood across the counter being scrutinized by the dapper salesman with the tidy silver mustache. "How may I help you today? Another gold chain?"

"Um, an engagement ring fit for Josee Riley."

The clerk's shapely eyebrows rose. "For Josee Riley or like Josee Riley? There is a world of difference."

"The actual Josee Riley." He started to say he knew he didn't look like a man who could afford such a spectacular ring or glamorous girlfriend, but he swallowed those words, looked Leslie in directly the eye, and waited.

"Ah, yes, another Billodeaux, the man who saved her life." Leslie's arch tone seemed to imply that explained the odd pairing. "Your brothers and their friends have been quite excellent customers of Schifferman's, and we have loaned Miss Riley jewels for gala affairs on several occasions." Leslie swept his arm around the showroom. "Nothing here is worthy of her. Let me bring a few samples out of the vault."

"Nothing honking big."

"Honking?"

"You know, ostentatious. She wouldn't like that."

"If you are sure," Leslie answered, a question implied in his emphasis.

Glad when the man left, Trin exhaled and wandered the room, peering into cases with gems sporting price tags turned over, though comfortable leather seating was available. Leslie took a moment too long. Trin's gaze rested on a case of milky stones, one in particular fairly large. He wouldn't have known what they were without the sign touting Australian opals. When Leslie reappeared and began to display several rings on black velvet for his consideration, he said as firmly as he'd ever spoken in his life, "What about this one?"

"Oh, a nice enough piece for a gift, but most young ladies prefer diamonds for their glitter and as they say, lasting forever. Now, consider this flawless blue-white, five-carat stone with two one carat pear-shaped diamonds on its flanks in a platinum setting."

Trin gave Leslie's choice a glance. "No, the real Josee isn't flashy. Tell me about the opal."

In the vein of the customer is always right or must at least be obliged, Leslie unlocked the case and presented the ring box. "It is a very fine stone, pear-shaped, heirloom quality, set in a halo of diamonds and mounted on an eighteen-carat gold band also encrusted with small diamonds, which enhance its luster."

"The price?"

"Two thousand dollars. However, diamonds are more traditional. Please look more closely at them. I am sure I can find one to suit."

"Josee isn't traditional, either." He held the stone up to the light. "Don't you see, under the milky surface are glints of blue like her eyes, the gold of her hair, some green too. It has depth. Besides, the platinum setting is too cold. Gold is warm like she is."

Leslie sighed as if conceding that his commission on this sale might be much smaller than he'd anticipated. "Perhaps both you and she have made the right choice. I've rarely heard a man wax more eloquent about an engagement ring, including your brothers. You appear to know your lady very well."

"Hardly, but I'm working on it. And she hasn't made her choice yet." Trin handed over his credit card, a black one he seldom used.

Leslie brows rose again. Twice he'd surprised the man. "I shall wrap this for you and wish you the very best of luck."

****

Trin retrieved his Tesla from the pay lot where he needn't worry about anyone stealing it. If they did, it would run out of charge and be abandoned somewhere. He headed across the causeway hoping Josee had returned home now that she thought he'd gone. Crap, the Lexus did sit in the Rileys' driveway, but so did his dad's black SUV, the one he drove when not hauling around a dozen kids. He found all of them, wine in hand, an antipasto tray on the table, sitting in the shade on the deck.

"Trin?" his mother said.

"Trin!" Josee exclaimed as if she'd been stuck by a needle.

The men simply exchanged glances.

Stevie stood, walked over, and gave him a hug. "So glad you returned. Don't you look nice. We're having Italian tonight. Chicken Alfredo is one of Eula Mae's specialties, her mama's recipe. You are going to stay? I'm trying to convince Joe and Nell to do the same."

"It depends." He scanned the large yard for a private spot and found none out of view of the table. "Josee, walk with me, please."

She rose without questioning his request. He held out his hand, and she accepted it. He led the way around the house and found no better place there. Out of the corner of his eye, he swore he saw the curtains move. Even retired football players moved fast—as did their wives and Eula Mae.

"Is the garage open?"

"Yes. I should put the Lexus away."

"Forget about that." He moved them into the building, turned on the lights, and sought out the backseat of the Benz again. Might as well invoke good memories and get them on his side. He opened the door for her.

“Trin, I’m not having sex with you while our parents are lurking nearby. Besides, that’s not what I meant. You have nothing to prove in that area.”

He allowed himself a smile. “I know. Just get inside. I have something to tell you.” Not ask, tell. She slid onto the cool leather seat. He sat beside her. No getting down on one knee in the posture of begging for her hand in marriage, even if he could inside a car, not the most romantic place, but high-class transportation.

“Josee Riley, you deserve a man who puts you first, who will defend you from bullies and bulls if need be, who is kind and thoughtful—or at least working on that, a man with a future he wants to share with you, and most of all, who will love you all the days of his life come what may. I am that man. Will you marry me, Josee?”

She didn’t answer. He groped for the black leather ring box tied with gold ribbon in his pants pocket. She’d know it came from Schifferman’s, the very best. He offered it to her and watched as she untied the ribbon and opened the lid, hoping the light in the garage would do the opal justice. He prayed she didn’t want a diamond and that he’d chosen well. He started to say she could trade it in if she didn’t like it but recalled X’s advice in time.

“Beneath the milky surface of this stone are many colors, blue like your eyes, gold like your hair. It has depth, like you, Josee. That’s why I chose it.”

She was crying, tears blurring her lovely eyes and rolling down her cheeks into the hollow where she’d been scarred. What had he done wrong now? He’d never understand women. But he waited. No blurting out his insecurities this time.

"I don't believe anyone has said more beautiful words to me in my entire life. Yes, Trinity Billodeaux. I will marry you."

"Oh, good." His eloquence had left him.

"More than good." Josee wrapped her arms around him and dried her tears on his expensive yellow shirt. She offered him the box and her hand. The ring fit a trifle loosely.

"We can have it sized, Leslie said."

"Leslie again? He has very good taste."

No way he was going to allow Leslie to take the credit. "He wanted to sell me some honking big diamond ring, but I chose this one myself."

"It's perfect."

"I guess we should tell the folks."

They emerged from the Benz and headed for the door, where they could clearly hear the debate on the other side.

"Should we disturb them? I mean, we don't want to walk in on anything intimate," his mom said.

Stevie's strong voice came through loud and clear. "I don't hear any sexual noises."

"Why don't we just leave them alone?" Connor suggested.

"Yeah, they need some space," his dad said.

"The chicken Alfredo is gettin' cold," Eula Mae's distinctive voice added.

Trin opened the door. Parents tumbled inside and regained their balance, if not their dignity.

"Like I said, dinner is served. Come along now. I see Miss Josee got a fancy new ring y'all can see at the table."

Sheepishly, they lined up and followed Eula Mae

to the house where, apparently, she'd set the table in the dining room for a special occasion and subbed the white wine with champagne. Far from appreciating her hard work, the chatter at dinner was all of weddings, how and when.

Trin helped clear the table as he did at home. When he had a minute alone with Eula Mae, he asked, "How did you know I'd propose today?"

"When I hugged you goodbye this mornin', I could feel you stiff with determination. Miss Josee, she came home early, missed you by a half hour because of some accident on the causeway, went to her room, and cried. Nice to see happy tears for a change. Besides, your folks arrived here to cook something up with the Rileys, but you didn't need them, no sir. Now, I have Neapolitan ice cream for dessert that you can dress yourself wit' nuts, cherries, and the like, but there's chocolate mousse left over. I don't mind the mess."

Chocolate mousse again? He'd definitely have to ask Josee about it.

Chapter Twenty-Seven

Three a.m., Trin lay side by side with Josee in his bed at the Riley's house. He'd told his parents he'd be at the ranch tomorrow for a brief visit, then back at his job Monday to present Joe's World to Jonathan Hartz and get the great wizard's opinion. He had no intention of selling the game, he assured Josee. Now to stick to that when a possible offer of millions lay on the line.

Though they'd had sex once already to their mutual satisfaction, Josee still seemed restless with endless wedding details running through her mind. While his dad and Connor had glazed over during the discussion of plans and retreated to the deck, Trin stayed and paid attention, adding his opinion if asked. Really, a whole year to plan a wedding. Why not May which knocked three months off the wait time? Josee thought May a possibility if they hurried to get a date for the reception. She wanted it held at the Roosevelt Hotel where Connor and Stevie had married when it was still the Fairmont, a good enough reason for turning down the ranch as a site. She also desired a private lakeside ceremony at her parents' house, exactly as they had done, though they could have filled St. Louis Cathedral with family, friends, and well, those who had to be invited like Marcello.

When the debate began about whether to have a Catholic priest, a Lutheran minister, or both, but maybe a justice of the peace, he spoke up and suggested that Rev Bullock unite them in marriage as his father had done for Josee's parents. Everyone around the table admired that idea. He made a mental note not to allow Mawmaw Nadine to bully him into a Catholic ceremony, even if she told him they'd never truly be married unless they took their vows in the Church, there being only one in her mind.

Having asserted himself, Trin drifted away to join the men outside watching the sunset and having a beer. He'd escaped during the discussion on which designer to choose for the wedding gown, as many would want to dress Josee, and the flowers, definitely not daisies both Josee and her mother agreed. After all that decision-making, his beloved should be exhausted, but she wanted to talk.

He steered her away from wedding minutia like favors to take home and what menu to choose. "Josee, honey, we have months to deal with that. Why don't you tell me about the significance of chocolate mousse in the Riley family?"

Not being sunburnt like her mother, Josee pinked up slightly. Her naked breasts flushed as well as her cheeks. "You must never tell my father I know. Once when my mom was trying to bond with me, she said she and my dad coated themselves in chocolate mousse and licked it off each other's body. Eula Mae had to strip those sheets in the morning and has teased them about it ever since. TMI about my parents. I can't stop imagining it."

"Neither can I, now that you mention it. There's still some left in the bowl if your folks didn't use it up last night when you weren't home."

"They didn't!"

"They did. Considering that Eula Mae wasn't grumbling in the morning, I suspect they changed their own sheets and washed away the evidence. Josee, I have a sudden craving for chocolate mousse."

"Me, too."

"I'll raid the refrigerator. Get ready to reenact family history."

"I'm ready now."

Josee kicked the spread on the floor and splayed her white body on the top sheet. For a moment, he considered skipping the mousse and simply going for it, but no, traditions must be upheld. Through the darkened house he crept and eased open the refrigerator door. The blast of cold air wrecked a fairly enthusiastic erection. He should have worn pants. Still, he had every confidence in raising another with a vision of Josee waiting in his bed. Victory! Quarter of a bowl rimmed with whipped cream and crowned with cherries remained. He cradled the fancy cut glass container in his hands and butted the door shut. Almost back to where his new fiancée waited with her opal ring on and nothing else, another door creaked open.

"I heard something, Connor. Maybe an intruder."

"The alarms are set, Stevie. Come back to bed—unless you want to bring the rest of that mousse?"

No, no, no! He managed to elbow into his room since he'd left the door slightly ajar. "I got it, but your parents are talking about going for a second round."

"Simple, we tell them we had the late-night munchies and wash the bowl before they get up in the morning. The sheets, too, I guess."

"I do love a smart woman, one who deserves

dessert. I don't think we have enough for full body painting, but let's start here."

He came to her side, dipped his fingers in the pudding and slicked it on her lips. After kissing most of it off and sharing with her tongue, he coated her breasts. Topping her pink nipples with rosy cherries, he sucked off the fruit because what lay beneath was a better treat. His tongue swirled round and round both mounds before he added a chocolate trail down her belly to that dainty patch of yellow fluff that he painted brown, then enthusiastically lapped back to the original color. Josee bucked and pleaded for him to stop. He didn't, not until she came for him like a swan taking flight. Pleased with himself, he went to lay his head next to hers on the pillow.

"Don't get comfortable. Give me a minute, and it's your turn." Her heart still beat wildly beneath his hand, but gradually slowed to a normal rhythm. "Give me that bowl and stretch out."

He managed to lie still while she massaged mousse onto his chest and ornamented his nipples with not only cherries, but a ring of whipped cream applied with a fingertip that both tickled and aroused, as if he weren't stimulated enough already. She made short work of the topping but took only a few laps of sticky chest hair before moving downward.

"Hair caught on my tongue. Mousse almost gone. Want to get to the best part," she explained with a catch in her breath. He had to agree, an erection being stroked with silky pudding and having the cherry balanced on the tip removed by her lips was definitely the best part—so far.

"Mercy, Josee," he cried out. "Mercy. I can't hold

out much longer."

She took pity on him, mounted, and took him inside that perfect body, scar or no scar. Leaning over, the mousse on his chest clung to her breasts as she moved back and forth, back and forth, making them slippery in his hands. He felt himself giving way, erupting into her with force—and she provided the aftershocks for both of them with a tightening of her internal muscles. She slid off to his side, her breath coming quick again. Once she caught it, she said, "We still have to strip the bed, take a shower, and wash the bowl."

"Give me a few minutes. My very masculine legs are still quivering."

"I do think you are the only man who would admit that. Maybe we'll do a traditional white wedding cake with a filling to keeping it from being dry. Should there be another dessert as well?

"Oh, definitely. Cups of chocolate mousse with whipped cream and a cherry on top. That's settled. Let's get a little sleep before we clean up this mess. Great family tradition by the way."

"I totally agree."

The sun caught them still naked but clothed in pudding. They dashed to strip the sheets, wad them into the hamper, and climbed into the shower, where they discovered washing mousse off was nearly as much fun as applying it.

As Trin helped Josee wash her hair, pausing to suck on the ends of the strands from time to time where the dessert remained, he asserted himself in a way that brooked no objections, "We're positively going to have a great marriage."

Epilogue

Trinity Billodeaux stood on the upper level of the Blue Room in the Roosevelt Hotel, once a supper club that had hosted the likes of Frank Sinatra and Louis Armstrong, now elegantly restored. He watched his wife, yes, his wife, dance with a man far taller and more handsome than himself. Jealousy did not disturb him in the least. The fact that her partner was his very married brother, Dean, helped out in that respect. Josee Riley had chosen *him*, not Mack or a movie star. He basked in the admiration of his peeps, the geeks of Hartz Technology's research and development team. They'd all rented tuxedos with more or less success and gawked like a flock of penguins at the scene below.

"You are the man, Trin. How did you get a supermodel to marry you?" one of them squawked. His pals eyed a clutch of Josee's friends, all leggy and beautiful, not to mention his own sisters and sisters-in-law dressed in their blush—some kind of pale pink—gowns as part of the wedding party. Jessie stood out in her wheelchair which didn't make her any less attractive than the others as X always said.

"Confidence and putting her first," he advised his worshipers.

"And creating a game that's bringing in millions," another guy shorter than Trin remarked.

"Josee helped create that game and Trinity

Enterprises. Marry a smart one, guys. You won't be sorry. Now, get down there and ask one of them to dance. Confidence, remember?"

He took a moment to recall Josee walking down the white runner between the rows of chairs for the especially selected guests by the lake. He hadn't seen the gown she'd finally chosen with its V-neck, strapless lace bodice. Yeah, he knew what a bodice was. He had plenty of sisters, after all. Beneath her breasts, the dress cinched in at the waist, then flared out in soft folds reaching the tips of the flat golden sandals she wore, though he'd told her she could choose four-inch heels if she wanted, a tribute to his confidence. As he'd specifically requested, she'd pulled her hair back but let it flow loose down her back beneath a simple veil as long as the gown, held in place with pearl-tipped pins rather than a tiara or headpiece. Her only jewelry—her engagement ring now wedded to a plain gold band and her grandmother's locket covering the scar it had helped to create. Simplicity itself. God, he'd married the most beautiful woman in the world, and to him, she always would be. He fingered the broader gold band he wore that still felt strange, but he had no desire to take it off at any time and relished its weight.

He'd had no input about the flowers because he knew diddly about them, but the tightly furled white roses tipped with pale pink reminded him of his wife's breasts. They dominated the cascade of her bouquet, the bridesmaid's nosegays, and the towering table arrangements on the head table, as well as smaller vases set on the others. He hoped no one else regarded the flowers in that way because now those breasts were his alone.

Trin checked his watch again. How much longer would this go on? They'd married at eleven beneath a bower where Reverend Bullock took up much of the space and ran on about the blessings of marriage until noon when all departed for a lobster and steak dinner at the hotel. Above them, a honeymoon suite awaited, still waited, as the clock approached six. If they'd fed them less, the guests, all four hundred of them, might be on their way home by now to get a snack. Some, he noted, dug into the little gold boxes of chocolate truffles filled with mousse intended as take-home favors. The cups of the dessert pudding had long been removed from the tables, but champagne and other alcohol still flowed.

Maybe there was hope of an ending in sight so they could begin their married life, not that they hadn't been living it the brownstone building where they'd taken a large apartment above Junior's abode. While Junior and Xochi filled their extra space with babies—and the nine-pound, eleven-ounce Knox Clinton Polk the Third, K. C. for short, took up a lot of room as he grew—he and Josee set up their computers and their company in the excess area. As Joe's World thrived, they worked on her game to be out in the fall. The fact that they sometimes went online to play with their customers didn't hurt its popularity at all. They chose various roles, but his dad always had to be the quarterback.

Oh, no. X-avier had mounted the blue-curtained stage and gotten ahold of the mike. Not that he had a bad voice, but people stuck around when he performed. Turned out, he had a whole set of duets with Caressa planned. Up 'til now, he'd been the perfect best man, a part in the wedding his brother Mack said he deserved more because of being one of the triplets, but Trin hadn't been pushed out of asking the wingman who'd helped him win Josee. Those hard feelings were assuaged as Mack worked his way through the bevy of models, undoubtedly planning to take one upstairs once the festivities ended—if they ever did.

He noticed one of his geek buddies, the boldest of the bunch, had taken his triplet sister out to the dance floor, though Lorena towered over him. Better a computer geek than the big Australian bloke who'd followed her home, tried out for the Sinners, gotten on the team, and now seemed to always be sniffing around her. There the Aussie, Jock Brown, was, making a pyramid of champagne glasses with the intent of pouring a bottle of bubbly down the sides to fill them as a rapt group of Sinners egged him on, his brother Tom among them and not the only redhead in the ballroom. Ty Beck, having doffed his Stetson, was easy to spot at a table with Bodey Landrum and Miss Eve. Trin reminded himself again that Josee had picked him, not the heroic rodeo clown.

Mariah's white wig and scarlet sequins competed for attention at a table where Corazon wore a more modest red dress and had tucked a rose of the same color in her gray braids. Although they'd asked for no gifts, but rather donations to Camp Love Letter, Corazon had crocheted them an afghan big enough for two, white and yellow yarns intertwined because Xochi told her that would be the most auspicious color combination. They cherished her effort. Eula Mae laughed, head tipped back at something Mariah said, and even Knox Polk cracked a grin. If only Mariah hadn't provided the cases and cases of good quality champagne that made the guests reluctant to leave.

He made his way down to the first level, stopped every few feet by well-wishers, football players past and present who slammed him on the back by way of congratulations or the more refined who shook his hand and wished the couple well. Jonathan Hartz and his Cajun bride of many years, a man who'd moved his entire headquarters to little Chapelle, Louisiana, for her sake, urged him to sit for a minute. Considering that Trin had turned down the man's massive offer for the new game and then allowed him to buy a non-controlling interest in the new company which Hartz considered a good investment, he had to oblige. No business talk tonight, however.

Hartz wanted to reminisce. "You know I took a bullet for my bride too."

"You did not! A crazy hunter's rights advocate shot you at the Ducks Unlimited banquet because you made Indian Lake off limits for all but a brief duck season. I was nowhere in sight." Celine Hartz's large, dark eyes sparkled with humor and love for her husband. She might be getting older, but neither her eyes nor her love had dimmed.

"Why would a citizen of Seattle be at that banquet if not to impress you with how Cajun he could be?" Hartz gave her that innocent, baby blue-eyed glance that often fooled his competitors into going easier on their deals with him than necessary.

Celine gripped her husband's hands. "I thought I'd lost you."

Trin knew the story, now a legend in Chapelle, along with their lavish wedding in a pecan grove draped with golden silk. Hartz continued, "The trick is to impress your gal, but not die in the process."

"I agree with you there." Trin strained slightly in the direction of the dancefloor where he wanted to be before a new partner seized Josee.

X made the perfect announcement at the right time. "The incomparable Caressa and me want to dedicate our next song to the bride and groom. Please clear the floor for Josee and Trinity and give them the spotlight for a while before joining them. Here we go with *Unforgettable*.

"Gotta go," he apologized to Hartz and his lady. Not that he wanted the spotlight as much as time alone with Josee.

He'd already done the opening dance with her briefly, then on to Stevie, his mom, and all of the ten bridesmaids who were mostly his sisters except for the two models asked to stand with Josee's brothers. The models hadn't been impressed by the groom and kept sending come-hither glances over his shoulder to Mack who eventually did, glad to ditch his wedding counterpart, his no-nonsense sister Jude, designated to keep him in line. That didn't bother Trin nearly as much as losing his bride when man after man lined up to dance with her. He'd retreated to the upper level and the guys he felt most comfortable among to wait for a moment to reclaim her. Good ole X had provided his opportunity.

Applause followed him to where his bride waited alone, slim white arms held out. As he stepped into her embrace, Josee lowered her head and whispered, "This should have been our first dance as man and wife. Didn't it all start at Mariah's Place when you defended me from Dirk?"

Denial sat on the tip of his tongue that he'd been no

hero with X backing him up, but he swallowed those words and simply said, "Yes." Looking up into her lovely blue eyes, he squared his shoulders and resisted the ever-present urge to rest his Tony Curtis haircut on her breast. "I wish this were over, and we were upstairs alone or lying on the beach at Musha Cay."

Josee kissed the curl on his forehead and the scar beneath it. "Relax and enjoy because this is the only wedding either of us will have, I promise."

Being the kind of people who kept their vows, Trinity believed he could hold out a little longer waiting for the festivities to end. A lifetime lay ahead of them, and everlasting love had true meaning in the world they would create together.

A word about the author...

Once a librarian, now a writer of romance, Lynn Shurr grew up in Pennsylvania Dutch country. She attended a state college and earned a very impractical B.A. in English Literature. Her first job out of school really was working as a cashier in a burger joint. Moving from one humble job to another, she traveled to North Carolina, then Germany, then California where she buckled down and studied for an M.A. in Librarianship.

New degree in hand, she found her first reference job in the Heart of Cajun Country, Lafayette, Louisiana. For her, the old saying, "Once you've tasted bayou water, you will always stay here" came true. She raised three children not far from the Bayou Teche and lives there still with her astronomer husband.

When not writing, Lynn likes to paint, cheer for the New Orleans Saints and LSU Tigers, and take long road trips nearly anywhere. Her love of the bayou country, its history and customs, often shows in the background for her books.

You may contact Lynn at:

www.lynnshurr.com

visit her blog:

lynnshurr.blogspot.com

or her web site:

www.lynnshurr.com

Thank you for purchasing
this publication of The Wild Rose Press, Inc.

For questions or more information
contact us at
info@thewildrosepress.com.

The Wild Rose Press, Inc.
www.thewildrosepress.com

To visit with authors of
The Wild Rose Press, Inc.
join our yahoo loop at
http://groups.yahoo.com/group/thewildrosepress/

www.ingramcontent.com/pod-product-compliance
Lightning Source LLC
Chambersburg PA
CBHW060534260626
47161CB00003B/891

* 9 7 8 1 5 0 9 2 2 7 0 6 8 *